Tangled Roots

a novel

Marcia Kemp Sterling

RIVER GROVE
BOOKS

This is a work of fiction. Although most of the characters, organizations, and events portrayed in the novel are based on actual historical counterparts, the dialogue and thoughts of these characters are products of the author's imagination.

Published by River Grove Books
Austin, TX
www.rivergrovebooks.com

Distributed by River Grove Books

For ordering information or special discounts for bulk purchases, please contact Greenleaf Book Group at PO Box 91869, Austin, TX 78709, 512.891.6100.

Design and composition by Greenleaf Book Group
Cover design by Greenleaf Book Group
Cover art by Thomas M. Hinton (1906–1975)

Publisher's Cataloging-in-Publication data is available.

Print ISBN: 978-1-63299-356-4

eBook ISBN: 978-1-63299-357-1

First Edition

Dedicated to the memory of

Dawn Elizabeth Arkema Kibler
(1972-2020)

whose passionate curiosity about our
tangled roots along Manada Creek
inspired this story

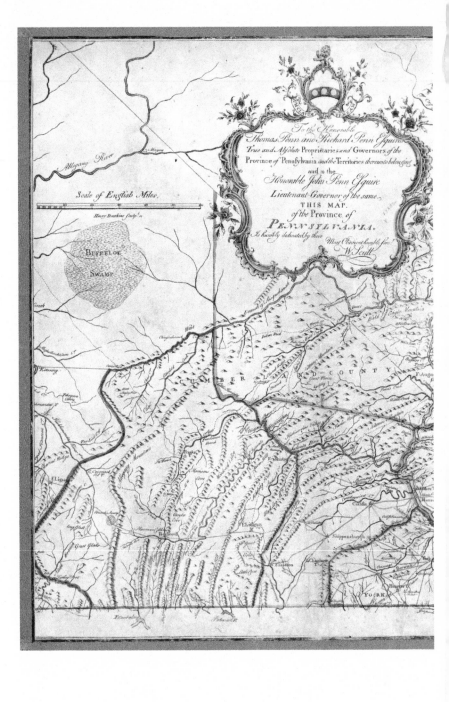

Scale of English Miles.

Henry Dawkins sculp.t

BUFFELOE SWAMP

Allegany River

To the Honorable
Thomas Penn and Richard Penn Esquires
True and Absolute Proprietaries and Governors of the
Province of Pensylvania and the Territories thereunto belonging
and to the
Honorable John Penn Esquire
Lieutenant-Governor of the same,
THIS MAP.
of the Province of
PENSYLVANIA.
Is humbly dedicated by their Most Obedient humble serv.t
W. Scull

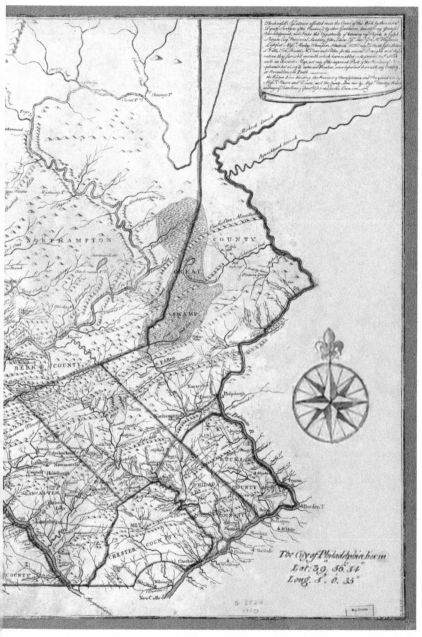

Pennsylvania Colony ca. 1750

Prologue

The Holy Land, 1191

A ribbon of armed men on horseback snaked through the dunes toward Jaffa, the rattle of steel armor mingling with the whinny of tired horses and the tinkle of booty from each of the great victories. Sweat dripped down grimy necks onto tunics so gray with dust that the crosses stitched in red were scarcely visible.

The Turk, exhausted like the others after so many months of travel and warfare, was nonetheless relieved to be travelling alongside the kitchen wagon instead of trailing behind with the other servants. Throughout the bitter months of hunger and fear, he had come to accept his changed circumstances and was determined to do what he could to improve his chances of survival. In the end, he had been saved by an ear for language and the culinary arts learned from his mother.

"Turk, go with Philip and Yusuf. We must supplement our provisions. There are date and fruit orchards in the valley to the south that Saladin forgot to burn." Like the other servants taken from the defeated Muslims, he was then, and to them always would be, simply "Turk."

He didn't mind the epithet or the orders or even the uncleanliness of these Westerners who wreaked havoc and mayhem in the name of God. He had been enslaved by one group of them or another since he was a child, since the first invaders from the West tore through his village and slaughtered all but the youngest children, including every single member of his family.

The mortal hatred he had borne toward the Western barbarians had dissipated over the years, as he became a trusted servant of those first crusaders from France. The tongue of his newest masters was different, but with each passing week he was understanding more of their English words and, in some mysterious way, felt proud to be part of the holy army of a king known as Richard the Lionheart.

The Turk followed Yusuf and Philip down the culvert road, a hand-pulled provision cart and mounted guards behind them. The inland hills were dusty and barren, laid waste by years of conflict between the Muslim tribes to the east and the Westerners who had rolled onto the shores of Palestine at the eastern edge of the Mediterranean in fleets of sailing ships too numerous to count.

The trade routes of Asia, Africa, and Europe had always brought strangers into this land, where so many religions had their roots, travelers from afar who had come to purchase spices and fruits and fabrics to take back to their homes. Christian pilgrims had mingled with the traders as they made their own kind of *hajj* to Jerusalem to touch the relic of the True Cross in the Holy Sepulchre.

But these warriors of the cross, merciless in their belief that this Holy Land had been promised to them by their god, had heard the call to jihad as a heavenly mandate for death and destruction and plunder. The Turk would cook for them and do their bidding, but he knew he was nothing to them and could be destroyed on a whim at any time.

As the foraging crew approached the stream responsible for this oasis of greenery tucked into the dusty hills, Philip sent Yusuf off in one direction and the Turk in another to gather provisions for the kitchen. Philip had come on the same ship as the king's closest knights and had proved his reliability during the voyage from Cyprus. This lion-hearted king was proving more effective than either of the other barbarian leaders—Philip II of France and Frederick Barbarossa of Germany—in this Third Crusade to take back Jerusalem.

It was surprising to find orchards still standing that had not been stripped and burned by the retreating Islamic armies. This land was connected to a large fortress on a nearby hill, one of many built after the First Crusade when French nobility established themselves in Palestine and made vast fortunes from the spoils of war and profit from export.

As the Turk made his way along rows of grape and citrus, he was enjoying the cool air and the heady aroma of mature produce. The sun slanted into the hillside with fierce intensity, but the ground was moist, and stands of plum and almond trees provided canopy shade. His breath slowed and for the first time since the siege of Acre he felt the tension flow out of his shoulders. Since he had been handed off to the English, there had been little time to get his bearings. This grove reminded him of the French monks who had taken care of him after his capture, providing education along with hard work. An eager student, he had picked up Latin and even some English during his captivity.

Tall and slender, no longer a boy but not yet a man, the dark-skinned Turk reached into the lower branches of the fruit trees, filling his sling without losing pace, even as his left shoulder was beginning to feel the weight of the harvest. The provision wagon was far behind, but the Turk was in a rhythm and so pleasantly engaged in his own thoughts that he was oblivious to the need to return his bounty to the cart.

The silvery timbre of water over stone drew him out of his reverie as he passed near the stream that fed the valley. After weeks of slogging through dusty hills, he couldn't resist the allure of fresh water and slipped down the ravine toward the stream.

It was dark and wet, a stand of oriental plane trees sheltering the narrow waterway. The Turk knelt and extended his fingers into the cool water, letting the stream push against his outstretched hand. He cupped his hands and drank deeply.

When he thought about what happened next, even years later when the attack was reenacted in slow motion in his dreams, the Turk had difficulty reconstructing the series of events.

He was leaning into the stream for another drink when all became shock and pain. A massive blunt force from behind propelled him forward into the water, from which he emerged gasping for breath, sharp pain shooting down his back. He could hear but did not see his assailant, a stream of French profanity filling the air. And then kicking and splashing, now on top, now pinned, blows to the head and midsection, the gleam of a silver dagger pressed against his throat, churning through the underbrush and mud. And then a rush of air, strangled moaning and a circle of red growing wider across the dying man's chest, dripping down the Turk's neck, the Frenchman's empty eyes staring in horror at his last sight of this world.

The Turk pushed the dead man aside, shaking from fear and shock, and fell to his knees to pray, prostrate on the ground. *"A'udhu billahi minash shaitanir rajim."*

So shaken was he that it was some moments before he felt the warmth of the sun on his face and turned quickly in the other direction towards Mecca.

It was the nicker of a horse that pulled him from prayer. He looked up to see a fully outfitted steed drinking from the stream. Sight of the magnificent horse caused him to look again at the body that lay at the edge of the water. With trembling hands, he felt for a pulse and confirmed what was already apparent from the astonished wide-open eyes.

As he approached the horse, the Turk had no plan. He felt pity for the animal, now without master. He pulled off the saddle and bridle and dismissed the grateful steed with a pat on the rump. He was still in shock and acting from instinct. Before dumping the saddlebag into a shallow grave, he opened it and rifled through the dead man's belongings.

The cross was wrapped in a small rough blanket. As the cloth was unfurled, the cross fell to the ground into a patch of small-leaved ground clover, in the one spot along the bank where a ray of sun had penetrated the tree cover. It lay there shining, its arms lit up like liquid gold, red and blue gemstones sparkling in the light.

The Turk gingerly lifted the cross from its verdant nest and clutched it to his heart. It was a sign. He knew it. The Christian god had reached out to him. He fell to his knees, this time with his back to Mecca, and prayed aloud the words he had learned in French from the earliest wave of crusaders: *"Notre père qui est aux cieux . . ."* Our Father who art in heaven.

Timeline

1189 – 1192   **The Third Crusade,** whereby the Christians of Western Europe strive to recapture the Holy Land from its Islamic rulers, sometimes returning to their homes in France, Germany, or the British Isles with booty and slaves.

1606 – 1650   **The Ulster Plantation,** established in the north of Ireland by King James I of England for the purpose of tightening England's grip on Catholic Ireland through the allocation of land grants to Protestant tenant-farmers brought in from Scotland and England.

1710 – 1770   **Scots-Irish Immigration to America,** when more than 200,000 immigrants from poor Presbyterian farm families with roots in Scotland but a century working as tenant-farmers in Northern Ireland stream across the Atlantic to escape poverty and oppression by their English overlords.

1774 – 1789   **American Revolutionary War and Independence,** when elected representatives of the thirteen colonies gather in Philadelphia to determine whether they share sufficient common purpose to join together as a single nation.

Genealogy

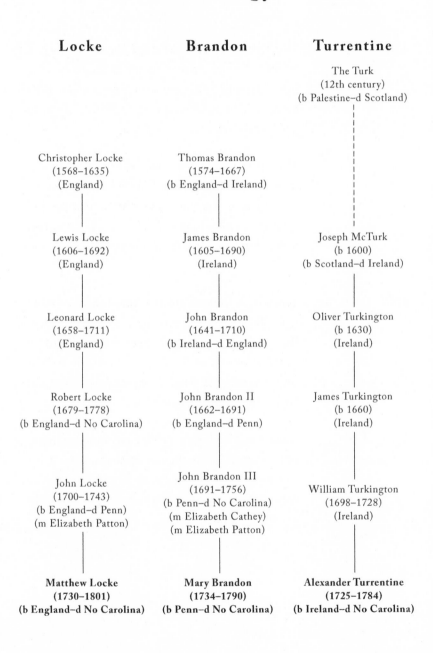

Locke	Brandon	Turrentine
		The Turk (12th century) (b Palestine–d Scotland)
Christopher Locke (1568–1635) (England)	Thomas Brandon (1574–1667) (b England–d Ireland)	
Lewis Locke (1606–1692) (England)	James Brandon (1605–1690) (Ireland)	Joseph McTurk (b 1600) (b Scotland–d Ireland)
Leonard Locke (1658–1711) (England)	John Brandon (1641–1710) (b Ireland–d England)	Oliver Turkington (b 1630) (Ireland)
Robert Locke (1679–1778) (b England–d No Carolina)	John Brandon II (1662–1691) (b England–d Penn)	James Turkington (b 1660) (Ireland)
John Locke (1700–1743) (b England–d Penn) (m Elizabeth Patton)	John Brandon III (1691–1756) (b Penn–d No Carolina) (m Elizabeth Cathey) (m Elizabeth Patton)	William Turkington (1698–1728) (Ireland)
Matthew Locke (1730–1801) (b England–d No Carolina)	**Mary Brandon (1734–1790) (b Penn–d No Carolina)**	**Alexander Turrentine (1725–1784) (b Ireland–d No Carolina)**

Book One

Mary Brandon

Fast Falls the Eventide

Salisbury, North Carolina, 1790

On a clear morning like this, propped up on two down pillows, Mary could glimpse the peaks of the Great Smoky Mountains across the Piedmont plateau. She knew she was dying but the span of green hills capped by blue haze somehow settled her mind.

She had never been a fearful person and she'd be damned if she was going to cower before death. She had left her mark on this land, after all, and that gave her satisfaction. Her husband and four of her sons had fought to win independence, young George resting in the ground at Kennedy's Farm. And now she too would soon join him on the other side.

With Matthew off again doing the work of the people of this new state of North Carolina, she had the house to herself, tended by servants and family, comfortable in the Locke home situated just five miles south of Salisbury on the road to Concord and Charlotte. Matthew had worked hard to accumulate worldly goods for her and the children—running those Conestoga wagons loaded with furs back and forth to the ships at Charles Town with his brother Francis—and he deserved the recognition he was getting as North Carolina delegate to the Federal Constitutional Convention.

In the legislature, they called him the "Honest Farmer." Matthew had voted against ratification of the Constitution, refusing to yield to the forces of power and money in Philadelphia, New York, and Boston. Forever at odds with the Federalists and brash young Alexander Hamilton of New York, Matthew worried about turning this new confederacy of colonies into a centralized power on the backs of the Southern growers.

But once he had accepted the rectitude of the Patriot movement, no man had worked harder to enable the birth of this new nation than Matthew Locke. And before his return, his wife was determined to complete the task that had hung over her head for forty years. There was too much history stuffed into these dusty trunks of family relics hauled all the way from Lancaster County, Pennsylvania.

"Here, Mama, I found another box in the attic. This one has to be yours. It says 'Mary Brandon' on the side."

Margaret settled the dusty case at the foot of her mother's bed, already cluttered with yellowing letters and rusty lockboxes, then leaned in to kiss her on the cheek.

"You've done enough for one day, Mama. Don't tire yourself. Can I help?"

The least adventuresome of the thirteen children of Matthew

and Mary Locke, Margaret was steadfastly devoted and terrified of the resignation she read in her mother's eyes.

"This is something I need to do myself, darlin'. I'll just take care of it a bit at a time."

As her daughter tiptoed out of the room, Mary sighed. *She will struggle when I'm gone, I know that. Margaret is a worrier like her father.*

Steadying herself on the side of the bed, Mary turned the lock on the old trunk. She knew what she was after. The cross slipped gently out of its hidden compartment in the back of the family Bible.

It was as spectacular as she remembered, the uneven gold surface soft to the touch, the colored stones emitting shafts of red and blue in the morning light.

Oh, Alex, she thought, *this belongs to you. Would I could find you to return it.*

Slipping the cross into her bedside drawer, Mary Locke released her head into the softness of the pillows, lost in memories of forty years ago and all that had led her family to the hills of North Carolina and to the winding down of her time on this earth.

The servants bustled in and out with tea and remedies, Margaret hovering as the doctor from Salisbury came round to check her pulse. Matthew had been hesitant to leave her, but he felt a deep responsibility to help shape policy that would make this new Constitution work for all the families of the land.

"And thanks be to the Lord for that," she said out loud. "I need time without him to make sure this one small task left to me is done right."

After the fighting had ended and life returned to normal on the farm, Matthew had turned most of the work over to the boys and set his sights on what he could contribute to proper governance of the new country. He had been a good husband and a good provider, if not an easy man to talk to.

I will not die and leave the secrets of my youth to be discovered by Matthew in loneliness and isolation. There is too much in these letters he could never understand.

All the same, she would not deny herself the pain and pleasure of reliving the sweetness of youth one last time before watching the brittle yellowed parchment flutter into the fire.

20 June 1750
Chester County, Penn

My beloved Mary,

For your own sake more than my own, I implore you to destroy this letter once it has been read. Keep it, my love, forever in your heart but let no one but yourself read these words.

The church has decided. I am banned from the congregation and from Lancaster County. Mister McClaskey has asked me and Sam to stay on here in Chester County after our indentures expire to get him through the fall harvest. In exchange he has promised us a wheat patch on the other side of the river where we can build a cabin and try our hand at farming.

Mary, I soon will be a free man. You know what that means to me. And yet I shall not lay eyes upon your beautiful face again in this life.

Dry your tears, lass. Matthew loves you too and he will be a far better husband than ever I could have been. This is our destiny and God's will. The cross is back in your father's custody and good riddance. It has brought nothing but suffering to me and my family.

When it is safe, leave a message for Kago in the clearing, signaling the hour when you can return to meet him in the usual manner. I trust you and God to make sure the infant is returned to him and to its native tribe when the time is right.

Your scarf is wrapped about my neck and I can still smell you and feel the salt of your skin upon my mouth. The wanting of you will never stop.

But greater yet is my love. You and Matthew will be the bedrock of this new land. Your children and their children will do the right thing to build a better world. I know this to be true.

Your own,
Alex Turrentine

Chapter One

Lancaster County,
Colony of Pennsylvania, 1749

I t was my fourteenth birthday and the September skies were as black and foreboding as the end of time. Just when we might have expected Indian summer to warm up the Pennsylvania countryside for harvest, a storm had blown in, rattling the shutters and peeling Father's hand-split white oak shingles from the roof of our farmhouse.

As a heavy, unrelenting rain began to fall, my brothers and sisters and stepbrothers and stepsisters, under orders from Father, were running in and out, tying down farm equipment, stacking sheaves, and rounding up the chickens. Even our house servants, Bella and Roxie, were enlisted to help their menfolk bring in the cattle from the outer pasture near Manada Creek.

Our big combined family of Brandons and Lockes lived together in a farmhouse built by my father John Brandon in 1740, before Mother died. I was only eight when I lost my mother and left my childhood behind.

Father would sell the produce we couldn't consume ourselves down on the Susquehanna River, piling buckwheat and Indian corn and potatoes onto a raft right here on Manada Creek and running it clear to Middletown, where Swatara Creek meets the river.

Mother had been gone for less than a year when our father met a lady from England who had just acquired ownership of a tavern in Middletown. Elizabeth Locke had scarcely arrived in the colonies after a long sea voyage from London to Philadelphia when she was widowed and left alone in a new land with seven children to care for. I guess neither of them could have lasted long out here without a helpmate. So John Brandon and Elizabeth Locke became husband and wife and doubled the size of our family.

"Mary, come help me bring in the wash before it gets any wetter," urged my sister Anne as she rushed toward the front door with our largest laundry basket in hand.

There was a sulfur smell in the air as the first steady rain saturated the earth that had dried out during the waning weeks of summer. Anne and I laughed as we slipped in puddles already forming, tossing the once nearly-dry breeches and shirts and undergarments into the basket and running for the house.

I had been counting on a special birthday dinner, with accolades from one and all, but victuals and celebration were forgotten in the chaos of battening down the farm as the unexpected storm set in. It was already well into the afternoon when my stepmother gathered the girls to help Roxie with dinner.

"Where is Lizzy?" my stepmother asked, surveying the assembled dinner crew.

Chapter One

The youngest of her children, seven-year-old Lizzy was hardly any help in the kitchen, but she always joined the other girls as we helped our stepmother and the house servants prepare meals.

"Perhaps she's in the parlor with the boys," Margaret suggested. "Let me go check."

Roxie, bent over as she tossed logs into the kitchen fireplace, her round bottom all we could see, leaned around in my stepmother's direction, rivulets of sweat streaming down her shiny black cheeks. "She over at the creek with them Cathey girls."

Roxie's high-pitched tone often implied without saying that whatever was going on in the world was beyond the pale and certainly not anything she would have approved of.

"Oh my Lord," Elizabeth shuddered. "Manada Creek is prone to flooding." She pushed through the kitchen door to find Father.

After an unsuccessful search of the farm, my father and several of the boys set out on horseback, William and Francis joining Father on the path to Manada Creek and Matthew and Richard heading off toward the farmstead of our Cathey cousins. Anne and I jumped into the smaller cart driven by Abraham, Bella's husband, and we took the road toward the upper creek to see if the children might have gone that way.

The road was already muddy and we were jostled side-to-side in the cart as Abe tried to keep the wheels of our wagon out of the soft spots. Rain was whipping through the open cart and we were soaked to the skin. Abe shook his head as we drove over the wooden bridge, muttering "Crick up to the banks already."

By the time we circled back east of Manada Creek, a crowd

was gathered near a sharp bend in the stream which was a favorite fishing spot for our cousins on the other side of the creek. The rain must have started earlier up near the gap in Blue Mountain where the headwaters were located, for the normally placid creek was rushing down the mountain at such a wild pace that the bend had become an island.

The three children were stranded on a bank that was now cut off from the road, with water flowing wildly all around them. Lizzy was straddling a moss-covered fallen log that extended out into the rushing water with her arms outstretched. Her mother's shouts were drowned out by the rushing water and pounding rain.

"Get back off the log, Lizzy, get back!" my stepmother screamed, as Father clutched her arm to restrain her from jumping headfirst into the roaring water.

It seemed to me everyone was shouting and no one doing a thing. I was tempted to jump into the water myself to try to reach my cousins and stepsister, but I was transfixed by the deafening roar of the water and everybody yelling at each other without being heard. It felt like one of those terrifying nightmares where you were about to be eaten alive by an ogre but could neither move nor speak.

I saw my father grab Matthew, screaming something into his ear that caused Matthew to run over to the cart, where old Abe was still sitting on the driver's bench. Matthew and Abe scrambled around in the back of the cart, pulling out a heavy hemp rope. The two of them worked quickly together without having to say a word, calm and purposeful in the face of a crisis.

From the day he arrived, my stepbrother Matthew, who was only a few years older than I and reserved in manner, had looked down on me as if I were a child. In our debates at the dinner table, it was always Matthew who tried to pull two ends of an argument to a middle place. He never got ruffled and never lashed out in anger, approaching every problem with a calm voice of reason that infuriated me. But I could see that Matthew was the one my father looked to first when he sought counsel and it was Matthew to whom my father turned in a crisis.

Abe wrapped one end of the rope securely around the thick trunk of a red cedar as Matthew grabbed the other end and slipped one leg into the roaring water, almost losing his footing. Father reached out and grasped his shirt, preventing Matthew from being swept downriver.

Abe slid into the stream beside Matthew, pushing him back onto the creek bank. "You stay outta here," he instructed. With one large hand wrapped in loops of hemp, Abe slowly started to make his way across Manada Creek to the fishing-bend-turned-island.

After each step, Abe paused to get his bearings, leaning upstream to avoid succumbing to the surging course of the waterway. He was like a stump in the middle of that wild stream, stoically settling each foot into the riverbed, extending his arms outward to maintain balance and waiting patiently until his footing was secure before taking the next step.

As Abe worked his way across the floodwaters, I was afraid to watch, certain he would be swept away to sudden death at any moment. He looked like one of the ancient gods, bracing against the force of the terrible rushing water, all for the sake of little Lizzy and our cousins.

A heavy branch in the churning water crashed into Abe. He lost his footing and was swept into the rapidly moving water. Someone screamed. Miraculously, he was thrown against the roots of a large elm at the edge of the island and was able to grasp a low-hanging branch, the biceps of his massive arms bulging as he strained to hang on. But he had lost his grip on the rope, which Matthew now reeled back onto the muddy creekside where we stood.

While Abe hauled himself up onto the island to join Lizzy and my cousins, Father gathered the older boys, leading them like a human chain across the water. As they began to extend their reach across the creek, each supporting the other from the force of the moving water, Abe stepped back into the stream from the other side and reached out to clasp Father's hand.

The old slave then took one girl at a time down into the water, as each held fast to every man in the chain as she passed, Abe supporting each child with his strong hands and providing shelter from the upstream water with his broad back.

As rain continued to pound the muddy riverbank, slanting into the roiling water like a steel blade, the bedraggled girls were wrapped in blankets, huddling with us along the shore, exhausted but safe.

By the time we were back in the house and changed out of our wet clothing, it was dark outside, rain continuing to pound the roof. Bella and Roxie were hastening to get dinner on the table, but my stepmother, usually the mistress of the kitchen, was too emotionally exhausted from the near loss of her youngest child and namesake to be bothered about feeding the family. She scooped Lizzy up in her arms and, holding her tight, tottered toward Father's study.

Chapter One

While my sister Anne and I went to help with dinner preparation, the boys joined Father, who was warming himself with a brandy in the parlor. When Roxie finally rang the dinner bell, everyone eagerly crowded around the table.

The door to Father's study was cracked open and I could see Elizabeth rocking little Lizzy and murmuring to her. I tapped on the door to let them know about dinner and saw Lizzy, hair still wet but cheerful and safe in her mother's arms.

"Will you be joining us for dinner?" I inquired, not wanting to disturb their privacy.

"We'll be there in a moment, dear," Elizabeth replied. "Do go ahead and start without us."

I of course understood my stepmother's relief at the safe return of Lizzy. But something about seeing them there together, in Father's study, unleashed a deep yearning inside me for my own mother.

Then I noticed Lizzy playing with the small golden cross that Father kept in the back compartment of the Brandon family Bible, which lay open on the desk. *That is not a toy, Lizzy*, I thought but did not say, feeling more resentment than I wanted to admit. It was the Brandon cross, an ancient relic that had been in our family for over a hundred years. Thanks to the protection of this cross, my grandfather's ship made it safely to America. Father kept it in his bedroom in the months after Mother died, drawing comfort from our own symbol of God's love and sacrifice.

Chapter Two

From our bedroom window on the second story of the farmhouse, as far as the eye could see there was nothing but forest, broken here and there by bits of cleared farmland, the hills rising in ridges above the valley. If you travelled as far as the southern ridge, you could almost see the Susquehanna, winding through stands of white oak and sycamore, the vast wilderness of western Pennsylvania and the Allegheny Plateau stretched out beyond the far shore.

Our little farm was backed up against Blue Mountain, and behind it a string of purple ridges—Second Mountain, Sharp, Story—stair-stepping into the Appalachians. The local Indian tribes had been pushed north of the mountains, but they were not happy about it and they made nighttime excursions through Manada Gap and Indiantown Gap to steal from our farms.

We were too far from the Susquehanna River to have easy access to the transportation system that connected cities like Philadelphia and Baltimore on the coast to Lancaster County. We were on the frontier, the river protecting our farm from the vast wilderness to our west, where native tribes fought for dominance and European settlers rarely ventured. The river and all its creeks and tributaries were our lifeblood, sustaining us as well as isolating us.

Manada Creek flowed past our farm, a constant source of life-giving water that murmured and splashed south to Sand Beach where it joined with the rushing waters of the Swatara which flowed west into the mighty Susquehanna. At certain times of the year, these streams were hazardous to cross, cutting us off from all the roads into Philadelphia or Lancaster. Then we would have to find a ford that was not too risky for a wagon laden with goods or travel to one of the rope-ferry crossings where we paid for assistance getting to the other side.

The farmhouse where we lived was built by Father and my older brothers, with the help of our Cathey kin across the creek. Father purchased the finished clapboards and windows in Lancaster and brought them up here by wagon. The stone facing came from our own land, gathered as rubble when Father was clearing the first meadow. The house stood two stories high, faced with stone up to the second floor and clapboard above, with a wide porch and a steep gabled roof.

It was a big house, meant for a big family, but since the arrival of the Lockes, there were brothers and sisters everywhere you turned, and it was almost impossible to find a moment alone or a corner of privacy anywhere in the house.

Between the house and the barn, there was, of course, a privy, as well as a smokehouse, a detached kitchen, and a bunkhouse for the temporary servants who worked for us under bond of indenture. The cabin where our four slaves lived was down close to the creek.

They had their own privy and an open fireplace out front where they cooked their meals.

We had access to a gristmill, as well as two sawmills, over in McAllisterstown, so we had everything we needed to get by well enough in the backcountry.

Father was proud of our farmhouse, and well he should have been since it was one of the finest homes in this part of William Penn's colony. When the cost of land near Philadelphia became too expensive for most immigrants, and taxes imposed by the English Crown too high, farmers had to travel far inland to find affordable land. We were more fortunate than most since Grandfather Brandon had been granted land in William Penn's colony back when Pennsylvania was still largely unsettled by white people. Father always said Pennsylvania was the best colony in the Americas because everyone was free to practice his own religion and live as he wished—everyone, that is, except the African slaves.

The scattered farms in Lancaster County were too remote to establish friendships with girls and boys my own age. We did, thank goodness, have my mother's kin, the Catheys, nearby. And, of course, an abundance of brothers and sisters underfoot in the farmhouse. Father said I had my nose in a book all the time, but in truth I was hard-pressed to find time to read, given all my chores around the farm. But for me it was a way to find a little privacy, lost in Robinson Crusoe's adventures or Gulliver's travels, trying to escape a loneliness I sometimes felt, even amongst so many people.

I had travelled as far away as Philadelphia, which was a grand city with people from every part of the world. Philadelphia was full of Quakers, with Friends' meetinghouses on every corner. The Quakers were big landowners who followed to the letter the mandates of the Penn family that townships be laid out in an orderly fashion. William Penn, who founded this colony, was a Quaker, and Father said he struck a fair deal with the native tribes in our part of Pennsylvania. But not everybody in our family was so sure. We belonged to the Church of England and had a natural suspicion of Quakers and all their talk of peace and goodwill.

In the parlor after supper, Father liked to engage everybody—boys and girls, down to the very youngest—in his debates about the politics and religions of the colonies, and what was right and what was wrong.

"Penn had a vision of this colony as a peaceable kingdom and he guaranteed the local Indians their own land which they could manage in their own way," Father argued.

"Oh sure," Francis countered. "He sold them that property they call Indiantown down near Lancaster, conveniently forgetting that all of Pennsylvania had belonged to the natives before King Charles gave it to Penn."

"In any event," Matthew added, "since Penn died, his sons have joined the Anglican Church and left behind all that Quaker peace-making. The Conestoga must know Thomas Penn cares nothing about his father's old treaty. That's why they're hunting up here in the mountains and making trouble on Lancaster County farms."

The Ulster Scots, who came in droves from across the sea, settled wherever they liked, ignoring all the rules made by the Penns, or so said Father. He called them Ulster Scots, a term I didn't understand because they came from Ireland, not Scotland, in ever-increasing numbers and ever-apparent poverty. They attended their own churches, called Presbyterian, and were inspired by charismatic ministers who worked themselves into a lather with talk of the devil, fire and brimstone, and the glory of salvation, all in a manner unseemly to those of us accustomed to the beauty and poetry of our beloved Anglican hymns and the King James Bible.

At the same time, I felt a bond to these Irish immigrants. My own mother and her Cathey relatives had roots back in the northern part of Ireland. Like many English people, they had helped to run the plantations in that papist country back in the 17th century, returning to England with a lilt in their speech and nostalgia for the superstitions and customs of the green island.

I had been born in this colony, a whole wide ocean away from England, which we had been raised to think of as our homeland. But I think my romantic notions about London had more to do with the loneliness I had felt out here on the farm since my mother died.

When I was feeling sad, I would often steal into Father's dark study and rummage through his old papers, always looking for a new book to read or something to touch that had Mother's imprint on it. Her old letters were tucked into the family Bible and, while caressing the smooth surface of the ancient cross which was hidden in a compartment in the back of the Bible, I would lose myself in the words written in her own dear hand. Maybe Father had forgotten her, but I never would.

After Mother took to her bed, having given over management of the household to my sister Anne, she and I spent hours together every day. She often asked me to read verses from the Bible or a favorite poem, which she would listen to intently, her eyes closed and her head resting on a pillow.

"Mary," she would say, "you are as clever a child as any I gave birth to. You took to reading before I even had a chance to teach you, sounding out even the longest words on your own. Darlin', you can do anything you set your mind to and don't *ever* let anybody tell you any different."

We still had many relatives in London—the greatest city in the world—and in my loneliness and longing for my mother, I would imagine myself living in London, having tea with ladies of style and hearing symphony music in a concert hall. I maintained a correspondence with my favorite aunt, who lived in London, whose letters filled me with a passion to learn about all the new ideas that people were talking about in the cities of Europe.

When I wrote to her about the terrible flood and the heroism of our slave Abraham, Aunt Agatha responded that there was an outcry among the Quakers of London against the enslavement of Africans and the immorality of depriving a man of his freedom for life. She told me that the big farms in the Southern colonies were bringing in black slaves from Africa by the shipload—free labor to harvest all that cotton and tobacco.

Father says it was the English and the Dutch who started the slave trade in the first place and now the whole Southern economy relied on it.

"The American colonies need more manpower to turn the forests into farms," he argued. "Even here on our little farm with our big

21

family, we need extra hands to clear the fields and bring in the harvest. If only we could attract enough immigrants, the rich farmland of these colonies would provide sustenance to families from all over the world who might have perished from hunger where they were."

But Abe and Bella hadn't decided to come here on their own. Surely they would prefer to make their own choices about where they lived and what they did. If they were free, they might decide to move to Philadelphia and start a small business. There's nothing Abe can't do, whether it's farming or building. And I'm sure Bella could get a job cooking at a tavern or an inn.

Maybe we could bring more indentured servants to the farm to take their place. Though our servants were poor Irish who had to work off the cost of their passage to America, at least they were eventually able to tear up their bonds of indenture. Then they could live where they wished and even marry and raise a family.

No one should have to be a slave forever.

Chapter Three

Matthew jammed the shovel into the soft earth behind the barn where he had been mucking out the stall.

"Mary, come speak to me for a minute."

Having grown up in London, Matthew spoke in the clipped manner of a proper Englishman, a formality that felt out of place on our little farm at the edge of the Pennsylvania Colony, where all of us Brandons had been born. Even Father had put aside the formality of high English in favor of the softer manner of speech of the American colonies.

I was on the way back to the house after gathering eggs and the last thing I wanted was a lecture from my stepbrother. Five years older than I, Matthew had decided to take me on as his special project. Like everything else, Matthew took seriously his responsibility to act as big brother to his adopted Brandon kin. Anne thought Matthew was handsome, but he was too stiff and bossy for my taste. True, he was tall and strong and polite to a fault. But so impossibly and tediously predictable!

As Matthew approached me, sweat dripped from his prematurely receding hairline past bird's-egg blue eyes and down his cheeks in grimy rivulets.

"I heard Mother and Father talking this morning. You're upset about not being included in the lessons we'll be getting from Master Fry."

The early morning sun was breaking through the morning mist and backlit Matthew's profile with yellow-white light.

St. James Church in Lancaster was starting a school for boys, but it was too far away for the young men of our family to attend. So a Quaker teacher—Master Elias Fry—would be coming to the farm twice a week starting on Friday. To my dismay and anger, Father intended that only the boys be included in his instruction. Disregarding my tears and pleading, Father's heart was hardened against me.

"Mary, you fight against every rule of the house and it worries our parents," Matthew scolded. "We couldn't survive the winter if everyone dropped their chores two afternoons a week. It isn't possible to keep the farm running that way."

I glared at him with all the venom I could muster.

"And why is it *you* deserve an education, but I am consigned to chores?"

"Because girls don't need the skills Master Fry can teach. Richard and William and Francis and I will have to manage farms, keep ledgers of accounts and understand politics and history to meet our responsibilities. Education is essential. I know you love your reading, but we're trying to run a farm here. We're not aristocrats who can afford to spend our afternoons reading and drinking tea."

"I am as capable as you are of understanding numbers and politics," I insisted. "And you haven't heard, I suppose, that there's now a school for girls called Linden Hall in Lancaster County down near Lititz run by the Moravians. Why do you think their parents would pay the money to see them educated? Maybe it's just that the German-speaking people are more advanced than the English, could that be it?" I delivered this closing argument as forcefully as my fourteen years would permit, glaring at my stepbrother for emphasis as I finished.

I could see that the truth of my unassailable position left him without response.

"Matthew, put down your shovel and sit with me for a moment."

Matthew's face turned a brighter shade of crimson at my offer to divert him from his chores, but he followed me over to the bench at the edge of the apple orchard.

"Here," I said patting the place beside me on the wooden bench. "Since you presume to be my superior in all matters of the mind, come and explain your politics to me."

Matthew sighed in consternation and futility and joined me on the bench.

"I was thinking about what you said last night, Matthew. You know, about the Penns and how things have changed now that the family business has been taken over by William Penn's children. Do you think the English have broken their promises to the local tribes?"

Matthew looked at me in that honest way of his and I could tell he was thinking about how to answer.

"I think my parents, like your grandparents, came over here to make a better life for their families," Matthew ventured. "They have worked hard to make this a place that will support families and build a just society. I don't think any of them wished harm to the natives."

"Well, whether they wished it or not, you have to think life was better for them before we came," I insisted.

I could tell he was thinking hard about this and I gave him a playful shove.

"Tell me what you think about the Crown's taxation of the colonies, Matthew. Share with me what Father keeps away from the delicate ears of his daughters."

"Mary, there's nothing you would find interesting."

"Oh yes I would. You so underestimate me, Matthew Locke. Are we a family of Tories? Does Father support King George?"

"We're a family of farmers. I don't think your father cares much one way or the other about Tories."

"Well we must care, Matthew. How else can we change things? Why should we support King George when I've heard Father say he is stripping hardworking farm families like ours of every bit of profit to fund his ambition for more and more colonies around the world?"

"Because loyalty to king and country is our duty. Would you prefer that the Pennsylvania land grants be given over entirely to the papists of France? Or to the Dutch?"

"It isn't Dutch, it's Deutsch," I corrected, laughing at his mistake. "It means German."

Matthew, never able to hide a feeling, tightened, embarrassed that I knew more about something than he did. Always so serious,

Matthew was, so blindly devoted to God and country and, heaven help us, King George II.

But I knew his soft side and gave him a shy smile.

"Oh, Matthew, can't you help me with Father? You know I'm capable of learning and I can't bear to be excluded from the chance to continue my education. What will become of me? I'm no better off than the servants. I will never have the chance to become an educated woman."

Matthew furrowed that golden-blond brow of his and studied the ground resolutely. When he finished his studious investigation of his feet, he turned to me and took my hand, the hint of a smile replacing that serious and fretful look he often bore.

"Mary, don't be sad," he cajoled, with a look of genuine concern and tolerant amusement on his face. "You should of course be educated. I saw you pouring over your father's copy of Voltaire's *Letters on the English* last night. You're just about the smartest person I know."

I assumed Matthew had taken my hand without thought, as he composed an appropriate response to my entreaty. But I noticed that he didn't remove his hand from mine.

At that moment, Matthew's older brother Francis, along with the young slave Peter, came around the side of the barn to put away tools they had been using to repair the ox cart.

Francis Locke was eight years older than Matthew and closer to him than anyone else in the family. He was not as tall or as fair as Matthew, and was more solid in build, but they had a similar look around the eyes and furrow of the brow when thinking about something. But where Matthew was circumspect and careful of his words, Francis was more apt to speak out, and sometimes without thinking.

Matthew still held my hand in his own, which caused his older brother to stop in his tracks and smile.

"So you're out here courting your sister, are you, Matthew?" he asked with a laugh.

Matthew dropped my hand, giving his older brother a glaring look, but didn't respond.

"I was speaking to Matthew about my desire to be included in Master Fry's lessons," I replied tartly. "And I'll thank you not to make smart remarks about courtship when I am trying earnestly to enlist Matthew's help."

"I'd be careful about that if I were you, Mary Brandon," he warned. "My brother may demand a high price for his services."

Then, after a wink at the two of us, he turned to Peter. "Come on, boy, let's stash the gear."

Peter lived in the slave quarters with Bella and Abraham and their daughter Roxie, who had still been a child when she and her parents were purchased by my grandfather to help him clear land for the family's first homestead in William Penn's colony. Peter had been the property of a neighboring Lancaster County farmer and had become Roxie's love when they were no more than twelve. And when the farmer decided to move south to the Shenandoah Valley, Roxie cried and carried on so that old Abraham had to plead with Father to buy the boy or else expect to lose his investment in a perfectly healthy slave girl as the result of a broken heart.

As Francis and Peter stowed their tools in the barn, I turned back to Matthew, eager to return to our discussion. "Peter is finally becoming a reliable hand in the fields, is he not?"

"He is improving, but he will never be worth the half of Abraham," observed Matthew.

"Well, who could fill Abe's shoes?" I asked, stating the obvious. "Did you see his strength and courage during the flood? He risked his life to bring your sister to safety. How can you put a price on that? And how can you justify holding a man of that character as a piece of property, never in his life able to go where he wishes or do what he wants?"

I realized I was getting worked up about this and angry at Matthew for something that wasn't his fault. But the injustice of it had stuck in my craw ever since the flood.

Matthew just shook his head. "Mary, who among us can go where we wish and do what we want in this life? Your father is trying to feed and clothe a large family. Sometimes you talk like a child."

With that, I took my leave of Matthew, throwing up my hands at any meager hope of bringing him around to a position of reason.

Chapter Four

7 October 1749
Lancaster County, Penn

Dearest Aunt Agatha,

I received your letter of 13 August a fortnight ago but have been kept so busy with the drudgery of cleaning up and drying out around the farm after the creek overran its banks that I am only now able to compose my reply. I do so sincerely want you to know the joy it brings me to hear from you and to get news of all the exciting things happening in London.

I was amused and delighted to hear of the uproar caused by Lady Montagu's Blue Stocking salon and I think when I reach an age of social maturity I shall form such a society in the backwoods of Pennsylvania, just to expand the horizons of this isolated land. How exciting to think about the ladies of London gathering for serious discussions of philosophy and politics and science. Science! Can you imagine it?

I rushed out immediately to tell my stepbrother Matthew all about the Blue Stocking Society. Matthew is shocked at almost anything I tell him, so shy and conventional is he. All the same, he is tall and handsome and gentle. So, though I pretend to treat him with great disdain and disrespect, he is truly my best friend here, except for sister Anne, and I only tease him because he is adorable when he blushes from head to toe. I honestly think, Auntie, that he's in love with me. But I have no intention of marrying and certainly not of settling on a husband before I have learned anything about men.

We had a frightful scare last Friday. This country is teeming with Indians who periodically breach the gaps in the Blue Mountain Ridge to attack the settlers who are farming the land east of the river. These incursions have been so worrisome that a new fort is going to be built at Indiantown Gap with regular patrols to warn the settlers of any trouble. We have heard for months that the natives encamped to the north of us are forming confederations with the French who are so plentiful in the Canadian settlements.

One of the servants who is helping us tend the fields during a term of indenture was working alone in the flax field to complete cleanup after harvest. He was a cheerful boy, Willie by name and not much older than myself, come to this country from the Ulster Plantations in the North of Ireland to escape the wretched poverty of that land.

He didn't show up for the servants' dinner, an event that brings in the field hands promptly at noon. My stepbrother Francis went out to the flax field to find him, but no Willie was to be found. His till lay askew in the furrows and his water canteen was left under an ash tree. In the field itself, thrust into the dirt, was an extraordinary artifact—a rustic wooden spear adorned with bright feathers and beads.

Auntie, we fear he has been taken prisoner by the Indians. Stories of hideous abuse of captives are rampant in these parts. We fear the worst for our poor Willie.

I thought he might have run away to escape the servitude required during the last three years of his bond. But Father says he would have taken his canteen and, anyway, there are stiff penalties for those who attempt to escape their bonds of indenture. He was treated well here and had given no indication of discontent.

Chapter Four

And now, as you might imagine, everyone is alert to danger and we never send boys out to the fields alone. This requires a larger pool of labor and Father says we must acquire the services of more field servants to complete the harvest.

I have thought much about your last letter and the movement you spoke of among Quakers to free the slaves. I can't imagine such a thing could ever happen, but I feel just as you do, that it cannot be right for one human to own another.

Father has turned a cold ear to my passion for education and denies me access to the boys' tutor. I am in need of your counsel, Auntie, as to how to overcome this unreasonable denial.

I think of Mother often these days. Do you remember our discussion about the family cross? Father keeps it in the hidden compartment of the family Bible. You once told me of its provenance in Ireland during our family's time managing plantation land there. Can you tell me more? Do you remember how Mother loved it? When I am missing her most, I take comfort from holding our cross, just as she did when she took ill.

Your most loving niece,
Mary

Chapter Five

Father and Elizabeth were seated near the window box in the parlor on a small sofa that looked out over the cherry orchard. I had come in search of my needlework, left on the end table near the fireplace, and decided to resume the task in a sunny corner of the room.

"I understand, my dear," said Father, his voice gentle in response to Elizabeth's concern, just as it used to be when my own mother was distressed about something. "But there are no affordable properties closer to Philadelphia. And we were given assurance that the Penns would prevail upon the king to provide sufficient military presence to keep the natives on the other side of the river and beyond Stony Mountain. They're building a new fort near the gap. Be patient, Elizabeth. This is where we must put a stake in the ground and show what we're made of—for the future of our children."

I knew they were talking about Little Willie, the servant who had disappeared. Elizabeth was scared to death and she kept all of us as close to the house as possible.

Chapter Five

I was equal parts scared and curious. On trips to Lancaster I had observed Indians around town, some who worked in the gardens of the Anglican Church and a few who came in from nearby villages to sell baskets and furs, but I understood nothing of their beliefs or practices.

Elizabeth was a handsome woman for her age, but her voice had a tremulous quality that made her appear more vulnerable than she was.

"John, I don't feel safe here with the children when you're away," she confessed. "There is talk of unrest among the tribes beyond the river. Just last week Andrew Cathey was accusing the French of getting the natives worked up to help them push British traders out of the Allegheny region."

Elizabeth was worried because she knew Father would be gone much of the next day when he and Francis were to pick up the indentured field hands who would fill in for our lost Willie.

"We will be back with the new servants before dark," he assured her, "and I've instructed Matthew and the younger boys to work close to the house tomorrow. You need not be afraid, Elizabeth."

"Of course you are right, my dear," she conceded. "And since you have all day alone in the wagon with Francis, consider the opportunity to talk to him about a match with Anne. He will be less likely to disregard the prodding of a father."

My needlework stopped cold as Elizabeth's words reached me. She and Father were conspiring to arrange a marriage between my sister Anne and Matthew's older brother Francis? This suggestion was shocking and fascinating to me, not so much because of the possible arranged marriage between a Brandon and a Locke, but for what it might portend for my own future.

At fourteen, I was of an age to consider marriage. But not so long as my older sister was unclaimed. It was understood that life on the frontier required the combined efforts of a husband and a wife to raise a family and wrest a living from the land. Perhaps they had discussed my own prospects, a thought which I found both alarming and intriguing.

"Dearest Elizabeth, he is your son, not mine. I know Anne is approaching an age when it may be more difficult to find a husband. Anne and Francis are friendly enough, though perhaps too much alike. Francis may prefer to wed someone younger, and frankly I've seen no spark of interest on either side."

"Well, given how far we are from civilization," Elizabeth countered, "I'd say beggars can't be choosers."

After we were in bed, Anne and I talked late into the night, whispering to avoid waking the other girls. Like always, Anne was trying her best to be a mother to me. But she was just a sister after all, though thirteen years my senior, and too conventional in her thinking to be a real confidante. Already well on the road toward becoming a spinster, she had little understanding of my passion for a life painted in vivid colors or my deep longing for education. I knew she loved me and understood how much I still felt the loss of our mother. But her efforts at comfort often wound up feeling like a lecture.

I turned back to our topic of the kidnapped servant boy.

"Anne, what would you do if you were captured by Indians and dragged off to their village?" I whispered.

Chapter Five

"Heavens," she shuddered. "What would cause you to ask such a thing?"

"They would make you marry a fierce, half-naked warrior who would ravish you every night after he came home from killing animals and scalping settlers," I proclaimed dramatically, before burying my laughter in my pillow.

"Stop it, Mary."

"I would bargain with him," I considered thoughtfully. "Make him my friend. Just to stay alive. Anyway, it might be preferable to wasting away on this farm. Maybe the Indians would let me learn something."

"Mary, don't be silly. Heaven knows, we've been taught well enough by both parents since early childhood. Even in London or Philadelphia, you would not be permitted to continue your lessons at age fourteen. The Good Book tells us about a woman's place in the world. Out here so far from civilization, women have the most important job of all—making a home and raising the children. You don't need an education for that."

"But I know I can contribute to the family's success as much as the boys can if I am educated. I'm pretty good at numbers and I already help Father in reckoning accounts for the farm. In Philadelphia many women are teachers and shopkeepers."

"Not proper women. Even our mother would not have permitted you to engage in such manly positions."

I turned away from her to hide the tears that were starting to well up.

Anne touched my shoulder, gathering me to her just the way

Mother used to do. That opened the floodgates and I cried hard, burrowing into her arms as she made soothing noises.

"Now, now, don't be so sad. You've nothing to be sad about. You're smart and beautiful. All the boys will want to wed you."

As my tears subsided in her arms, I knew my sweet sister was thinking of her own circumstances and how time was quickly passing when she might find a husband.

"Anne," I said. "I overheard Father and Elizabeth talking about you today."

She sat up and gave me a hard look. "What about me?" she asked.

"About . . . about you and Francis, you know, getting married," I stammered in response.

"What a perfectly absurd idea. We are kin. It wouldn't be proper," Anne huffed.

"Well, you're not really kin. Just by marriage."

All the warmth had turned to chill as Anne stiffened at the thought of parental matchmaking.

"I'll not be married off to a brother just to save me from the crime of spinsterhood," she insisted.

"Anne, if you don't marry first, I may never have a chance!"

Father was set on keeping our large brood intact, and that included our own mother's clan of Scots-Irish cousins, the Catheys, who owned the land across Manada Creek. He and my stepmother had been diligent in seeking brides for the older boys by setting up visitations with parents on neighboring farms, and they were pleased to see our tribe expanding. While the Ulster branch of our family might not object to a union of cousins, Father was opposed to marriages between close blood relatives. That definitely cut back on the limited supply of husbands available to Anne and myself. But I could tell Anne wasn't convinced by my petition that she wed our stepbrother Francis just to clear the path for me.

"Mary," she said, drawing herself up and giving me that older sister look, "I know you well enough to be certain you'll wed when someone comes along who captures your heart, with or without my own marriage first."

"I don't want a husband, Anne," I replied. "Just an education. But if you won't marry Francis, Father will probably offer you up to one of the Catheys."

"Oh, good Lord," she retorted. "I guess I would have to become a Presbyterian."

"Anne, did you hear Father talking to Matthew last night about our own family's history in Northern Ireland?" I asked.

The great-grandparents on both sides of our combined family—our Brandon ancestors and the forebears of Matthew and Francis Locke—had once owned land in Northern Ireland, granted by the king to the guilds of London and others owed favors, with the understanding that they would populate the land with solid English or Scottish tenants who would help stem the rebelliousness of the native Irish with their pagan roots and papist allegiances. But when taxes had to be raised to support England's worldwide colonization and its perpetual warring with France, it was naturally the Presbyterian Scots, and not the English stakeholders, who bore the brunt of that financial burden.

Having stayed awake so late talking to Anne, I was slow to rise the next morning and behind in my chores all day. Late that afternoon, there was much excitement as Father and Francis, sitting in the driver's seat of the old wagon, pulled up to the house in a cloud of dust with two passengers in the back.

Father jumped down, with a hug for Elizabeth and enthusiastic scratches behind the ears for the dogs. He walked to the back of the wagon and gave a hand to two young men who crawled out with meager bags of gear.

"Sam and Alex," he said, extending his arm toward the new arrivals. "These boys are brothers, newly arrived in the colony from Ulster Province in the north of Ireland. We've picked up their contracts for the next six months or so from two farmers in Chester County. Francis, show them the bunkhouse."

The older of the two new arrivals tipped his hat without looking up and followed Francis down the path past the barn. His brother slid out behind him, flashing a smile to the gathered clan, and walked right up to us.

"Alex Tur'in'ton," he said, with a heavy brogue that revealed roots in the Scottish Lowlands, with an Irish lilt at the end. "Your humble and obedient servant."

I couldn't be sure whether he was being cheeky or respectful in his use of this common greeting, given his position and ours. But whatever he meant by it, any awkwardness was instantly dispelled by his disarming smile.

"It is our pleasure to be here at the Brandon farm and we are grateful for your warm welcome."

He looked to be about Matthew's age, maybe a little older, with clear hazel-green eyes that seemed to be almost transparent, wind-swept hair that curled around his ears in shades of ginger and carrot, and a smile that lit up our little farmyard the way the sun flashes from behind a cloud after an April storm. He was slender, but well formed, and moved with grace and confidence as he met the family.

He passed around the circle of onlookers, shaking hands and bowing. When he came to me, with a slight inclination of his head and what for all the world appeared to be a wink, Alex said gravely "Your servant, ma'am."

The new servant exhibited such warmth and enthusiasm that I was looking forward to his cheerful addition to our little community.

Chapter Six

When harvest was completed, plans were made for the biggest excursion of the year, a trip to Lancaster to stock up on provisions: replacement parts for aging farm equipment, cloth for new garments, staples for the kitchen. From my vantage point on an isolated farm, this town at the hub of activity for the entire Susquehanna Valley was as thrilling as Philadelphia or London.

With more than 750 people living there, Lancaster had become one of the Pennsylvania Colony's centers of commerce. Father bragged that it was one of the biggest and most successful inland towns of the whole British Empire. New farms were popping up everywhere along the Susquehanna River and farmers needed mills, ferries, and tools. As settlements spread west and with Indian incursions on the rise, local militias had constant need of guns and ammunition, which Lancaster's merchants were able to provide. And the skilled German-speaking artisans in and around Lancaster built the finest covered wagons in all the colonies.

We always left behind a small crew to manage the farm, while most of the family and many of the servants, all of us packed into two wagons, would journey in tandem through forested countryside and across rippling streams before we joined the well-travelled road into Lancaster, where we camped near town on the farm of a family related by marriage to our Cathey cousins.

For weeks ahead of the trip, our dinner table conversation turned to cheerful debates about which shops in Lancaster were essential to our shopping, which relatives we must visit along the way, and what to pack up for the journey. Our big dinner meal was midday on the farm, with a smaller supper in the evening after our work was done.

One afternoon as we cleared the table after dinner, Matthew pulled me aside. I could see that he was much pleased with himself and eager to share some exciting news.

"Well, Brother Matthew," I said, "since it's urgent to speak with me, perhaps you're going to help me clear the table. Since you wasted yesterday afternoon practicing your Latin with Master Fry, it is indeed time for you to do some honest labor."

If he thought I had forgotten about the personal affront in being excluded from the lessons, he was misguided.

"It wasn't all that interesting, Mary. You didn't miss much," he assured me, gathering a handful of dinnerware.

"And you would tell me if you learned anything interesting?"

"Of course I would. You have my promise."

"I'm just frightfully bored out here, you know."

"I know you are. But I have some news that may cheer you up. We have been petitioning your father for permission to go to a dance in Lititz, a little Moravian town outside Lancaster. He has finally consented. And, Mary, I have finally convinced him that you are old enough to go. I promised to keep you out of harm's way. I wanted to be the first to tell you."

And, with that, Matthew smiled and headed out the door to return to the fields, leaving me utterly speechless.

My head was spinning. A dance? Out here in this wilderness? Where did he say it was? And what on earth would I wear?

The days that followed seemed to drag on endlessly as I impatiently awaited the journey to Lancaster and my first dance.

As we loaded the wagon for our trip, I was surprised that Alex and Sam were climbing into the servants' wagon and commented to Father that I hadn't expected them to travel with us, so soon after their arrival.

"They are much engaged with their Covenanter Presbyterian Church back where they regularly work. Alex asked if I would consider letting them come along to help out in Lancaster, then spend a day or two with their church community before we head back," Father replied. "I could see no harm in it."

Although it was a long uncomfortable journey into Lancaster, nothing could diminish our excitement about an adventure away from the farm. The family wagon, though not as large as the new covered wagons being built for settlers in Lancaster, which people called Conestoga wagons, had a barrel frame and heavy sailcloth covering that kept us dry in inclement weather. It accommodated ten passengers, along with two drivers up front, and we entertained ourselves with guessing games and stories as we rolled through the green Pennsylvania countryside.

Chapter Six

Once we were south of the Swatara Creek crossing, it felt like a different world to me—not at all like the isolated farmland where we lived. People were coming and going as if late for an engagement. We passed well-dressed gentlemen on horseback headed toward Philadelphia to deal with important matters of commerce or governance. So many questions kindled my imagination. Who are they going to meet? What news of the colony will they share? What are the secrets hidden in their hearts?

The rumble of passing wagons picked up as we approached Lancaster, where a constant stream of carts laden with grains and produce made their way into town, sharing the road with farmers headed back home with plow parts and bridles, cotton and wool fabric from the cloth spinners of northern England, and muskets to protect the farm from marauding natives.

As we entered Lancaster, there were excited exclamations about changes in the town since our last visit.

"Look at the size of that!"

"What is it?"

"A church of some kind."

"Look at the steeple."

Lancaster had churches on almost every corner, serving the Anglican, Lutheran, Calvinist, Moravian, and Catholic communities. Many of the settlers had come to the colonies in search of freedom to practice their own kind of worship, and it was these churches erected by the community that provided the social center and moral foundation for their lives.

"Father, will the new servants meet their friends here in Lancaster?"

I asked, wondering whether we would stop to let them off at one of these churches.

"No, they're going to help us load up first. Then we'll leave them at the White Swan, where they will be picked up," he responded. "There is not yet a Presbyterian Church in Lancaster since most of the Irish towns are south of here in Chester County, but I understand there is one to be built soon. The boys will meet us back in Lititz," Father added.

I felt a thrill as we trotted into the thriving town, with its impressive courthouse on Centre Square, a real prison, and substantial dwellings along King and Queen streets.

Matthew pointed to a two-story brick home at the corner of Lime and Grant which could well have stood along any London thoroughfare.

"You know," he offered as we drove past, "when James Hamilton laid out the town, there was nothing out here. His father bought the tract for 30 pounds 10 shillings back in London as an investment for his son. The only activity in these parts was over at Wright's Ferry by the river. Still, James was able to sell the lots without any trouble at all, what with all the Germans flooding into these parts, and to this day they still have to pay him seven shillings a year ground rent for each lot."

We always looked forward to seeing Centre Square, where the brick-faced courthouse soared skyward to a bell tower that had a working clock on each face and a large bell in the cupola imported all the way from Italy, which rang every hour on the hour.

As we passed St. James Church of England, with its spire visible from all around the countryside, Father reminded us how important it was to maintain our British traditions here in the colonies. In spite of our family's modest means, Father always saw the world as an Englishman, somehow assuming that other peoples were less capable and less deserving.

"The Anglicans sent Reverend Richard Locke to establish this church," Father reminded us, "ensuring that our English traditions are not overwhelmed by the influence of German and French and Irish immigrants."

"Is the priest a relative of yours, Matthew?" I wondered.

"No, but a theologian of renown in England. Richard Locke is a scholar who can make something of this new church in Lancaster."

I was surprised at the number of native people walking the streets and selling goods in the market. The townsfolk didn't appear to be frightened of the Indians, as we were out on the farm, but they weren't on personal terms with them either. I was curious about these natives. What must they think of this splendid city, arising on ground that was once merely forest and river? Surely they must be astounded by the magnificent bell towers and mills. Once wandering aimlessly through empty lands, they could now see with their own eyes the emergence of a city square with a brick courtyard, tall spires that emitted musical tones across the city, and barracks that could house fifty British soldiers.

Studying the faces of the Indians as we passed them, I didn't see the expressions of delight and admiration that I expected. But perhaps their culture taught an impassiveness of expression to maintain privacy of intent.

After Father pulled up alongside the courthouse, we split off into groups to begin our shopping. Anne and I walked down Vine and up Duke, admiring the sturdy buildings and the well-dressed residents of Lancaster.

"Anne, look at her bonnet," I whispered in amazement.

"I think I could make something similar if I gathered enough beautiful feathers," Anne suggested.

I had to laugh. "Anne, you would be a sight to see in that."

We strolled and commented on people as they passed, keeping our eyes appropriately lowered when young men, whom we guessed to be lawyers or ministers based on their splendid attire, hurried past.

The Lancaster barracks housed the militia that provided protection to farms all over the county and we saw many handsome soldiers who seemed to take more than a little interest in Anne and myself.

I was carrying several empty canvas bags over one arm in anticipation of the wonderful fabric and yarn I planned to pick up in town. Anne and I were peering into the window of a leather shop when someone tapped me on the shoulder. "I think you dropped this, mistress."

He was a ruddy young soldier, plump and cheerful, looking splendid in his uniform, and grinning ear to ear at his nerve to approach us.

Anne and I both blushed, but once I gathered myself together, I made a proper curtsy to the soldier, retrieving my bag gratefully. "Thank you kindly, sir."

His friends were sniggering in the background and Anne was mortified.

Chapter Six

"Perhaps you young ladies would care to join us for a glass of ale?" he offered, to the appreciation of his friends.

Anne grabbed me by the arm and pulled me off in the opposite direction with such force that I could only shrug my shoulder as I looked back at the disappointed soldiers.

We picked up a copy of the *Lancaster Journal*, which was published twice a week, and were fascinated to read about local disputes and upcoming sales at shops carrying cloth and books, teapots and pans.

"I saw you talking to Francis outside the apothecary's shop," I confessed to Anne. "What did he say? Is he going to ask for your hand?"

"Of course not, Mary," she brushed me off, turning to the next interesting sight.

When we returned to our meeting place near the general store, Anne went inside, but I continued to wander down the block, past a tavern with a lively clientele and into a street market where several Indian women were offering goods for sale, which were laid out upon woven blankets on the ground.

I was curious about these native people who had kidnapped our poor Willie and who were reputed to hang the scalps of victims on their tents as décor. What made them so murderous and savage? And why did they hate white people?

Lancaster was the perfect place to observe the habits of Indians. As I had learned from Father's lessons in the parlor, this was the site of the 1744 treaty between the Six Iroquois Nations and representatives of the colonies of Maryland, Virginia, and Pennsylvania. Lancaster was at the very heart of the fragile peace between the European settlers and native tribes.

After checking to see that no one had emerged from the store where Elizabeth and the children were measuring cloth, I studied a plump old woman with leathery skin who was seated on the ground, tightly woven baskets made of long grasses, straw brooms and an array of colorful beads spread on a blanket before her. Two native boys scampered nearby, laughing and tossing a bag of some sort. The woman, whom I took to be their grandmother, would occasionally reprimand them, using words I did not understand. The children ignored her for the most part, which didn't seem to bother her.

I pretended to be shopping to get a better look at her. I think she knew what I was up to. After ignoring me for a while, she looked up with a disarmingly sweet smile, muttering endearments in her native language, and winking at me as she spoke. I had such a longing to communicate with her, so tried my hand at making some sort of contact.

"Lovely goods you have here," I murmured softly, afraid to look her in the eye.

I was leaning over the blanket to feel the texture of a geometrically patterned carry basket so tightly woven that its design looked like it was painted, when I felt a sharp blow to my arm and was literally knocked off my feet, falling face first into the object of native art. I looked up into the horrified face of an Indian boy of about ten years. Like me, he had been thrown to the ground from the force of the collision. He was still clutching the rough branch which he had been swinging at an airborne bean bag but which had instead connected squarely with my left forearm.

Chapter Six

The tumble knocked the breath out of me. After making sure I hadn't destroyed the basket, I attended to my arm, which had a scrape with a few drops of blood dripping down my wrist, more stunned by the unexpected collision than physically harmed.

Suddenly there were Indian grandmothers and aunties descending upon me from everywhere—tending to my wounds, reprimanding the boys, and jabbering away with clucking tongues to one another in their incomprehensible speech.

The elderly woman who had been tending the stall when I arrived helped me gently to my feet and urged me to demonstrate that I could still walk unattended. She studied the abrasion intently and apparently concluded that there was no serious damage, which she communicated to me in mime, patting me on the head from time to time to attest to her sympathy and my resilience.

Then an angry young matron with black braids to her waist and a strong hand on the neck of the boy who had caused the collision drug him over to me like a sacrificial lamb and deposited him at my feet. In a very soft voice, he appeared to be expressing his remorse while keeping one eye on the woman I assumed was his mother in case he should need to fend off a blow.

I gathered myself together and paid my respects as the circle of Indian ladies showered me with pats and sympathetic murmurs.

When Elizabeth and the children emerged from the store, my stepmother took note of my disheveled condition with a look of utter astonishment and took me by the arm, guiding me safely toward our wagon.

Though I had heard all the stories about the two wild Indians who had stormed Samuel Betel's tavern, knives drawn and demanding fire water, the natives we encountered in town hardly seemed capable of the fearsome barbarity attributed to them. They bore more resemblance to the poor of Philadelphia and London—downtrodden and fearful of looking you in the eye—than to the murderous savages of literary fancy. And the women who had attended to me with gentle concern made me understand for the first time that maybe we weren't so different after all.

Chapter Seven

My heart had been racing all day. The long-awaited dance in Lititz was finally to happen. Father would drop us there on the way to his cousin's, to return at ten o'clock. Anne and I had been practicing dance steps for weeks in the privacy of our bedroom. We were clumsy and usually fell laughing onto the mattress after stumbling over one another. Anne had a sweet, lyrical voice and she would hum familiar tunes that set the rhythm for our movements.

"Mary," she would warn me, "don't be upset if you aren't asked to dance. The boys may think you are too young."

We had been given access to our host's quarters to wash and dress and put up our hair. I wore the blue and white chintz dress I made last summer—open in front to show the white bodice with lace and blue ribbon, as well as the petticoat I wore over my shift and stays. When I saw myself in our host's looking glass, I couldn't believe it was me.

I wasn't a beauty, by any means, but with my hair pulled up, you could see a well-proportioned face with dark brown eyes and arched brows and lips that had grown fuller in my fourteenth year. I tried out my most alluring smile and concluded that I would surely be asked to dance by someone.

It took Anne and me a good half hour to lace each other up, and I couldn't take a full breath for the rest of the evening, but we looked like two angels gliding above a heavenly feast.

As our wagon pulled into Lititz, the whole village was alight with energy—torches blazing, wagons turning into the school grounds, and music in the air. Though we had no Moravian neighbors near the farm, we had heard tales of their prosperous towns and the beautiful music that spilled out of their churches. They had come to the colonies from lands near Germany with a knack for farming and a rich tradition of music and dance.

I had heard stories of the new Linden Hall School for Girls in Lititz and I studied every girl we passed, wondering whether she was one of the lucky ones whose parents had seen fit to send her to Lititz for an education.

The evening air was crisp and cool and, as we disembarked from the wagon, the strains of fiddle and fife filled the air. Matthew offered me his hand as I climbed down from the wagon and we followed Anne and the boys in the direction of the schoolhouse, sparkling with light and song.

People were darting back and forth in the gardens around the Moravian compound, the gay sounds of laughter and music stirring my heart. The dance took place in a large wooden building with carved figures on the portal that appeared too big and too grand to be a schoolhouse. The band was gathered at the far end of the hall with an assortment of horns and strings, fiddles and fifes. Not since the concerts in Philadelphia had I heard such glorious sounds, but in this setting it was not the subtle beauty of strings and minuets, but a pounding energy that made my heart beat and brought a warm flush to my face.

A plump man with a large mustache and ruddy cheeks stood near the musicians and called out directions to the dancers in a German accent. The dancers were arranged in circles by pairs, swinging and swaying to the music in parallel dips and spins.

Our little clan of Brandons and Lockes moved to the side of the room closest to the music, joining dozens of other party-goers tapping their feet and watching the experienced dancers with envy and admiration. Oh, the warm passion that such music aroused in me!

Anne, Matthew, and Francis appeared to be mesmerized by the sounds and sights but also seemed embarrassed by our inexperience in the social world. I turned to Matthew and pleaded for an invitation to dance.

"The girls aren't supposed to ask, Mary," he said, turning beet red and giving me a look of disapproval.

"If you won't ask me, I'll have to find someone who will," I retorted, much to his horror.

"Well then," he replied, taking my arm. "Let's give it a try."

So we made a leap of faith and joined the dancing, though we had to watch the others carefully. It was exhilarating to spin around the room and sway to the music. Matthew was a little awkward on his feet, but he smiled shyly as he spun me around in accordance with the caller's instructions. I was giddy from exertion and happiness, and

I could tell that Matthew was aware of the flow of my blue dress and how womanly I looked with my hair pulled back.

Our cousins joined our circle and even Anne and Francis participated, though both with eyes averted. The room was increasingly crowded with local villagers from Lititz, as well as settlers from all along the Susquehanna. Most of the guests were English speaking, but the locals spoke with a German accent and many of them in their native tongue. There were even young Presbyterians from the Irish settlements in Chester County, rough in their dress and their heavy brogue, but joining in the dance with lively spins and hops that were as athletic as they were graceful.

I was sipping a glass of cider and chatting with my cousin Susannah Cathey when the musicians broke into a particularly charming Irish tune. Our Cathey kin shared blood with many of these poor Irish immigrants, and they also understood the culture of Northern Ireland and could explain the intricacies of Irish dance.

"Do you see, Mary," she whispered, "how they spring to life with the rhythm of the tune? Isn't it lovely?"

The group from the Irish Settlement had formed their own circle and, instead of following the caller, they seemed to have their own form of dance, with a good deal of fast footwork. And it seemed that the fiddler knew many of them, as he responded to their requests for certain tunes with a friendly nod and tap of the foot.

I had revisited the table for another bit of cider, when someone tapped on my back, and I turned to face Alexander Turrentine, the new field servant who had just arrived on the farm.

He greeted me warmly. "Mistress Brandon, is it not?" he queried with one eyebrow raised, as if we were old friends. "I wasna' expecting the family of our new master to be here at the dance."

"Please, call me Mary," I offered with as much sophistication as I could muster, as if bestowing a great favor upon him. "You are Alex, I believe."

"Oh aye, that I am. At your service, Mary Brandon," he offered with a little bow, as if mocking my feigned propriety.

In spite of the teasing tone, his voice was warm and friendly, and his hazel-green eyes gazed at me with such lack of artifice that I felt immediately this was someone I could trust. He seemed older than I first thought when he and his brother arrived at the farm and was not at all shy about talking to a girl. I could see he was enjoying this event as much as I.

I liked the look of this lively Irish servant of ours. He was small in stature, not much taller than I, and though dressed in a simple gray homespun shirt over his linen breeches and woolen stockings, he made an attractive figure, tidy and graceful in movement, given to bursting into laughter, both at others and himself. His skin was slightly freckled from days in the sun, giving him an irregular color that was not displeasing to the eye. But his most striking feature was his thick unruly hair. I guess you would call him a redhead but his hair was really more ginger-gold than red, pulled back in a queue like a French soldier and tied at the neck with a strand of leather, which did little to constrain the extravagant curls of color that sprang up around his face.

The Irish lilt in his voice and his passion for the moment quite charmed me, though I was not accustomed to such direct address from someone I didn't know well. Our lack of formal introduction didn't seem to bother Alex Turrentine for a minute, as he began to chatter away about his prior workplace, the Irish jigs and reels that were so popular, and his pleasure at being brought to our farm in this developing part of Pennsylvania.

"We're so pleased to have you and your brother with us at the farm," I offered cheerfully, stumbling for words that would give the impression that I knew how to make casual conversation at a dance. "We think Lancaster County is the best place to be in all of Pennsylvania. And Father says Pennsylvania is the best of all the colonies."

"Well, I should not presume to doubt your father's word on any subject, lass," he responded with a wink, somehow giving the impression he saw right through me.

"Father says it's hard to find help out here on the frontier, especially after the way our poor Willie disappeared. We fear he was taken by the Indians."

This appeared to be surprising news to Alex, though it didn't seem to frighten him particularly.

"Indians, you say. What nation of Indians lives hereabouts?"

"The Susquehannock mostly," I responded. "Some people call them Conestoga. They have generally been peaceful toward the settlers, but my father says they are growing concerned about so many Europeans moving in and interfering with their hunting patterns. They resettled north of Blue Mountain to avoid our farms, but our neighbors keep telling us about cattle that have been taken or crops stripped."

"Well, ye can't blame them, can you, lass? This was their land before we came, after all."

As we were speaking, an older girl with lips blushed and a soft green shawl over her shoulder came up to Alex quite boldly, she with a manner of speaking similar to his own, and said "Come dance wi' me, love. They're playin' my favorite reel."

And at that, Alex gave me a rueful grin, bowed low before me and intoned with playful artifice, "It has been my pleasure to speak with you, Mary Brandon." And off he went to join a lively circle of Gaelic frolickers, who stomped, hopped, and clapped in time to the music, a stark contrast to our subdued circle of English farmers.

As the evening progressed and in spite of every good intent to show reserve, my eyes followed Alex Turrentine, who seemed to make his presence felt in every part of the room. He surely must have had prior experience at dances, that flashing smile of his responding to a word from here and there, as he reveled in the music and spun in joyful abandon with the rest of them. Though he had just arrived at our farm, he seemed to know everyone in the Irish community, all no doubt poor farmers or servants like himself trying to redeem their indentures for passage to the colonies.

Susannah Cathey nudged me from behind.

"Cousin Mary, you have your eye on that bonnie red-haired Irish lad just sold off to your father, do you not?" Susannah poked at me playfully.

I was startled and irritated that my cousin would imagine such a thing.

"Of course not," I huffed. "I try to be friendly and welcoming to all the hands who work on the farm. I'm not a snob after all."

"Ah, but this servant is more bonny than most, if you ask me, cousin," she teased.

It was just like Susannah to notice everything that went on between a girl and a boy. Even though she was about my age, she paid a good deal of attention to the boys.

Susannah and I had just returned from the outhouse, which was down a long path behind the dance hall, when Alex came up to me and extended his hand.

"Would you do me the honor of a dance then, young Mary Brandon?"

This took me by such surprise that I was speechless for a moment. I looked to my cousin for counsel, but she was as shocked as I by the invitation and I had to laugh.

"But I don't know how to perform the Irish dances," I stammered.

"Och, well, there's not a thing to it. Come and I'll show you," he said, gently pulling me onto the floor with a bemused look on his face. Whereupon he began a patient and elaborate lesson in the fine art of Irish dance, which I stumbled through as my astonished kinsmen looked on in horror and amusement.

Sometimes I would turn left when everybody else turned right and sometimes I stumbled into Alex in my clumsiness. But it didn't seem to bother him a bit and we laughed at the missteps and reveled in the spinning and weaving, as light from the hanging lanterns flickered across the room like sparkling jewels.

"Aye, now you have it, lass," he complimented me when on rare occasion I spun the right way, his eyes studying my performance with candid interest and approval. On one occasion, keeping my hands in his, he stepped back and looked straight into my eyes, not saying a thing but just looking. He was different from anyone I had ever known in that honest way of looking. Then he narrowed his eyes, shaking his head a little as he laughed to himself—heaven knows what about—before guiding me back into the next dance step.

Throughout the long ride home, there was much chatter and joking about my adventuresome fling with the servant boy and my ineptitude in the fine art of Irish dance, but I could see that neither father nor Matthew found it very entertaining. For my own part, I would live off the excitement and joy of that magic evening for weeks to come.

Chapter Eight

15 December 1749

Lancaster County, Penn

Dear Aunt Agatha,

Each year as we approach the twelve days of Christmastide, my heart is heavy with memories of Mother's warm presence. But my week was brightened immeasurably by your letter. Mother loved you dearly, and you are like her in so many ways. In spite of protestations from the rest of the family, I refused to open your letter in the parlor for consumption by one and all but scurried off to my room to relish every word in private.

I know you will tell me that was selfish and impolite, but there is so little in this large family that is mine alone and I wanted to savor each word of your letter in my own time.

We have recently returned from our annual

pilgrimage to the city of Lancaster. It is the most interesting and prosperous of all the towns near the river in this part of the Pennsylvania Colony, separated as we are from the coast by vast forested wilderness. You would doubtless find Lancaster quaint and sleepy with none of the majestic beauty and energy of London. But Auntie, to me the growing town is a sight to behold, bursting with brick-faced mills and soaring church steeples and tree-lined neighborhoods of lovely homes.

And, best of all, I attended a DANCE. Yes, me, Mary Brandon of the chicken coop and the spinning wheel. There I was, on a dance floor, the rise and fall of music filling the air as skirts swayed and adornments sparkled in the golden light of lanterns.

The gathering took place in a small village near Lancaster inhabited by the Moravian people who speak the German tongue and worship in a way which is unfamiliar to us but known for its splendid song and the thrilling tones of brass and stringed instruments. They are a people who place great value on education—EVEN FOR GIRLS—and have large, well-tended farms that bring traders and merchants from around the colonies.

Do you remember the blue and white chintz dress that Anne and I worked so hard on last summer, with delicate ribbons along each tier? I wore it to the dance and I believe it displayed my figure to advantage. My hair was gathered and pulled back in the French style, making me look at least sixteen. And I danced with a young man who couldn't take his eyes off me—an Irishman with red-gold locks and green eyes and a smile that makes you think he has just heard a wonderful story that he is about to share.

His name is Alex. I can assure you, Auntie, that he did not make any improper advances, but I could see that he was observing me with some interest. And though he was gallant and polite, there was a look in his eye when he regarded my person that was not a bit modest. And he didn't seem to care a whit that I, and probably everyone else in that room, could see that he was smitten.

If Mother were still alive, I would tell her about Alex. But I'm glad I have you to tell. When I pass him in the farmyard, I feel a little flutter in my heart and the sky is brighter and the birdsong sweeter. Oh, I almost forgot to tell you: He works on the farm. He and his brother came to us on a temporary contract of indenture. I do not know his age, but he is older and more worldly than I. So perhaps you will conclude that it is not proper to feel about him as I do. Probably Father wouldn't approve.

Chapter Eight

If you wish to impart to me any words of wisdom regarding matters of the heart, be assured that Father is very respectful about the privacy of personal correspondence and will not have access to any of your letters except what I might choose to share with him.

With love to you and a song in my heart,

Mary

Chapter Nine

My humdrum existence on the farm was quickly reestablished, with one exception. Every time I ran into Alex Turrentine, he greeted me warmly, often with a wink or a knowing smile, and my heart would explode in confusion and excitement as I remembered the evening in Lititz.

I had responsibility for the kitchen garden and took pride in the tidy rows of lettuce and herbs, free of weeds and insects, and in the artistry of the cages I constructed to keep my beans and squash properly constrained. About a week after the Lititz dance, I was removing weeds from among the wild thyme when Alex and his brother Sam passed by the garden on their way into the midday dinner. Sam was more reserved than his brother and looked displeased when Alex turned off the path to join me by the bean poles.

"May I be of assistance to you then, lass, in getting rid of some of these godforsaken weeds?" he cheerfully asked, brushing a red-gold curl out of his eye and settling beside me in the dirt without waiting for a reply.

"I shouldn't want you to miss your dinner, Alex."

Chapter Nine

"And I shouldn't want you to get your pretty hands dirty, Miss Mary," he teased.

I who was so clever and quick to retort with my own family again found myself flummoxed and at a loss for words around the cheeky servant. So we worked at the task companionably without a lot of chatter in the bright sunlight.

"How did you come to be a servant here?"

"I guess the farmer who holds my bond didn't have enough for me to do, so when your father came looking for temporary help, he offered me up. Me and Sam, though Sam was working for another farmer on the next plot. I think we're supposed to go back there after spring planting."

"But, no, I meant why are you a servant?"

"Och, that. Well, Sam and I were at the fair outside Lurgan last March, when two lads came through with drum and fife, stirring up interest in ship passage to America."

"Lurgan?" I asked.

"In County Armagh. Ireland. The land of my birth. We were at a fair when the ship captain's crimp sunk his teeth into us," Alex added.

"What's a crimp?" I asked.

"Why, that's a lying, cheating sinner sent by the captain to fatten his purse by tempting poor boys like us to sign on," Alex replied matter-of-factly. "The captain's crimp was stationed near the animal pens with broadsheets tacked up on trees. 'Voyage to America,' 'Children Half Fare' and such like—with the music drawing people in, touting the benefits of transporting to America. You know, good work, plenty of money, free to do as you please. Truth is they needed hands over here in the colonies. And they knew we were sick and tired of getting played by the landlords, the king, and the whole bloody mess in Ireland. Tired of working all the time and still half starving. They were eager to sign us up, but of course didn't mention anything about loading the ship with twice as many bodies as it was meant to carry or being owned as somebody's servant. That wasn't announced to us until we tried to leave the ship in Philadelphia. The captain said we owed more money for passage and would have to work it off."

"And what if you had simply refused to be someone's slave? What could he have done?"

"Lock us up in the Philadelphia gaol as paupers, I imagine. Anyway, we went along. The city clerk of Philadelphia signed a piece of paper certifying we were servants, and so we were. Captain didn't even put down our names right, so now we're called Turrentine. Who would have such a name? I told him very clearly it was Turkington."

I laughed. "Sounds just the same when you say it, Alex. You Irish speak in a brogue that's not too far removed from the Gaelic."

"We're not really Irish though. My family is from Scotland originally. It's not my fault that the Philadelphia clerk was hard of hearing."

"Okay, Alex Turkington, I promise to use your proper name from now on. That sea captain *was* a wicked man, deceiving you and your brother like that."

Alex had a bemused way of looking at me, as though he weren't entirely sure I had meant what I said. For my part, I couldn't decide whether he was trying to take the measure of my character or simply couldn't believe an English girl capable of kindness or sincerity.

"Why are you looking at me like that?" I asked with a smile, trying not to sound defensive.

He continued to study me, in that direct way of his. Sometimes it felt like he was trying to see straight through me. Gradually his quizzical face brightened into a smile.

"Maybe I just like the way you look."

Though Alex and Sam spent most afternoons in the fields, they were assigned chores closer to the house in the morning and Alex and I had many opportunities to see each other as we came and went around the barn, the chicken coops, and among the vegetables and herbs that were contained in the kitchen garden. Unaccustomed as I was to receiving notice from the men on the farm, he always brightened up my day with his attentions.

Alex's stories of his journey to America, and how he was tricked by the captain, evoked such outrage in my heart that I could scarcely bear to hear him speak of it. As I came to understand better the plight of these indentured Irish servants, I felt deeply the moral wrong in taking advantage of their desperate poverty back in their homeland. And I couldn't help but wonder, in spite of Father's high notions about this new world, just what kind of new world we were building here, resting as it did on the backs of the poor and the desperate.

Chapter Ten

O n the days when Master Fry came to give lessons to the boys, everyone pushed to finish the afternoon chores early and the farm became unusually quiet. Tempted though I was to position myself under the parlor window and listen, I exercised better judgment and busied myself elsewhere. I didn't take up the needle because I preferred to be as far from the house as possible, knowing the resentment that was sure to arise while Master Fry was teaching the boys of our family about subjects of such burning interest to me.

I stomped off to the wooded marsh beyond the horse pasture to seek out mushrooms and was foraging under a conifer when I saw Alex in the distance, walking alone without his farm tools toward an adjoining part of the forest. I knew him well by now, his natural joy in all things, eyes open to the little miracles of nature. But even from that distance, the way he carried himself, shoulders squared, lost in thought, made it immediately apparent to me that he didn't care to attract attention.

Drawn by curiosity, I decided to follow the parallel path above

Chapter Ten

the trail Alex was taking into the woods. A morning rain had passed through and softened the leaves enough to muffle my footfall. I could occasionally catch a glimpse of Alex some twenty feet below me and kept just behind him to avoid detection. He was moving rapidly toward a mossy clearing where Anne and I as children had built imaginary castles and pretended to be ladies in waiting to the Knights of the Round Table.

Positioning myself behind a tree with a perfect line of sight into the clearing, I settled down to watch. Alex was pacing back and forth and would look up each time he heard the snap of a branch from the surrounding undergrowth or a whistle of wind through the oak canopy. This watchful state seemed to go on for quite some time when suddenly without warning an Indian appeared from the bush.

My heart began to pound with terror, fearing that Alex was soon to be struck dead. The Indian had straight black hair, pulled back from his face in a band, high cheekbones, and a glow about his complexion, still reflecting the unblemished blush of youth. His face was blank, showing no emotion, and he watched Alex carefully as if expecting him to spring into attack at any moment. The Indian wore a decorative strap woven in geometric shapes of red and blue across his lean muscular chest and the fur of an animal with feet still attached slung over his shoulder.

The Indian moved with such ease and grace through the underbrush that even though Alex had been listening attentively, he was clearly as surprised as I when this fearful apparition stepped from a bush. At first, the two of them, about the same age, stepped back from one another warily, but then Alex broke into one of his charming smiles and the Indian boy smiled back.

At first, they didn't appear to be saying much, just friendly nods of greeting. I could hear laughter and a gentle give-and-take like two friends who had run into each other at a village fair. Then they sat on the ground facing one another and appeared to be having a friendly chat, pointing here and there, occasionally using a stick to draw something in the dirt, murmuring to one another. This conversation went on for quite some time until both of them stood, gave a nod to the other and, as quick as that, the Indian disappeared.

I could not tell anyone what I had seen—not even Anne. I was afraid for Alex and for our family when I thought of his meeting with the Indian. Yet somehow I knew, when I was watching them, that they had reached across some kind of invisible barrier to know each other and that there was no real danger. I never spoke a word to Alex about his meetings with the Indian. But from that day, each time Master Fry came for a lesson, I slipped into the forest and spied on Alex and his native companion.

It was wrong of me to eavesdrop, but these meetings in the forest clearing were so dramatic and so far removed from my humdrum life on the farm that I was curious and couldn't help myself. I watched them every week. They seemed to be playing at school—one week teaching each other new words, the next discussing mathematics or history. It may not have been as rigorous as Master Fry's rhetoric, but they were approaching it in all seriousness. Sometimes they scraped stick figures into the dirt to illustrate a concept and sometimes they seemed to be debating ideas with a good deal of emotion. Something about this friendship and their effort to share knowledge and learn each other's ways seemed magical to me, and I was fascinated.

One day several weeks later, as I leaned against a scrub pine, straining to hear the language lesson below me, I noticed the Indian had left the clearing while Alex worked on an elaborate sketch. Before I knew what was happening, I was snatched off my feet by strong ruddy arms and hauled ruthlessly through the undergrowth, scraping my bare arms as thorns and sticks tore at my clothing. I was dumped unceremoniously onto the ground in the clearing as Alex looked up from his work in astonishment.

"Mary Brandon, what in God's name are you doing out here?"

Alex gingerly released the Indian's hold on me, awkwardly brushing the twigs and dirt from my dress.

Alex straightened himself and stepped between me and the Indian brave, pushing him away and giving him a threatening glare.

"MY friend," Alex protested with an emphatic thump on his chest, pointing toward me as I remained in an undignified posture on the ground.

The Indian broke into rapid speech which I could not understand, pointing from time to time up toward the perch where I always watched them, with the occasional gesture in my direction which suggested criticism of my behavior.

"This is HER farm, for heaven's sake," Alex scolded. "She's the landowner's daughter."

The Indian looked at him with disapproval.

"HA," he exclaimed as he moved almost chin to chin with Alex, turning redder than ever as he had to endure this outrage. "This is

NOT White Man's land. Indian land. From the first moon and for more moons than there are leaves in this forest."

After that speech, he glared at Alex with such ferocity that I was certain they would come to blows.

Alex made an effort to return his fierce look, but I could see that he was thinking about what the Indian had said, and a thoughtful smile crossed his face.

"Aye," he said with a conciliatory shake of his head. "You're right of course. But it's not her fault. The bloody English always assume everybody else's land is theirs by birthright."

And so began an unlikely threesome. The Indian, whom Alex addressed as Kago, at first resented my intrusion into his friendship with Alex, and neither of them approved of a girl like me hanging around with them in the woods. But Kago got used to me and we became friends. At first, I was surprised that he spoke English so well. He patiently explained to me that the white invaders were already in control of his tribe's land before he was born. I soon joined Alex in sharing ideas with Kago. He was curious about everything. Like Alex, I learned more from Kago than I taught, as he corrected our misunderstandings of the order of the natural world, enriching our vocabulary with Susquehannock words for which there was no English counterpart. For the first time I came to understand the pride and gentle dignity of these native people—their connection to the land, their almost-religious feeling of responsibility for it, and their puzzlement about some of the practices brought with us from Europe that led us to treat the bounty of the earth and its creatures as ours to consume.

Chapter Eleven

Alex and I could never have become such close friends if we had only seen each other around the farm, where you couldn't turn around without a nosy brother or sister or servant eavesdropping. Of course, we chatted in a friendly manner when we passed one another in the course of our daily chores. But it was in the forest clearing where we became friends and really got to know each other.

We were quite a bit alike, Alex and I, both quick to say what was on our mind and quick to laugh at all the nonsense going on around us. Though not formally educated, I had learned from my father to appreciate this moment in history and how we were all part of something new, a time and a place where people from all over the world, rich and poor, preacher and farmer, German and Scot, saw the opportunity and left everything behind to take a chance here.

I had been troubled from the beginning by the financial peril that could have led Sam and Alex to abandon hearth and home without any means upon which to build a future. Time and again, I would ask Alex to describe the squalor and claustrophobia of their crossing.

Each time I heard the story, I would be freshly outraged by the trickery of the shipping companies and colonial landowners in enticing poor Irish youth to risk their lives to fill the pocketbooks of colonists short on manpower.

"Aye, and maybe we were just too stupid to ask the right questions," Alex would say, rolling onto an elbow to face my endless queries.

The story was always the same. Like all poor Scots-Irish immigrants, Alex and Sam, and their father and grandfather before them, had been used and abused by the English over the generations. Alex was a good storyteller and he filled my head with tales of storms at sea and treachery on the northern shores of Ireland as the afternoon sun would filter through the oaks onto our secret meeting place.

"Och, lass, I wish you had known my Grandda. He was the storyteller of the family. Never had two ha'pennies to rub together, but full of love and life."

His grandfather's grandfather, Joseph McTurk, left behind his farm in the Scottish Lowlands in the early 1600s to move to Northern Ireland after King James came up with a plan to develop that land for the benefit of the English. Just like Alex and Sam, Joseph was recruited by the English with lofty promises of freedom and prosperity in a new land. *Join the Ulster Plantation and escape the poverty of your father's life as a tenant-farmer. Work hard and in a few years, you'll own your own farm.*

"The English changed his name too, just like mine," Alex complained. "No McTurks on the plantation. Everybody had to have a nice English name, none of this Scottish nonsense like Mc and Mac. So 'Turkington' it was on the plantation records and Turkington it would remain, at least until Sammy and I arrived in the colonies."

When Alex was telling his stories about the old days on the English plantations in the north of Ireland, Kago would listen intently, his eyebrows almost meeting in the middle, so wrinkled was his brow as he tried to understand the historic power struggles among the English-speaking peoples.

"Why?" Kago would ask every time Alex told a tale of abuse by the plantation stakeholders, sometimes bursting into laughter at a competition for property and wealth that made no sense to him.

Kago understood power well enough, its force manifest among native tribes as well, but he couldn't fathom a system of private land ownership. To him, it was obvious and should have been crystal clear to any simpleton that land belonged to everybody and that its bounty was to be shared.

We could never predict the things that would impress him or the things he found ridiculous. But when it came to mathematics and to the new understanding of motion and matter we described coming out of the scientific breakthroughs in Europe, Kago couldn't get enough of it. He would ask us over and over to explain these theories, but neither of us had deep enough understanding to satisfy his curiosity.

Alex and I would often stay and talk in the clearing after Kago left us, his departures as abrupt and unceremonious as his arrivals. He would glance up to see the angle of the rays of sun cutting through the clearing and suddenly he was gone.

Alex would make fun of Kago's ability to move so fast without making a sound.

"I wish Kago could teach me how to do that. I could slip out of the barn before anybody missed me, leaving Sammy to do all the chores."

"You and your brother are very close, aren't you?"

"Och, aye. Course we are. Here in a strange land with no other family to care for us."

"I think he's a different kind of person than you are. Not so sociable."

Alex chuckled. "Do you think I'm too sociable, lass? Cavorting with the landlord's daughter?"

"Hardly cavorting," I protested. "Doing our part to improve relations with the natives maybe."

I gave him a stern look to establish my serious intent, but as always, when I looked into those laughing hazel eyes, I had to smile.

"We are friends, truly, Alex. I don't think it's improper. I feel I know you better than I know most of my kin."

He took my hand in his. "And I will always be a friend to you, Mary Brandon, for as long as I live."

I didn't object when he held onto my hand longer than necessary. I wanted him to know that I too felt we had a special bond between us and I wasn't going to let old-fashioned social rules get in the way of that.

We would often stretch out side by side on a gentle slope covered with soft, creeping thyme and talk about where we came from and our earliest memories of childhood. I could talk to Alex about anything. He understood how I missed my mother and longed for a life of meaning. And he in turn filled my head with images of Ireland, its brooks and loughs and green hills pitted with leprechaun caves.

Alex told me stories that had passed down through generations of his family and his telling was so vivid that I could almost smell the lamb roasting over the open fire and hear the music of the bagpipes and fiddles drifting across emerald moors. The characters in his family narrative were like the heroes in my favorite books.

Joseph McTurk and his wife Sarah had grown up on neighboring farms outside Galloway in the Scottish Lowlands, each the youngest of large families. Longing to wed but without prospects for work nearby, they had jumped at the chance to cross the Irish Sea for a new start on the plantations being built near Ulster.

Each land grant on the Northern Irish plantations was parceled out to Scottish or poor English tenant-farmers. The English landowner was lord of that plantation, recruiting farmers to tend each parcel, often spending part of the year overseeing the property and part of the year back in England.

Old Thomas, as he was always referred to by Alex, was owner of the parcel where Joseph and Sarah settled. He had recruited Joseph to Northern Ireland, along with dozens of other Scottish farm families, under a land grant from King James. He didn't mind moving from his ancestral home near London to help settle this remote Irish farmland because, with luck, he would accumulate enough financial power to re-establish roots in England that would leave a real legacy for his children and grandchildren.

"Grandda picked up all the stories about Old Thomas from his own grandfather. Thomas and his family lived in luxury in a huge fortified manse made of stone which stood atop a hill, visible from all the crofts and thatched-roof hovels scattered across the plantation. When Grandda's father was still a boy, he would climb the hill up to that manse with his father Joseph at the end of each month to report on the crops and pay rents and taxes."

Joseph and Sarah, poor as church mice, had worked hard over the years and eventually saved enough money to pay Old Thomas outright for their parcel. As a result, the title to their small farm was transferred to Joseph's name and the family had finally achieved security and a stake of their own in Ireland.

It was the firstborn son of Old Thomas who was the villain in Alex's tales. James took over the record-keeping as his father aged, and it was he who "regularized" the tenant-farmer's names to proper English, thus erasing the Scottish history of the McTurk family and imposing a new Turkington identity, and it was James who took advantage of the Turkington family when the English king increased quit-rents, driving them into poverty, reclaiming the land, and stealing from them everything they had of value.

"Aye, Grandda used to talk about the treachery of the son James. He said Old Thomas would never have acted so cruelly. Up to that time, our family had been spared the worst of the perpetual Irish famine and fighting, thanks, as we were always told, to the special protection of our family cross, a religious icon which dated back to the time of Christ and had been blessed by St. Francis of Assisi himself."

"A holy relic, Alex? Hard to believe it could have been blessed by St. Francis. I doubt he ever made his way to Scotland."

Chapter Eleven

Alex sat up and gave me a quizzical look. I think he never quite got used to my free opinions on subjects of which I knew nothing. But then he shook his head with a rueful smile, leaning over gently to touch my cheek.

"Oh aye," he murmured, "you're probably right, come to that, lass. Given the luck of my kin, it wouldn't speak well of St. Francis at all."

Chapter Twelve

15 March 1750
Lancaster County, Penn

My dearest Aunt Agatha,

Everything about my life on the farm has changed so much and so fast that I scarcely know where to begin. I will simply say to you, Auntie, that not only have I lost my heart to Alex Turrentine, but I have become close friends with a native Indian boy of about my own age—Kagogararo by name, but we call him Kago—all of which seems the most natural thing in the world.

Lest you think I have lost my mind along with my heart, let me assure you that both Alex and Kago are as smart and as kind and as respectful to me as any young man I might meet at one of your London coming-out parties. This may seem unlikely to you, given that neither of them was born into the good fortune of title or wealth or education.

Chapter Twelve

We meet regularly, deep in the forest, and no one else knows of our friendship. Be at your ease, Auntie, there is no danger to me from either of them and they look out for me with the intense concern and protective benevolence of kindly older brothers.

It is shocking to me how little we English understand of the native peoples of America. Before we came, the Indians enjoyed a peaceful and abundant commune with nature, which provided amply for their every need. I wish you could know Kago, Auntie. He is nothing like the savage redskins you read about in the London broadsheets. He is curious and proud, sometimes angry at the devastation inflicted on his people by the settlers, sometimes fascinated and awed by the tools and inventions we brought to his homeland. And he's funny and smart. What he loves more than anything else is— if you can believe it—mathematics!

As for Alex, he is the last person I think about before I fall asleep at night and my heart skips when I catch sight of his figure at work across the field. He speaks with a gentle, rolling Scots-Irish lilt that is more like a song than a statement, and is so heartfelt in his expression that every sentiment he feels is manifest on his face. Alex takes delight in every new thing he encounters, his mind endlessly curious, his eyes taking on a sparkle, one eyebrow raised in surprise, when he learns something new about another person. And all this in spite of the fact he is wretchedly poor and is not even a free man.

I have read and re-read your last letter so that I might understand your counsel, which is always wise and loving. I always feel that Mother is still speaking to me through you.

You describe the feelings one might have for a young man like Alex as "a passing fancy" that might lead astray someone of my age and inexperience. I promise you, Auntie, that Alex would never attempt to take advantage of my innocence. It is true that he sometimes looks at me with such longing that his eyes become soft, and when our hands brush past each other, there is a connection that causes both of us to step back. He has taken my hand in his only two times, in each case to comfort me in confiding some sorrow or fear, and the warmth between us is so real that I am never willing to let go. It is always Alex who releases my hand.

Though I lack worldly experience, I am not so naïve as to imagine I could obtain my father's consent to marry a poor servant. But remember, Auntie, we are in a remote colony where social custom often gives way to the practical necessities of life. I feel Father will come over time to appreciate Alex as a person of high character like himself.

Chapter Twelve

I hope you do not feel disappointed in me, Auntie. I of course do not wish to cause heartache or concern to my dear father. But my heart seems to have a mind of its own.

I pray about this every night, Aunt Agatha, and my pillow is wet with tears. Your love and support mean everything to me.

With deep affection,
Mary

Chapter Thirteen

E ven though our midday dinner was the main meal of the day, suppertime on the Brandon farm was a boisterous affair and often the only time of day when Father and Elizabeth had the entire clan of Brandon and Locke children in one room. Everybody could relax after the day's labor was done. And it was not unusual for one or two of our cousins from the neighboring farm to join in the meal.

Our farmhouse was large and well made, but not luxurious in the way of homes in the cities on the Eastern seaboard. By late afternoon, the kitchen, managed under my stepmother's supervision in a separate structure, was a beehive of activity, with tasks assigned to all the girls in our family, as well as the help.

The dining room housed a massive hand-hewn oak table, slightly irregular but sanded smooth and soft to the touch, where the dishes were passed along after a Bible reading by one of the children and a prayer by Father. After blessing the food, Father returned the Good Book to the shelf in his study, our family doubly blessed by the Scripture and by the old cross tucked away in the hidden compartment inside the back cover of the large leather-bound family Bible.

When our family broke bread together, it was not a time for idle chatter. Father led us in formal discussions of history, politics, and books. He was interested in the monarchies of Europe and the tensions between England and France. He loved to quote from *Poor Richard's Almanac*, a serial publication by a printer in Philadelphia named Benjamin Franklin, with witty insights into virtue and wealth and everyday life. We were too busy with the day-to-day challenges of running the farm to have time for a lot of reading, but Father strove to keep us informed in matters of the world. After supper we would often gather in the parlor to talk over matters of importance, both on the farm and beyond, with particular emphasis on happenings back in the British Isles.

"Listen to this, children. London was shaken to the core by a huge earthquake, those magnificent buildings swaying as the ground shook. And look! A glorious new bridge across the Thames—Westminster Bridge they call it. It's grand."

And, his favorite, the latest edition of Samuel Johnson's *The Rambler*, published on Tuesday and Saturday of each week. Father always asked us to interpret Johnson's latest maxim. "'Join both profit and delight in one,' Johnson says. What do you think he's getting at, Mary?" And we would make our pitiful efforts to explain the latest thinking in moral philosophy coming out of London.

Our dinner table discussions often continued in the parlor after supper. How I loved Father's passion about events going on in the world and his conviction that children should learn about politics and philosophy and develop their own opinions. He may not have wanted to give me a formal education, but I knew he cared about my ability to understand the explosion of intellectual activity going on back in our homeland.

One evening my uncle James Cathey was complaining to Father about the rate at which immigrants were pouring into Pennsylvania, particularly out of Northern Ireland, where English domination of the plantation estates was driving out the Scottish farmers. The American colonies offered new hope of a fair break which the Scots-Irish farmers had given up on back in Ulster.

Uncle Jim, with his own roots in Northern Ireland, understood the ups and downs of farming and feared a similar fate out here on the western edge of the colony. He complained of the rising cost of land and goods in the Susquehanna Valley due to the flood of immigrants. For him, it awakened bad memories of unfair treatment of his father and grandfather.

"It's a promise made and broken to those tenant-farmers, John. You know it is," Uncle Jim argued. "Those plantations were a cynical scheme by the English to control the heathen Irish papists and bring them under the yoke of the English."

"Not at all," Father argued. "Those plantation farms, with all that rain watering the flax and oats, provided a good living to the Scottish transplants for years, including your own ancestors—and mine."

"Aye, my Scottish ancestors and your English ones. Guess who carried away all the profit from that partnership?" my uncle goaded him.

"Ah, brother Jim, so much like your sister. Throughout our marriage, she was always for the underdog, blaming the English for everything. She was captivated by that history, the plantations and all that, and hung onto all the records—still stuffed away with the family Bible—about how our families became intertwined there in the northernmost reaches of Great Britain. She had a soft heart, that woman. I still miss her, you know. But, as for me, I don't care to look back. I'm thinking about the future for this family. And here, in the green hills of Pennsylvania, we have put down a stake in this new land that we can pass along to our children and grandchildren."

"You're an optimist, John. We're under the thumb of England and the foot of King George. The English will always scrape the cream off the top of any profit we make," my uncle insisted.

"It's not in their interest to do that. England of all countries understands that immigrants to the colonies must be allowed to prosper," Father argued.

"We're too far out of the stream of commerce up here by Blue Mountain to prosper," Uncle Jim said. "Can't get our harvest to Philadelphia from here and the time it takes to get down Manada Creek to the Swatara and then down the river into Baltimore is killing us."

I loved listening to them talk about the business of farming. I was convinced I could learn how to run a farm if Father would just take me under his wing and let me help.

"You haven't been reading the broadsheets out of Philadelphia," Father insisted. "There is talk of a canal that would connect the Swatara with the Schuylkill River, giving us a straight shot into Philadelphia."

Uncle Jim just shook his head. "I'll believe that when I see it. I hear cheaper land is opening up in the fertile hills of the Carolinas. I'm not sure our future is here in Pennsylvania."

After my uncle left for his neighboring farm, I took my place beside Father on the sofa.

"Father, I thought our family came from England. What did you and Uncle Jim mean about our family's history in Ireland?"

"Ah, my Mary, you don't miss much, do you? Well, you've always known that your own mother, and all the Cathey relatives, have their roots back in Ulster. And of course prior to that in Scotland. It was my family that came from England, our Brandon roots all the way back to the Middle Ages.

"My great-grandfather was granted land on the Ulster Plantation as a guild member in London. He rented tracts of land to Scottish farmers and even lived there himself for a long time. But those Scottish farmers, they were poor as dirt—no prospects and never enough to eat. It's no wonder it was so easy to recruit them to come to Ireland."

I tossed and turned that night, questions about family legacy mingling with romantic fantasy to trouble my repose.

We had Brandon ancestors who owned land in Ireland? Ancestors who walked those magical green hills Alex was always talking about?

After sleeping fitfully—visions of leprechauns merging into images of Alex Turrentine, his eyes sparkling as he spun me around the dance floor—I woke up thinking about Ireland and the plantation owned by my ancestors.

I was curious about those ancestors and the Brandon family papers Father had referred to.

Why were they so important to my mother?

Chapter Fourteen

Since the day had been set aside to clear the south pasture, the farmhouse was quiet and I begged off quilting, blaming my absence on a bad case of the ague. I knew I would have the day to myself in the still recesses of Father's study.

This was not my first time to steal into Father's private work corner. I loved the quiet darkness of the study, the smell of Father's leather-bound books and musty papers piled on shelves. But I always reached first for one thing—the gold cross. I loved the smooth feel of the cross in my hands, believing that it enabled me to commune with my mother. I had stumbled upon the cross on the day of my mother's death, seeking solace from words in the Good Book. It was then that I discovered the letters, written in my mother's own hand, tucked into the Bible. From that day, any time I felt the need for her comfort, I would steal into the study and read her notes and letters in the quiet privacy of that room, away from the curious eyes of Father or my stepbrothers.

The longing to commune with my mother was not now so much an act of mourning. Like Father, I had determined to manage without her and was even coming to accept Elizabeth as an asset to our family. But I longed for the comfort that came from my mother's belief in me. Having entered my fourteenth year, I felt the changes in my body and mind, with turmoil in my heart about the attentions of my stepbrother Matthew and my growing closeness to Alex. I guess I still needed a mother.

Because Father's study had a door that locked from the inside, this was a place where I could pray or weep without notice. The windows were high in the walls, letting in slants of light sufficient to permit reading in certain parts of the room. Except where the light cut through from the upper windows, the room was dark, cool and quiet, slowing the beat of my heart as I drifted from memory to longing.

I slipped a letter from its resting place marking one of Father's favorite Bible passages. I liked the smell of the old writing paper and the grace of Mother's fading script, penned to Father when both were young and in love.

As I followed the sunlight to read Mother's letters in a well-lit corner of the room, I saw on the bottom shelf of a nearby glass-front bookcase an old leather box tied in pink ribbon, a sure sign of my mother's touch. Opening the glass shelf, I retrieved the dusty box and unfastened the stiff ribbon to find a trove of ancient letters and documents. Most didn't appear to be in my mother's hand, but on top was a note from Grandfather Brandon to my father: "John, please hold safe these records of the Ulster business in case needed for future verification."

I would have laid the packet back into its resting place had I not spotted the name "Turkington" on the very top document. Given

Chapter Fourteen

Alex's recent lamentation about the English tendency to change his family's name at will, I was intrigued by the coincidence and began to leaf through an amazing array of formal documents and personal letters, most of them dated more than a hundred years ago. There were land grants in the name of Brandon with the seal of James I, King of England, Ireland, and Great Britain, property leases with both the Brandon and Turkington names on them and an embossed land grant issued by the Parliament of Scotland dated 1650, awarding eighteen acres of plantation land in Ulster to one Joseph McTurk.

Book Two

Alexander Turrentine

And So the Troubles Began

Ulster Plantation,
Northern Ireland, 1650

J oseph McTurk turned to his wife with a look that was not so much irritation as resignation.

"No, luv, he willna'boot us off the land. He just wants to talk. We'll work something out to get us through to the next harvest."

Joseph and Sarah had been in Ireland for almost thirty years and it hadn't gotten any easier. Their speech still reflected the throaty Gaelic of the Scottish Lowlands, where they had grown up on neighboring farms outside Galloway. Each was the youngest of a large family. Longing to wed but without prospects nearby, they had jumped at the chance to cross the Irish Sea for a new start on the plantations being built in Northern Ireland.

Oliver pulled his wool scarf from the corner and rose to join his father. "I'm comin' wi' ye, Da," he insisted.

Hard to conceive that Oliver, now at twenty, was the age Joseph had been when they boarded the sloop for Ulster and was just as eager to carve out a living that would permit him to wed.

Father and son set off together toward the stony fortified manse on the next hill where the Brandons held court to collect fees from the tenant-farmers and oversee the estate.

They walked shoulder to shoulder along a dirt path that wound through a grove of wild rhododendrons and across emerald hillocks, Oliver as tall as his father. Fifty-year-old Joseph still had a full head of curls that shimmered with shades of red beet, cinnamon, and fresh hay, his skin ruddy from long days in the field under the Irish sun. He had changed from his work clothes to a clean shirt and vest for this meeting with the landowner.

"Da, you've got to make it clear to Old Thomas that the security of his family is tied to that of the leaseholders. We have been under the boot of the English for thirty years as they break promise after promise. If we starve, he fails as well."

Oliver had his father's untamed curls but without the flashes of red. He was fair, his freckled face giving a first impression of timidity, which dissolved the minute he flashed his perfect smile, full of mocking affection and mischievousness. Oliver could be brash in his youthful confidence, but Joseph trusted his son's good sense to show deference in front of the landowner. "I will speak for us, Oliver, and you will hold your tongue."

Old Thomas Brandon had received the land grant in 1615 through his power in the London guilds. Three thousand acres of fine tillable soil, fed by the waters of Lough Neagh, in the northern reaches of County Armagh. In return for the bounty from King

James, he had only to conscript forty-eight adult males, twenty with families, from England or Scotland to build homes, farm the parcels on the estate, and win over the "rude and barbarous Irish" to the civility of English rule and Protestantism.

For Joseph and Sarah, it had been an adventure of faith as well as fortune. They had committed themselves to the new Protestant religion taught by John Knox and were prepared to undergo hardship to help spread the Presbyterian version of Protestantism to the heathens of Northern Ireland. How could they have anticipated that English suppression would expand from the pagans and Catholics still scattered throughout the northern reaches of Ireland to the Presbyterians who had been imported from Scotland as well? All the opportunities went to the English-born and English-churched settlers and undertakers, while the Scots were taxed to starvation and treated scarcely better than the native Irish.

While the Brandon manse with its fortified walls and hilltop perch contrasted sharply with the cottages on the surrounding farms, it was not an opulent estate and Thomas Brandon had maintained a cordial relationship with his tenant-farmers. Joseph and Oliver were shown down drafty corridors into the library where Thomas Brandon and his eldest son James were warming themselves before a fire.

Thomas stepped forward with his hand extended to Joseph and a friendly nod to Oliver. "Thank you for coming by, Joseph. It has been some time since we've had a chance to talk, has it not? And, with both our boys here, we can speak of the future."

Thomas Brandon spoke perfect boarding school English, his words clipped as carefully as his thinning sandy hair, which at age seventy-five still showed no sign of turning gray. Though his callers on the plantation were mostly tenant-farmers like Joseph, he was dressed as carefully in waistcoat and breeches as he would have been for the club in London.

Joseph was not surprised that James would be brought into the discussion, given his greater role in management of the estate and his father's age. But he would have preferred to have this discussion with Thomas alone.

"Sire, thank you for seeing us. I know we are overdue in payments and I've come to you trusting in your understanding of the corner we're put in by the increase in taxes."

James Brandon stepped in front of his father and directed Joseph and Oliver to the oak chairs in front of the massive desk that dominated the north end of the hall. "Have a seat, please, both of you, and we can go through the records."

Shorter and darker than his father, James Brandon never let cordiality get in the way of profit. Having been born in Northern Ireland, James had acquired a Gaelic lilt to his speech, inevitable after thirty-five years in County Armagh, but in his case the tone was characterized more by mockery than gaiety. His father had been one of the original undertakers with a land grant from King James, and Thomas had populated the farm lands with hungry tenant-farmers from Scotland, the McTurks among the first to lay claim to a plot of land watered by River Bann south of Lough Neagh.

James took a large bound register from the shelf and flipped through its pages. "Let's see. Stanhowe, Symonds, Tence. Here we are. Turkington."

It still grated on Joseph. The English insistence on forcing everybody else into the bloody Anglican way of doing things. The name was McTurk, not Turkington, wasn't it? But Shamus O'Neill had learned to live with Neal and the MacMurrays had soldiered on in spite of being, in the eyes of the English, plain old Murrays.

"Your payments have been well behind for over a year, Joseph, as you can see," James said, flipping the ledger around for Joseph to inspect. "Quit rents are due on the first and we have an obligation to the Crown to transfer taxes on time, an obligation to which you too are bound by oath."

"But, sire, every ballyboe on the estate must be in the same position. The oat and barley crops were devastated across the whole of the plantation and the last harvest can hardly sustain families through the winter. I'm tryin' to apprentice our youngest lad to a bricklayer in Lurgan but it will be another year before he can bring home any money."

Joseph turned to Thomas, still standing near the fire. "Sir Thomas, you know I am good for my debts. You'll have all we can spare at the next harvest."

It was clear that management of the estate had passed from father to son. The elder Brandon made no response as his son escorted Joseph and Oliver out of the library, passing them along to the doorman.

Oliver could see that his father was in no mood to talk, so he walked just behind him in silence, wondering whether he and his beloved Katie would ever be free to wed, given the failed harvest and the overdue rents. At the creek, he moved along next to his father.

"Da, I must stop by Katie's but I'll be home to finish the orchard clean-up before supper."

As he approached the Cathey croft, with the kitchen garden neatly framed by yellow iris tended lovingly by Katie's mother, Oliver was greeted warmly by the twins who were chasing a puppy down the path but stopped to chat with their sister's frequent guest.

"How goes it with you, Oliver Turkington? Come to see our Katie, have you?"

Oliver gave a perfunctory greeting to the twins and proffered a hand to the hound before a raven-haired lass of sixteen rounded the corner of the chicken coop and greeted her beau enthusiastically.

"Come in then, Oliver, and let me find you a wee bit o' somethin' to drink."

A frequent visitor to the Cathey cottage, Oliver was soon surrounded by Katie's kin with questions about their meeting at the manse.

"It's a sin before God, I swear it," opined Katie's older brother Andrew. "Brandon knows we canna' pay the tax with too little grain harvested to feed the weans. We can probably sell a hog in Lurgan, but I know your da is still tryin' to make up for last year."

"What did Old Thomas say when James made the demand?" asked Katie's mother as she spun long strands of wool deftly through a spinning wheel.

"He said nothin', silent as an empty tomb," Oliver reported. "It's clear he's given the reins to James."

"So we feared," said Andrew. "James Brandon cares naught whether it be us or some other poor sap lured from Surrey or across the sea, so long as his coffers are filled."

"Da believes James doesna' enforce rents so strictly against the English farmers," Oliver responded, as Katie took his hand in hers, hoping to distract him from the gloomy topic of poverty and politics.

Katie's father sighed with frustration. "Aye, that's so, lad. The bloody English dinnae care much for Irish or Scots either. I took the Oath of Supremacy like everybody else. But it's one thing to swear allegiance to the English king and quite another to have the Book of Common Prayer shoved down our throat, isn't it? Our people have kept this land out of the hands of the bloody papist Irish for thirty-five years. Cromwell's fanaticism aside, we were promised the right to worship God Almighty in our own presbyteries as our fathers did back in Scotland."

Oliver and Katie were hanging on every word, anxious about their families' future in Northern Ireland. In order to marry, they would need realistic prospects of sustaining a family from the proceeds of whatever small lot was passed to them.

As opinions flew about the cottage, all expressing some form of dissatisfaction with the intrusion of English dominance in their lives, Oliver stroked Katie's hand and whispered in her ear.

"God means us to be together, Katie. You're destined to be my wife. Dinnae fash yersel' about this, lass. God will provide the means."

Katie had to smile at Oliver's lovely spirit, always grounded in hope. She lifted his fingers to her lips and kissed them.

"I believe you, Oliver. I'm going to put my trust in the lucky McTurk cross, just like you do. It always seems to pull your family through, even when all looks hopeless. I pray we can wed before the next harvest though. I think they can make room for us here if that's better for your family."

When Oliver returned home, his father was resting on a straw mat near the fireplace.

"Are ye not well, Father?" The tremor in Oliver's voice betrayed his alarm. Joseph was not the sort of man to be wrapped in a wool blanket before the hearth on a fall afternoon.

"He just took a chill," Sarah insisted, moving past her son to take her place at Joseph's side. "He'll feel right as rain after a good cup of honey cider."

The strain in his mother's eyes was not reassuring.

"Son, go out and finish bundling the cuttings," she urged. "I'll not have your father out again in the cold."

When Oliver returned to the croft, Joseph was propped up on pillows, sipping the warm cider, a bit of color returned to his cheeks.

"Sit with me here for a moment, Oliver," Joseph said, patting the blanket. "There's a thing I wish to speak to you about."

Oliver noticed right away that his father was gripping the old family cross, its gold arms and colored stones reflecting the warm glow of the fireplace embers. Seeing it in his father's hand, Oliver felt overcome with a sinking sensation.

"Oliver, my lad, should anything happen to me, you're going to need this cross to pay our arrears to the Brandon house. It's the only thing of value I own. I showed it to Old Thomas last year and he understands its value. No matter what your mother says, if we must sell this cross to save the farm, it will be to you to go to Thomas and strike a bargain."

Joseph fell asleep by the fire and Sarah decided not to wake him for supper. After she too had fallen asleep at her husband's side, Oliver picked up the cross and examined it, turning the ancient relic from side to side.

He had heard so many stories from his father about the old cross and wondered how many of them were true. Probably just family myths, passed along from father to son.

The fire was dying, but the glowing embers still warmed the small cottage, the only home Oliver had ever known. The gold of the cross took on the deep red of the smoldering fire, evoking the suffering of the Son of Man to save souls.

Surely not, Father, Oliver thought to himself. *I couldna' bear to let it go.*

Chapter Fifteen

Lancaster County,
Colony of Pennsylvania, 1749

When we pulled into Mister Dickey's farm to pick up Sam, he was waiting under a tall chestnut tree, his goods wrapped in the same plaid knapsack he had brought onto the boat.

"Hey, little brother. You're a sight for sore eyes, sure," he said with a broad smile, pulling himself up into the back of the wagon.

Sam had played the father to me since we left Belfast. When they sold us off to two different Chester County farms, him to Dickey and me to McClaskey, I knew he worried about how I would do on my own. He tried to argue with the captain that we shouldn't be separated, but there was no point in speaking reason to that English bastard.

For myself, I didn't so mind being a servant. Granted, it had never occurred to me that I would begin my life in this big, beautiful, free land being owned by somebody. But Mister McClaskey was a good enough man and I truly didn't mind the hard work. But big brother Sammy had never gotten over the trickery played on us by the ship captain and his men who had sold us a bill of goods on life in the colonies.

"So, Alex boy, we may have a new master for the next few months, but we'll be together, eh?"

"Do you know where we're headed to?"

"Not exactly. A farm close to the river, I think, where they need help to finish off the fall harvest. We'll meet up with the new master in Lancaster, then he'll drive us up to his farm for the season. After that, we'll be sent back to Dickey and McClaskey to finish our service."

"Is he Irish, the new master?" I speculated.

"Don't you wish," Sam responded bitterly. "He is English. And guess what his name is?"

I had no idea what Sam was getting at.

"Brandon," he sighed.

I had heard all the stories from our Grandda back in our cottage in Lurgan. How his grandparents had been recruited by an English landowner, one Thomas Brandon, to leave their families in the Scottish Lowlands. And then were cheated and taken advantage of by Thomas Brandon's son, who took everything our family had worked for.

"How long will we be working for the Englishman?" I asked.

"Och, I dinnae ken. But how bad could it be, with the two of us together again?"

Chapter Fifteen

When Sam and I were separated at the ship in Philadelphia, I feared I would never see him again. We had survived the rough crossing, thanks to God's mercy and our reliance on each other. I didn't care to face the uncertainties of a new continent without my brother at my side. Once we got down to Chester County, we were happy to discover that our masters had emigrated from the north of Ireland, just like us. Here in America only one generation separated servant from master. The Dickey and McClaskey farms were only five miles apart and Sam and I were able to see each other when we gathered with the Londonderry congregation of the Fagg's Manor Church on Sundays.

For all his fatherly attitude towards me, people were generally surprised that Sam and I were kin. He had Da's look—tall and rangy with thin brown hair and skin a shade too dark for a respectable Scot; whereas you couldn't mistake me for anything else, what with shades of Ma's unruly chestnut tresses, and not enough bulk to put the fear of God into anyone.

In Belfast they had called Da Black Irish, but he wasn't black and he wasn't Irish either. He always complained that it was the English who forced Grandda to use the name Turkington. They tried to make the whole of the plantation sound English, so as better to trick the local Irishmen into thinking we were there on behalf of the bloody English king. But our family knew we were Scots of the long-standing and proud McTurk lineage, no matter what the damned English overlords said. Thank God poor Da can't hear the way these English bastards pronounce our name in America.

I was glad to be reunited with my brother and excited to be

setting off on a new adventure. It was a bright and beautiful day and we didn't have to work as we rolled along through the green hills of Chester County. This was God's country all right. Small farms and villages could be spotted in the occasional valley or ravine, but for the most part it was meadows and forests as far as the eye could see.

I loved it already, this bonny colony of Pennsylvania, founded by a Quaker who thought all men had a right to their own churches and towns and their own way of life. Many of the settlers here had come from the woods of middle Europe—Germans and Moravians and others, all speaking a language they called Deutsch. Of course, the bloody English were everywhere, trying to run things as usual and stealing land and power from anybody who wasn't careful.

As we headed northwest into Lancaster County, there were fewer farms and villages until we approached the rich farming lands near the river. Here settlements were flourishing, with towns fueled by mills and ferries and taverns providing services to the farmers who brought their produce to the river to ship to Baltimore or Philadelphia and from there on to London.

Mister McClaskey pulled up in front of a tavern on the outskirts of Lancaster. Sam and I waited in the cart as he approached and shook hands with a tall gentleman with distinguished-looking gray around his temples. He had the bearing of a gentleman but was attired in the clothing of a working farmer.

"Come on down, boys, and meet Mister Brandon. This here is Sam Turrentine and his brother Alex."

John Brandon, the new holder of our indentures, greeted us cordially, without any outward impression of rank because he was

English and we Irish, or because he was master and we servants. He showed us to the inn's privy and provided us with water, bread, and cheese for the journey.

When we were ready to go, Mister Brandon introduced us to his stepson Francis who had remained in the wagon and rode with our new bondholder up front. Settled in the back of his wagon with our sparse belongings, Sam and I shared stories about the farm work we had been doing and considered our changed circumstances.

"Our new master looks to be a decent chap," he said. "But he is English and Brandon by name. You'd do well to stay in your place and keep your head down. Our family has been cheated by the English every time they've had us under their thumb."

Sam still carried in his heart the bitterness our Ma and Pa bore toward the treacherous English. Joseph McTurk before us had been promised ownership of land in Northern Ireland when he pulled up stakes and left his da's farm in Scotland to join the plantation. And he had a gold medallion from the Scottish Parliament to prove it. But of course Oliver Cromwell found a way to strip the Scots of their land and reallocate it to the Anglican guilds. Their English overlords demanded rents, jacked up taxes, favored those who practiced the religion of the Church of England, and ruled the roost like someone with a stick up their arse.

Our trip on the boat was more of the same. The Kouli Kan, she was called, as fine a brigantine as lads like us had e'er seen. She had quite a history already, having survived a hurricane off Jamaica and captured a French ship off the coast of Nova Scotia, relieving it of furs worth fifty thousand Pounds British.

But with every passing week at sea, the provisions grew thinner and the work harder. Below deck everything smelled of regurgitated gruel, masked only a little by the dim yellow fumes of the lanterns. When I would crawl in beside Sam at night, I would find my brother's musky-sharp scent a comfort and shield from the rank odors that emanated from every corner of the sleeping quarters.

We toiled from daybreak to dark every day on the ship, thinking that was paying our way. And then of course when we landed in Philly, our fine captain gave us the big news that we'd have to be slaves for four years to pay our passage.

Mister Brandon pulled the wagon off the road near a landing beside a broad creek. Clear cold water was moving over stones of brown, gray, and white, filling the air with music. There was another wagon ahead of us, paying crossing fees to ford the creek at this shallow point.

"Jump down, boys, and help us set up for the crossing. This is Swatara Creek and once we're across, we just follow Manada up to the farm."

I was glad for the chance to get out of the wagon and stretch my legs. The hills north of the Swatara Creek ford were green and peppered with oaks and maples that jumped with color against the blue sky.

"Come on down, Sam, and see this fine country. It's as bonny and green as Ireland."

The four of us guided the horses through the shallow ford and onto the far bank.

"In the winter this crossing can flood out and you need to hire a

Chapter Fifteen

ferry to get across," Farmer Brandon explained as we waded through the moving water, holding the horses' bridles firmly and speaking softly to calm them as we crossed.

"Is it still a ways north of here, then, to your farm?" I asked.

"Yes, a few more hours. But it's fine country up here. So enjoy the sights."

Sam was starting to drift off to sleep but was jostled awake as we hit some rougher trails that led toward the foothills of a mountain range. Sam never did adjust well to change and had become withdrawn and moody as we travelled farther west into Indian country, just another reminder of all the difficulties we had experienced as we settled in this land.

"Cheer up, brother," I cajoled. "We're in a free land with opportunity to be whatever we want to be. The sun is shinin' and fish are jumpin' in the streams and we just passed a Scots Presbyterian Church where we can go and worship the Good Lord in our own way and praise him for bringing us to America."

Chapter Sixteen

By the time the wagon rattled into the Brandon farmyard, the sun was low on the western horizon and I was itching to get out and explore. We were pretty far out in the woods and visitors would be rare at such a farm, so the sound of our wheels throwing up rocks and dirt along the path brought folks out of every corner of the house and orchard.

The Brandon farmhouse stood out among the settler cabins in the Lower Susquehanna Valley. Its rough-hewn frame sat atop a rock foundation of local gray stone which extended well above ground up the side of the house. The raw wood was covered in overlapping rows of clapboard, which had been whitewashed and set off at the windows by dark green shutters. The two-story house was topped by a gabled roof with dormers that accommodated attic sleeping quarters.

Farmer Brandon appeared to have quite a large family as lads and lasses of every age gathered outside the house, sizing us up, and giving welcome. They were a handsome family, were the Brandons, strapping lads with fine-looking sisters, all with an appearance too lovely and refined to be working on a remote colony farm. Hard to believe Mistress Brandon, a handsome woman with a no-nonsense look in her eye, could have borne them all.

As I was having a look at this engaging English family, my eye kept returning to a stunning lass with big brown eyes who must have just come round from doing chores in the garden because she was damp with sweat from her work. As she wiped her brow with one sleeve, a line of moisture trickled down her chest in a direction my eyes couldn't avoid. She had dark hair that was full but straight as an Indian's, one side falling across her forehead in a way that almost covered one eye. She wore her hair shorter than the other women on the farm and, as she gazed at us with curiosity, she would periodically flip her head to one side in order to clear her line of vision. Likely one of Mister Brandon's daughters, she looked at me with such directness, a hint of amusement at the corner of her mouth, that I instantly wanted to know her better.

The field hands slept in a small bunkhouse behind the barn. We had our meals in the kitchen, which was housed in its own small structure alongside the farmhouse. Mister Brandon owned four slaves—Abraham and Bella and their daughter Roxie and her husband Peter—who lived in a small cabin down by the creek and cooked their meals over a firepit out front.

After a few days working on the farm, we were starting to know the family who owned the farm—and *us* for the time being. I was told that the Brandons, the master and mistress of the house, had each been widowed with a houseful of children, so their marriage resulted in quite a large clan. Though they were a friendly enough lot, Sam was naturally wary of the English and kept his distance. I, on the other hand, found the Brandons quite congenial, especially young Mary, with her shiny brown hair and cheeks as pink as roses, a sassy lass who looked you in the eye and said what was on her mind.

The work was hard, but we didn't mind. Sam was worried when we heard about the Indians snatching one of the indentured farm-hands before we came. We hadn't much exposure to natives in our time in America, but we were now farther west than we had ever been and heard plenty of stories about their raids and scalpings and all such as that.

We were up early every day and out in the far pastures, clearing or planting or harvesting. Sammy always kept one eye on the gap where we imagined the Indians snuck through at night to steal chickens or horses and, when they could, the scalps of white settlers. Once we spotted a couple of braves winding their way up the northern hillside on bareback ponies, but they were going about their business and paid us no mind. I watched them ascend the hill, graceful on their small horses and unconcerned about two farm boys down below.

Chapter Seventeen

A few days later after finishing up in the fields by myself, I wandered down to the creek to rinse off the dirt before heading back to the bunkhouse. The farm got quiet in the late afternoon. The owners would retire to their house, their children often occupied with studies or personal letters, and we field hands, whether slave or indentured servant or hired help, had some time before supper to get off our feet.

I don't know what made me look up. It was still as death. But as I shook the water from my face, there he was, about twenty feet downstream. Staring me down. A wild Indian. Eyes as black as a crow. Neither of us moved.

He had a knife in his hands and I had nothing. He seemed to size that up about as quick as I did. He showed me the blade, then stuck it back under his belt, raising his arms in a shrug as if to say "I sure don't need any weapons to defend myself against a skinny Irish whelp."

In an effort to reciprocate the positive gesture, I stood facing him and offered my most ingratiating smile and an outstretched hand. "Friend?"

The Indian could have been my own age, maybe younger. He glanced over his shoulder toward the hill, looking for a companion, I guessed. My Irish smile hadn't won him over just yet.

I eased myself onto a rock, taking care to make no sudden moves, and swished my hand through the water.

"Bloody hot today, isn't it?" I offered by way of casual conversation.

He kept his eyes on me but moved to take a seat himself. I could tell from the sparkle in his eye that he found me somewhat amusing and certainly non-threatening, but he didn't say anything.

I fluttered my hand through the water and proclaimed proudly, "Water."

The Indian didn't dispute my definition at first, but when I splashed a bit of the cool liquid his way, he smiled, and returned the favor, stating in a strong voice something that sounded like "Oneega."

I repeated his term as best I could, gathering a palm full of water to make the point, and he nodded in approval of my quick learning.

His next word "Kagogararo" was stated strongly as the Indian thumped himself on the chest, repeating the word several times. I could see that he was referring to himself, but the name was long and it took me a while to get the hang of it. Realizing that "Alex" sounded too diminutive in comparison, I gave him the full-blown "Alexander Turkington of Ulster County in Ireland," an identification that left him speechless.

It took me a while that first day to realize Kago was playing with me. I had been raised to think of the American native people as uncivilized and unlearned. I assumed Kago would not speak English. As he patiently taught me over many weeks, his people had endured a

Chapter Seventeen

hundred years of sustained cultural exchange with the invaders from across the sea and by this time the tribe's sovereignty and economic sustainability depended upon integration into the colonial system. He spoke English well enough to be understood if the conversation didn't get too complicated and had learned to affect proper English manners to the extent necessary to survive, a skill we Scots-Irish had yet to acquire.

From that day, we let down our pretentions and became Kago and Alex, communicating as best we could and learning what we could from each other. When we parted that first day, I thought never to see the Indian again. But when I went into the forest, he would often appear out of nowhere and we soon fell into a rhythm of meeting late in the afternoon toward the end of a week when my work was done.

Although we had little in common, I felt I understood Kago. He was nothing like what I expected of a native Indian. He laughed a lot and found my earnest struggles to learn his language amusing. He found almost everything about me amusing, including my hair, which he liked to muss up with his fingers, chuckling at the unruly curls that emanated from my scalp, which I hoped didn't reflect Kago's wish to display that particular scalp as a souvenir on his tent post.

He was the one who realized that Mary was spying on us. One Friday I was waiting for him in our usual clearing and he didn't show up on time. When he finally arrived, he had begun to draw figures in the wet dirt along the creek, a method he used when we didn't have enough words in common to share complicated ideas. He drew a female figure and kept moving his head in the direction of the thicket on the ridge above us. When he saw that I had no idea what

119

he was talking about, he slipped out of the clearing, only to reappear five minutes later with Mary Brandon under his arm, one hand covering her mouth.

"Mary Brandon, what in the name o' God are ye doin' out here?" I scolded, loosening Kago's hands from around her.

I immediately regretted my harsh rebuke. I could see Mary was shaken by Kago's assault, believing as she must that all Indians were deadly savages and that she was being carried off to slavery or death.

"There, lass, you're all right. Kago won't hurt you."

Mary's lower lip was quivering and I had to smile at the plight of my cheerful, bold friend being reduced to tears.

"Kago is my friend. He just didn't like the idea of being spied on."

Mary eyed the Indian with suspicion and moved a little closer to me. I took her into my arms as the tears began and tried to calm her down with some comforting pats, mindful all the time of how lovely her young figure felt pressed close to me.

Kago saw at once that I was enjoying this situation more than I should, giving me a hand signal that I took for an obscenity.

Once Mary calmed down, she began to take an interest in Kago. That was the Mary I knew, curious and open-minded. I don't think Kago had really known a white girl before, and he was as interested in her as she in him. I bade Mary take a seat on the ground next to me, thus forming a circle there in the clearing.

Reaching out to touch the Indian's knee, I turned to Mary.

"Kago," I said pointing to him. "This is Kago, my friend. He lives with his tribe on the other side of Blue Mountain. Well, sometimes there, sometimes down near Lancaster."

She looked at Kago and then at me, one eyebrow raised in surprise.

"Kago," she said, turning to him with a smile.

Even the wildest Indian would have melted in the warmth of that smile. Kago looked her over with some interest and a good deal of caution.

"Mary," I informed Kago with more formality than I intended, extending my arm in her direction.

"Mary Brandon," she added with a nod to Kago.

"Mary Brandon," he repeated carefully.

"Kago is teaching me some words in his native tongue—that of the Susquehannock tribe, which some around here call the Conestoga. Their language is derived from Iroquois, but it's apparently a little different. It's very hard to mimic what he says, but I'm trying. Kago is quicker than I am and he has learned quite a bit of English."

Mary laughed. "I hope he doesn't think that Gaelic brogue you speak is English."

After a while, we settled into our usual rhythm and from that day, Mary found her way to our lessons and we were a threesome.

Chapter Eighteen

I hadn't told Sam about meeting the Indian or our lessons in the forest or the fact that Mary Brandon now joined us on a regular basis. Sam knew that I was smitten with Mary Brandon and he didn't like it.

"She'll tell her da and we'll be sold off in two different directions," he worried.

Sam took our indentures to heart, angry that we'd been put in the position of African slaves. I didn't see it that way. We weren't slaves. We were just paying off a debt. This wasn't the way we had planned it, but we were here after all, weren't we, and once we got some land of our own, we'd take our place in this new homeland like everyone else.

I didn't much mind the hard work in Mister Brandon's fields, but meetings in the forest with my two friends were what kept me going. Kago was a quick study and his facility with the English tongue grew stronger each week. He was serious and earnest and generally perplexed when Mary and I burst into laughter over some misstep in his speech or manner.

Chapter Eighteen

I've come to believe that the Indian people are a sincere, kind-hearted people and in all the years since my friendship with Kago, I have remained cynical of the European view of the Indian as a blood-thirsty heathen. Kago couldn't have been any less like that—a gentle soul, smart, curious, and reliable.

After several months of our meetings, Kago showed up with a box of implements—stones, feathers, knives. He kept repeating "Friends, all time" as he pointed to Mary and me and to himself. When he drew a sharp knife and laid it across his wrist, Mary gasped with alarm, unclear about his intentions but not liking the look of it. He took my arm and turned it upward like his own.

"Alex and Kago brothers," he repeated earnestly, touching each of our wrists with the knife.

I began to sense what he had in mind and was not o'er pleased at the prospect. The sharp edge of the knife slipped over Kago's arm, leaving a trace of blood seeping out. He looked at me for a sign of assent and I extended my open arm towards him. The cut could scarcely be felt and he then turned the open wounds toward each other, chanting something in his native tongue as he held the cuts together by wrapping a colorful woven tie around our arms.

He was looking me straight in the eye as he performed these ministrations. At the end of the chant, he unwrapped the tie and said simply, "Blood brothers."

Mary watched this ceremony with fascination. Before Kago could return the knife to its compartment, Mary had pushed up the sleeve of her blouse, exposing her own arm to the Indian.

Kago was taken aback by Mary's offer, which was, both in its aggressiveness and its unabashed egalitarian impulse, inconsistent with his experience of the female role in the world. But, after looking to me for a sign of assent, Kago cut Mary's arm and bound it, first to his own and then to mine.

Mary's eyes shone with pride as she took part in this ritual. I knew her so well by this time, admiring her brave determination to pledge her blood bond to our friendship.

Each time we gathered in the forest clearing, Kago kept a precise schedule and always seemed to know when the sun had descended to the point where he must return to his village. He never explained why he left or where he was going. Mary and I too had chores waiting for us at the farm and we were cautious about ever being seen together returning from the forest.

But we had taken to spending a few minutes together each week after Kago left, often to debate what he had meant by a particular word or a cultural practice. On the day we shared blood with Kago, Mary regarded her marked forearm with awe, moved by the solemnity of the ceremony.

"You should cover yourself until the wound heals," I advised. "Someone in your family may become suspicious."

"It's easy enough to explain this away as a scratch from picking berries," she responded, dismissing my concern by studying her arm with not a little pride.

"Alex, what we did today—with Kago—what do you think it means?"

"I guess we're kin now, lass. All three of us."

I took Mary's arm in my hands, rubbing gently on the tender

Chapter Eighteen

skin. For a girl so strong and self-sufficient, her skin was surprisingly soft and warm. I would happily have held onto her arm forever.

"We should get back," I mumbled, not daring to look at her. "You go ahead and I'll take the upper path."

That day was not the beginning of my love for Mary Brandon. I had loved her for months, maybe from the night I danced with her at Lititz, cheeks flushed with exertion and giddy with pleasure as she swirled around the dance floor.

But I had no illusions about my place in the world and hers. I couldn't have her and we both knew it.

Chapter Nineteen

I was forever changed by an intimate friendship with someone of another race and of a history so very different from my own. And I think Mary was too. Kago was wiser than we were in so many ways, in spite of his ignorance of world history and modern philosophy as understood from the perspective of Europeans.

As his ease with the English tongue increased, Kago was better able to delve into more complicated questions than the names of flora and fauna in the forest. He was particularly interested in race and skin color, which was often the way European immigrants and natives described each other as a group apart from their own people.

"At your house . . . your farm . . . some people white like snow, some black like night," Kago ventured with a furrowed brow. As he made this observation, he held his arm against Mary's to point out his own middle ground.

"You mean our slaves?" Mary asked. "Have you seen them working on the farm?"

"Small house by creek," Kago nodded.

I was once again surprised by how much he had observed of the comings and goings on the farm and wondered how many other Indians watched the daily lives of settlers from a safe hiding place.

I could see he was thinking hard about how to ask something.

"Slaves?" he asked Mary carefully, studying her face. We had not progressed in our lessons to the point of discussing slavery, but I knew it was a concept not unknown among native tribes.

I held my hands together as if bound by a rope. "Slaves," I explained. "They canna' leave. Master paid gold coin for them."

Kago looked distressed and nodded his head in understanding. "Slave," he repeated.

He was quiet for a moment and then asked, "Their tribe will come and make war? Rescue slaves?"

"Their tribe is far across the water. They cannot come," I said with certainty and some relief.

Kago was thinking about an earlier conversation where I had tried to explain my own situation as an indentured servant. He said, "You slave too, Alex," giving me a poke in the chest.

"No," I protested. "I'm not a slave. Just working off a debt."

Kago studied me warily, having heard my explanation of indentured servitude several times and not quite understanding the difference.

Then he smiled and lifted my freckled pale arm. "No black," he concluded with certainty.

But as much as we valued our friendship with Kago, my time alone with Mary was always too short before we had to return to the farm. We looked forward to those few minutes alone after Kago left. I think he understood this.

Though I couldn't judge Kago's age, I think he was younger than I and perhaps closer to Mary's age. Yet I always felt that Kago had lived more and was closer to maturity than ever I would be. He had seen less of the world, knew nothing of commerce, and had never read a book. But he understood the world around him—the earth, how the light and the seasons move and change—and in the same way, I think, he understood the feelings between a man and a woman.

"Kago seemed somber today," Mary noticed, as we moved to our usual talking place where the late afternoon sun warmed the earth.

"I thought so too. He seemed to be worried. I wish we had the language to talk about such things. We are making progress on plant species and birdsong, but I have no idea how to speak of matters of the heart."

Mary smiled. "Ah, matters of the heart. Now I should have thought that was a specialty of yours."

There was a sparkle in her dark eyes when she teased me, though she said such things with a straight face, leaving me confused about whether she was serious.

"Do you think so then, Mary Brandon?" I put my hand on her shoulder and turned her toward me. "And what matters do you think are in my heart?"

She touched my cheek softly. "I think you like me well enough."

She said it in a soft way, not teasing this time, and she didn't avert her gaze from mine.

I felt soft inside, as if all the strength it had taken to leave home and cross the ocean had turned molten.

Our lips moved very slowly together and time seemed to stop. I would have stayed in that embrace forever, but Mary moved back, studying me earnestly with those curious, endlessly deep eyes.

"That was my first kiss," she confessed, marveling at what we had just done. In that confession, as in all things, there was no artifice about Mary Brandon and no hesitancy about acknowledging what had just happened. In that moment, I so much wanted to confess my love for her, but I was afraid it would frighten her and I didn't want to spoil the magic of the moment.

"Alex, I must talk to you about something."

Those words gave me a foreboding of something that would tear her away from me and I didn't want to hear it. But I said, "There's nothing you can't tell me."

"I discovered something yesterday," she explained, "in my father's study. While I was reading some of Mama's letters."

"It's good to remember your mother, who carried you in her womb for nine months and bore the pain of your birth. I believe she still watches over you from on high and knows how much you still love her."

Mary's eyes moistened up briefly before she returned to her discovery.

"Father keeps her letters in the family Bible. I don't want him to know that I go into his study to read them. I don't know why exactly."

"Well, your da is a practical man. I'm sure your mother's death was a great sorrow to him. But he has determined to continue to live."

"Yesterday I found a box of old family legal papers in Father's study. My great-grandfather and his father before him lived in Ireland."

"Are you Irish then, Mary? Do you think we're kissing cousins?"

She gave me a friendly shove. "No, I'm not Irish. But for several generations, the Brandon family owned land on the plantations in Northern Ireland. And one of the papers contains the name of Joseph McTurk."

My attention was still focused on the kiss, so it took a few moments for her words to sink in. "Joseph McTurk? That was the name of my great-great-grandfather."

"I know. You have spoken to me of him. How he was made to change his name and all that. It shocked me to read his name in those papers. Could there have been another Joseph McTurk on the plantations?"

"I dinnae ken, Mary Brandon," I responded, truly not knowing, or caring about anything but losing myself in those deep eyes of hers.

None of this made sense to me. Nor did it seem important at that moment. All I wanted was to have this beautiful English girl in my arms again and my ancestors could go hang themselves. All that surrounded us in the clearing that afternoon faded into blurred shades of gray except for Mary Brandon.

She looked up at the shafts of light, sunbeams through the wooded forest, ever lower in the sky.

"Alex, we must leave. It's late."

"Go, lass. I'll follow after a safe time."

Chapter Twenty

Sam and I sometimes worked under Mister Brandon's direct supervision but more often we were assigned to one of his sons or stepsons. It was a big family and Mister Brandon's boys worked the fields alongside the servants.

Sam had been part of Francis's crew since we got here. Being younger and skinnier, I got more of the odd jobs in the orchard and the small fields close to the house. But for spring planting Matthew took me and another boy out to the western edge of the farm, closest to the river, to finish clearing and preparing the field for planting.

We took turns driving the mule team and breaking up the clods of dirt kicked up behind the cart.

Matthew was pretty close to my own age, maybe a few years younger, and he stood out among the family members on the Brandon farm. He was a bonny lad, tall and fair-haired, with a courteous manner and a blush to his cheek. He never asked the servants to do anything he wouldn't do himself and worked every bit as hard.

Until Mary explained the family history, I hadn't understood that she was not a sister to Matthew or Francis, who bore the surname

Locke and were children of Missus Brandon from a prior marriage, her first husband having died shortly after the family crossed the ocean. Mary's father too was widowed and I had come to understand that Mary still grieved her mother and resented the imposition of her father's new wife.

Because I worked so closely with Matthew, I had often observed his interactions with Mary, never quite understanding the brother-sister relationship. Now it became clear that they were not blood kin at all and I could see that the flush in Matthew's face when he spoke to her and the teasing tone in Mary's voice reflected something different altogether.

Springtime on the farm meant hard work for everybody as we prepared the land for the crops that would see the family through the next cold winter. This time of year, the Susquehanna heartland of William Penn's colony was bursting with life and I was happy being out in the bright sunshine with its long days as the squirrels and starlings scurried about to feed their young.

As the sun rose higher in the sky, the coolness of early spring gave way to a hint of summer to come and we were all dripping wet from throwing aside rocks and breaking up lumps of clay.

"Let's break for lunch," Matthew instructed, and we made our way over to the shade under a chestnut where we had left the food packs and the jug of cider. We were glad to be off our feet and ate in silence, Matthew not being one for idle chatter. His fair skin was beginning to redden after a morning in the sun.

"Is this the field where they took the boy who worked for you before we came?" I asked.

"Just over there, this side of Manada Creek," Matthew responded, pointing toward the north where the field met an oak grove at the foot of Blue Mountain. "The Indians make camp on the other side of those hills, using trails through the woods to get over here and steal anything that's not tied down."

"I guess that includes servants," I speculated, with trepidation. Now that I had an Indian friend of my own, I didn't conceive of the natives as bloodthirsty heathens, as I had before. But I didn't have any illusions about kindly treatment of captives either.

"Since Willie was taken, nobody works out here alone," Matthew assured me. "And I keep a rifle nearby, just in case. Nothing to worry about."

"Have you ever shot an Indian?" Maybe it was too personal, but I was curious.

"No, but with what they've already done on this farm, I wouldn't hesitate," Matthew insisted.

"But this was their land after all. Before we came, I mean."

Matthew looked at me warily. "It's true they were here first, but in all those years they couldn't manage to turn the wilderness into useful land."

"How long has your family been here?"

"My stepfather was born here in the Penn colony, but my own family, the Lockes, emigrated from England when I was ten."

"So Mary Brandon, then, is not really your sister?"

Matthew gave me a sidelong glance. "We're now family and that's all that matters."

"She's a lively girl, is Mary Brandon," I volunteered, taking a bite from the chunk of bread in my pack and watching for Matthew's reaction out of the corner of my eye.

He turned in my direction, studying me with cool blue eyes. "And?" he asked.

"Och, just thinking . . . how lucky you are to have such a charming sister," I replied innocently.

He gave me a look that was not necessarily friendly.

"Charming, yes, but still a girl and not a woman. And though she became my stepsister through marriage, I feel responsible for her just as I do my own sisters. Mary can be impulsive and strong-willed, but that's just because she finds every new thing interesting. She doesn't much care for being treated like a child, nor should she be, but I would protect her with my life."

At the conclusion of this declaration, Matthew looked me straight in the eye and it was clear as it could be that he understood there was something between me and Mary Brandon and he didn't like it a bit.

When we went back to work, Matthew had no more to say to me, but I couldn't help but wonder why he felt it necessary to explain how he felt about Mary. Could he know that I loved her as much as he did? Surely he didn't think I would ever do anything to hurt Mary. I wondered if John Brandon intended for her to marry her stepbrother, a fearful thought that prompted an instant flash of jealousy and dismay at the thought that it could be Matthew Locke and not myself who would share Mary Brandon's bed and know the delightful mysteries of her soft skin and her indomitable spirit.

As the sun descended near the horizon after a full day of

preparing the fields for planting, Matthew called me over. "That's enough for today. Grab your pack." We headed back to the farmhouse side by side, though I had to move at a fast clip to keep up with his long strides.

Chapter Twenty-One

Kago leaned over and plucked a handful of small red berries from a prickly bush that crept along the ground near the path, popping them into his mouth.

"You can eat but . . ." he paused in his explanation, grimacing as he searched for the English word.

"Bitter," I said completing his sentence.

"Bitter," he repeated, playing with the sound as he committed it to memory. "But good for sickness of the belly. Put in hot water, then drink."

Kago's knack for English had far outpaced my poor efforts to learn the long, complex words he patiently repeated to me in the Conestoga version of Iroquois which his people spoke. When he spoke to me in his native tongue, his words came quickly and fluidly, including sounds which had no analogy in the alphabet I had been taught in my plantation schoolhouse back in Ulster, where speaking the Gaelic was sure to land you a crack across the wrist from the schoolmaster's ruler.

At the end of a day's work in Mister Brandon's fields, I would often follow the trail alongside Manada Creek deep into the woods, just to get away from the bunkhouse, sometimes to pray, longing for the time when I could go where I wished without being accountable to Mister Brandon or anybody else. It was not unusual for Kago to emerge from behind a tree and walk with me, which made me wonder whether he hunted near our farm every day, even when we weren't having our regular lessons with Mary, and whether he kept his eye on me as I toiled in the fields.

Walking by the creek with my native companion was as good as prayer for my peace of mind. He treated all things growing with a reverence that was near like being in church and he filled my head with stories of how the headwaters of this stream or the outcroppings of that rock were intended by the Great Spirit to protect the people of the land or to warn them about some impending danger. When he spoke of "the people," I had come to understand he meant his tribe and that such protections or warnings were not inclusive of other tribes and certainly not of the invasive European immigrants who were filling the land and treating its bounty as their own entitlement, to be taken or destroyed.

We had just passed a bend in the path when he stopped our progress with a firm hand to my midsection, urging me to silence with a finger first to his lips, then to mine. Turning deftly on one moccasined heel, he pointed toward a tall cedar to the right of the trail ahead, reached over his left shoulder to pull an arrow from his pack and took aim at a branch that extended across the path. His arrow flew into the tree at a speed which was hard to follow, and then with a thud a gray squirrel impaled by his arrow dropped to the ground in front of us. Kago picked it up, pulled out the arrow, wiping it clean on his deerskin breechcloth, and slipped the kill into a pouch slung over his shoulder, all without missing a step in the rhythm of our footfall.

His figure moved down the path in front of me with a natural grace that was completely in tune with the forest we were walking through.

"Alex," he said, turning back to me suddenly, "I want you to come to my village tonight. For the festival."

This stopped me cold, bringing to mind the frightening tales I had heard of white slaves taken by the natives and scalps collected to decorate their tents.

"You want me to come to your village?"

This was about as likely as an invitation from Mister Brandon to Kago's family to come over to the farm for Sunday dinner. I understood right away that Kago was going outside the usual boundaries between natives and settlers and I knew he wouldn't have suggested it without a good deal of thought. But I couldn't fathom how it could happen and the very thought of it frightened me near to death.

"Och, that is very kind of you, Kago, but I cannot," I responded, hoping to quickly put the matter to rest.

He took my hands in his with an earnest gesture of friendship. "I want you to see my people. And I want my people to know my blood brother." He was struggling to explain something to me that was perhaps too complex for the words we shared.

"In the time of my ancestors, we were a mighty people, feared in all the land. Now we are few and many are sick. But the spirit of the ancient mothers lives on . . . in the heart," he explained, thumping his chest for emphasis.

I had to shake my head with amusement that Kago thought I was brave enough or naïve enough to pay a visit to his village. Come to that, it would be like volunteering myself for the kind of captivity the servant Willie must be enduring. Trying to explain this to him with the help of mime to demonstrate my mop of auburn hair being unceremoniously removed from the rest of my head, I restated my position firmly.

Kago finally understood what I was trying to say and laughed out loud at my fearful imaginings.

"No, Alex. No scalpings," he laughed. "You are my brother." He held our arms together to reenact the blood vows. "This is something special for my people."

I could tell he was struggling for a word.

"False face," he said, circling his face with his hands.

"False face?" I repeated. This made no sense to me, but I could see that it meant something to Kago and he wanted me to understand it.

He frowned and wrinkled his nose the way he did when I tried to explain the English aristocracy or the need for private ownership of property.

"Alex, we make this false face, this picture of angry man, to call on the spirit of the great healer. He promised us his protection. But since the white man came, there is too much sickness.

"I want you there—my brother, my white friend—to call on the great healer with us. Special medicine, I think," he winked and nudged me with his hip.

Chapter Twenty-Two

Later that night, as I rode behind Kago on his pony up towards the gap in Blue Mountain, I kept wondering what in bloody hell made me agree to come. I had scribbled a note to Sam, left in his boot where he would see it if I failed to return before dawn. Time had weighed heavily on me there in the bunkhouse as I waited to be sure Sam and the others were asleep before slipping out of my bunk and into the dark woods where Kago awaited me.

I was fearful and excited at the same time, wondering if I would ever again see the Brandon farm or Mary or my brother. The forest was still as death and it felt like a dream, rocking silently through the dark pines as I held onto the bare waist of a mate whose entire experience was closer to that of the bear or beaver than to my childhood years in the rolling green hills and thatched cottages that overlooked the North Sea of Ireland.

I began to hear a distant thumping and not long after, I could see light from a burning campfire in a hollow ahead of us. As we rode into Kago's village, Indians of all ages gathered to observe our arrival.

"Do not be worried, Alex," Kago turned to assure me. "They know you are coming and they are just curious to meet my white brother."

We dismounted and Kago led me toward an older man and woman, both magnificently attired in robes woven with elaborate patterns and adorned with beads and porcupine quills. The man's tattooed face was weather-worn but his eyes shone with warmth as he greeted his son in their native tongue. Kago's mother was studying me from head to toe, curious about what manner of friend her son had acquired. I could see she was the more wary parent, but her intelligent eyes softened when Kago took her hands in his, murmuring to her as he appeared to be defending my character and pulling his mother in my direction.

They welcomed us into their longhouse, one of several large structures in the village built over bent softwood frames covered with bark. I was surprised that there were so many people inside.

"My family's house," Kago said, with a sweep of his arm. "We are many because each of my sisters and their husbands and children live here."

Kago's father invited me to sit with a group of the men of his house before a small fire, set just below one of several openings in the roof, where we shared tobacco. Kago did most of the talking as his brothers-in-law eyed me with considerable suspicion.

"Alex, come and I will show you where I live now," Kago said, striding toward the door of the longhouse.

"You don't live here?" I asked, following him outside.

Kago led the way to another longhouse, smaller than the first but also crowded with families. As we entered, a light-skinned lass with straight, shiny black hair down to her waist and a hint of mischief in her eyes came up to us, giving Kago a nudge with her hip and a look that told me all I needed to know about their relationship. She whispered into Kago's ear and the two of them chattered back and forth in words I couldn't follow.

"Alex, this is my woman . . . my wife, Osha," he said, nudging her toward me. I instinctively reached out a hand to the lass but withdrew it quickly when I saw the shocked look on her face. She glanced at Kago, then returned her gaze to me and said tentatively, "Al-Leeks," quickly covering her mouth to suppress amusement at having to recite such an improbable name.

"Your humble and obedient servant, ma'am," I countered with a little bow in her direction.

Kago explained his living arrangement. "Here, in my tribe, when you take a woman, you move in with her family."

It was a surprise to learn that Kago had a wife, a fact he had never mentioned in all our discussions. Both of them seemed young to be married and, come to that, I wondered why he had not spoken of her in our lessons about family.

I could scarcely divert my eyes from all that was going on around me. Natives were coming and going with purposeful composure as they tended to everyday life in this cedar-lined valley—preparing food to cook, reprimanding children who were playing a game with sticks and rocks too close to the fire, braves competing for the attention of girls who pretended to ignore them.

As the tribe prepared for the evening festivities, Kago and I found a comfortable resting place on a boulder at the edge of a creek where we could watch the ceremonial fire being built in the center of the village. It seemed to be important to him that I understood the way of life of his people and how much had changed for them in recent years.

"In the winter we leave this camp and go closer to the river to escape the cold and live off the fish. There on the river we have our own land, given us by Onas."

"Onas?" I did not understand his meaning.

"Onas," Kago insisted. "You know him as William Penn. He sought a peaceable kingdom with us and we honor his memory."

"Oh, you mean the land we call Conestoga Indiantown that William Penn reserved as a settlement for the Indians, down near Lancaster?" I asked, recalling that Penn had signed treaties with most of the local tribes. "You know that he is dead now—William Penn, I mean."

"Yes, but the children of Onas will honor their father's word," Kago assured me.

I wondered if the rumors I had heard about Thomas Penn's rejection of Quakerism in favor of the Church of England reflected a changing perspective within the Penn family.

"In old times, we were the most powerful tribe in these lands," Kago continued, "striking fear in the hearts of the Iroquois who travelled these paths. But we lost many warriors in the Beaver Wars. Now every winter many die from sickness brought by white people. Tonight is ceremony of healing. False face, like I told you."

Kago moved his hands in front of his face as if that explained everything.

"False face," I repeated, still mystified by this aspect of Kago's tribal tradition.

This time he gave me that look which often crossed his face when he was finding me particularly dense.

"Alex, you speak of your people's god and many ways to honor him—English, Catholic, Scots. For our people, Great Spirit of Orenda is same. Invisible force at center of every man and woman, alive in land and trees and all creatures of earth. We honor Great Spirit as you honor your god."

Kago led me to the edge of the village where a young man was painting a wild-looking face that had been carved into the trunk of a tree, then chipped out to form a mask depicting a fearsome old man with a crooked nose and pouches of tobacco tied onto his horsehair toupee. I could not for the life of me ken how such a dreadful mask could heal the sick or show honor to the spirit Orenda, but I expect Kago found the sacrament of communion equally strange. I nodded appreciatively at the young Indian's creation.

"Tonight we call upon Great Spirit to end the sickness that has brought death to so many of our tribe," he explained.

Kago always bore an expression of deep concern when he spoke to me about the decline of his people. I wanted him to understand that my people too had lived through troubles of our own.

"My grandda's grandparents were born in Scotland, where they spoke Gaelic and lived on a small farm. They had hard times too, just like your people. They were tricked into working for the English on a plantation beside Loch Neigh in the north of Ireland."

Kago was trying to follow me. "Loch?" he asked. "Not lake?"

"Oh aye, that's the Scottish word. We Scots and Irish speak the English tongue, but in our own way. Kind of like your Conestoga tribe and the Iroquois."

"Mary thinks you do not speak English correctly," he pointed out, grinning.

"Mary knows little about the Irish," I retorted. "Ireland is a green island far across the ocean, where wee crofts are built into the hillsides and the farms are separated by stone walls. It's a bonny land, is Ireland, but not enough food and not enough freedom.

"It wasn't so much the Great Spirit that brought us here," I explained. "We were just sick and tired of being cheated by the landlords back home, that's all. We wanted a chance to work and keep something for ourselves.

"Everybody in his right mind gets out of Ireland."

I could tell he was thinking about this and not understanding much of it. From his perspective, the white man's arrival in America was such a great disaster that it could only have happened as punishment visited upon his people by what he understood to be God.

"I know that your tribal home is called Ire-Land," he repeated, careful to say the name correctly. "But why did you invade *my* people's land? This has been our home for more winters than there are stars in the sky."

Kago knew nothing of European history and he had no bloody idea why the English and Scots and Irish couldn't just get along. But he did understand that we were tribes, and tribes went to war to protect their families and their hunting rights. As for the thriving cities and inventions and industries that had given Europeans the economic power to build huge ships that carried entire populations across the sea, all that just left him scratching his head.

"You didn't tell me you had a wife," I pointed out.

He smiled, fully aware that he had skipped over this very important part of his family.

"My father does not approve of Osha and my mother mourns my move to Osha's longhouse, as every brave must do when he marries. Osha's family, they are not leaders of the tribe like mine. My people do not speak loudly or draw attention to themselves. They show courage through actions, not words. They do not respect Osha's family.

"But I have loved Osha since we were children," he continued. "She has always been wild and beautiful. Her people fight too much and drink too much fire water. But the heart does not always choose wisely. Just like you and Mary. What can you do?"

Kago laughed and gave me a nudge, suggesting the universal helplessness of men who have lost their hearts to the wrong women.

After food and tobacco, the men, women, and children of the village moved closer to the campfire and the insistent pounding of drums grew louder. Indians emerged with wooden masks of demonic faces painted red and black and began whooping and dancing around the fire, shaking turtle shell rattles, a sight as colorful and fearful as any I had encountered in my life. Soon all were dancing—men, women, and children, myself included, if you could call my poor efforts to move ferociously to the beat of the drums dancing. It was not what you would have considered proper dancing such as you might engage in with members of the opposite sex back in Ireland.

Chapter Twenty-Two

I couldn't help but notice Kago's young wife Osha, moving her hips rhythmically around the circle, drawing attention from many of the men—not surprising since her lovely form, adorned with colorful ornaments that sparkled in the light of the fire, was exposed so that one's eyes could not move away from the silky golden skin undulating seductively to the rhythm of the pounding drums.

My attention was drawn to Kago's parents who were watching the swirling figures from the other side of the raging campfire. Kago's mother was tight-lipped as she watched her daughter-in-law exchange glances with many young men. And then Kago walked into the circle and took Osha by the arm, speaking to her with a stern word. She responded sharply, with a flip of her head, continuing to spin around the fire.

Riveted as I was by Osha's beauty and her willfulness, I couldn't keep my eyes off her as she gave herself over to the passion of the dance. Yet something felt out of balance, in spite of the girl's loveliness, and I couldn't think why. Then it became apparent to me.

Osha was pregnant.

By the time Kago pulled me behind him on the horse that carried me back to the bunkhouse, I was exhausted, but my mind was spinning with all I had seen. My friend was quiet as we rode for a second time through the still, dark forest.

Kago took my hand warmly after I dismounted at the edge of the woods near the farm. "So, my white brother, you see my people. Now you know who I am."

As the sun started to glow on the eastern horizon, I was still staring at the bunkhouse ceiling from my bed, reliving the evening and wondering how in the name of Jesus, Mary, and Joseph I would be able to drag myself out to perform my morning chores. Thanks to a ray of light that entered the bunkhouse through a crack between logs and illuminated the ground between my cot and my brother's, I remembered the note I had put in Sam's boot before leaving to meet Kago and quickly slipped out of bed to retrieve it so he wouldn't know where I had been.

Chapter Twenty-Three

Sam and I were assigned to different crews for the week. I had to get out to the barley patch early, so I didn't wait for the farmhouse bell to roust me out of bed. I was out of the bunkhouse, face washed at the pump, and enjoying a chunk of brown bread on my way to the fields before Sam was up.

That was just fine with me. Sam had been in a foul mood all week and I was weary of his lectures and complaints about our dismal fate as servants in the new world.

I didn't see it that way. I felt about as free as I ever had since there was always something to eat on the farm, which was more than you could say for our meager fare back in County Armagh, where there were always too many hands reaching for too little meat.

It wasn't that I didn't miss my ma and da. But they had given their blessing for us to leave hearth and home to make a life in America. My mind always turned to them in the prayers I said each night before falling asleep, asking that God watch over them, as well as each and every brother and sister, naming them one by one in order of birth. But as time went on, my family back home seemed less and less real to me and my prayers for their well-being were recited more from habit than anything else. Mary Brandon was real to me and so was Kago. But County Armagh seemed like another world.

I knew it was wrong and a sin to be avoiding my brother, who was really all I had in this place. He looked out for me every day, just as he had during the long sea voyage. But I was not a child and I didn't need Sammy playing the father to me. I had been to a celebration in an Indian village and I loved a girl in a kind of way I didn't care to explain to my older brother.

On Friday I had spent the morning thinning apple trees and looking forward to dusk in the forest clearing with Mary and Kago. Sam had become suspicious of my regular disappearances, and for some reason I canna' explain I didn't want him to know about Kago, a native of this land, a person of a different race and a culture I couldn't begin to understand, and yet who had become as true a friend to me as I had ever known. With his quick and physical wit and his kind and expressive face, laughing gaily at my lack of understanding of things that to him were second nature, Kago was every bit as much a brother to me as Sam.

But most of all, I didn't want Sam to see into my heart which was bursting with love for Mary Brandon.

"Roamin' in the woods again, are ye, brother?" he asked as I headed toward the bunkhouse door.

"I won't be out long. I need to be by myself sometimes."

"I guess I never realized you were such a lover of nature," Sam replied, with more cynicism in his voice than I would have expected.

Chapter Twenty-Three

"Look, I don't like being cooped up in here. Reminds me of the ship."

"You aren't meeting the Brandon girl in the woods, are ye, Alex?"

That got my attention.

"You think I haven't noticed you and Mary Brandon wanderin' into the woods at the same time every Friday. I'm not daft, am I? Are you out o' your feeble mind, Alex? We'll be sent away from here if you're found playin' around with the owner's daughter. A lass still of tender age."

"I don't know what you're talking about."

Sam raised one eyebrow as he gave me an accusatory look.

"I'm not blind, brother. Do you think I didn't notice your empty cot the other night? What has got into you, ye wee shite—spending the night rutting in the woods with the owner's daughter?"

I didn't have an answer to Sam's discovery of my overnight absence from the bunkhouse. But the very thought that he would accuse me—and most of all that he would accuse Mary Brandon—of lying together without the benefit of marriage made my blood boil.

"Shut your trap, Sam. Ye dinnae ken anything about it. And don't you dare bring Mary Brandon into this."

"Do as you will, brother. But don't blame me if you get hauled before the church board."

"What are you talking about, the church board?"

I didn't care for my older brother sticking his nose into my affairs and I also didn't care for the fact that our Presbyterian congregation got pulled into the debate every time Sam called me on behavior he didn't approve of.

"What in the name of Jesus does the church have to do with who my friends are?" I sputtered.

"Well, eejit, ye may not be aware of it, but over here they don't have so many legal courts like they did back in Ulster. So it's your local congregation that's going to hear the case if you've been stepping out of line. Such as you have been doing with the landowner's daughter. The church knows a bit about that, don't they—what's a sin and what isn't."

"The church has nothing to worry about," I grumbled. "What I do on this farm is none of their concern. And your life would not be so miserable, brother, if you tried to make friends once in a while."

"Is that what she is, Alex? A friend? Is that why you follow her into the woods every week where you can't be seen? And keepin' your darlin' girl out all night in the forest? Good God, her father will kill you."

At that point, I tore into my brother with a rage I had no idea was simmering inside me. "Stay out of my affairs, you bloody shite," I sputtered, pushing him back toward his bunk.

Not expecting such a reaction, Sam was caught off balance and fell against the wall, scraping the side of his face against the rough boards.

Now he was mad and he charged me with his full force, both of us rolling on the floor in a death lock.

"Want to be an Englishman, do ye? Big shot landowner, eh?" He was out of breath and furious, pinning me to the floor as he leaned over my face.

"Mother of God. Think she'll wed a servant, do ye? Do ye

honestly believe her da will keep you around once he gets wind of this? You're a fool, brother."

I rolled out of his grip, pulling myself up against the wall before making another lunge at him. Sam was bigger and stronger, but I landed a blow to his nose that made full contact and it was now gushing blood. The sight stopped me cold. This was the brother who had looked after me all the way from Lurgan.

He glared at me. "And to make it all worse, she's a bloody Brandon."

I had no idea what he meant by that. "A Brandon? I know that."

We were both breathing heavily and our anger spent. Sam eased himself onto his bunk, staunching the flow of blood with a dirty shirt. He stared at me.

"After what they did to our family? Do ye not remember Grandda's stories of old Thomas and his son? How they stole our land and laid claim to everything our family had saved on the Ulster plantation? Took everything we had of value 'for unpaid taxes,' including the cross. The cross that our family had passed down over all our generations in Scotland?"

It was Da's grandfather Oliver who had been forced to give the cross to the landlord's son to keep his family alive during the worst winter in Ireland's history.

"You probably can't remember him," Sam said, "but I can—old as the hills. How he hated Old Thomas Brandon and his greedy son James and all the Brandons that came later. They broke his heart."

"Jesus, Sam. There must be people named Brandon all over the world. What on earth makes you think this family has anything to do with Old Thomas?"

Sam sat on the bunk, catching his breath and tending to his nose. He looked at me with considerable disgust. "It's a name I will hate forever, that's all."

"Good lord, all that was a hundred years ago. You'll never see Ireland again. When are you going to begin to make a life for yourself here?" And with that, I turned and walked out, the rough door slamming behind me.

Chapter Twenty-Four

"What happened to your face?" Mary exclaimed, gently touching the purple swelling around my eyes.

"Nothing worth talking about, lass."

"You look terrible."

It was Friday and Mary and I were alone in the clearing, surprised that Kago hadn't stepped out from behind a tree to join us. He generally arrived first, but he could move through the brush like a cat and preferred to watch the clearing from a hidden place before exposing himself.

"It's not like him to be late," Mary worried. "I know he likes to hang back, to be sure it's us and nobody else. But he should be here by now."

For my own part, I never minded a few minutes alone with Mary Brandon, her dark eyes sparkling with interest and amusement every time I said a clever thing.

We talked about nothing and everything, and I often thought to myself that this was the only time of the week when I could say whatever was on my mind.

"I can see that Matthew is sweet on you, Mary Brandon, but I think it improper for a brother to have such attentiveness toward his sister."

She was quiet for a moment, surprised that I had noticed her stepbrother's attentions.

"As you know very well, he is not my brother, and anyway he has no such feelings for me."

"I am a man, Mary, and I know well what a man is feeling."

Mary laughed. "You're not that old."

"I felt like a boy when I left my home in Ireland, but not anymore."

How could I tell her, daughter of the landowner who also owned me as surely as he owned the land, that I too loved her and saw her stepbrother as my rival?

Kago burst through the bushes in his usual manner, appearing out of nowhere. He wore a sling around his chest and had a look of concern on his face that I had never seen.

"I ask big favor from friends."

Kago knelt on the ground between us and gently unwrapped the bundle he carried on his chest. As he did so, Mary emitted a murmur of gentle astonishment.

Except for Mary's exclamation, we were dead silent, the three of us, contemplating a perfectly formed newborn infant, looking up with raven eyes fixed on Kago's face.

Finally, I emerged from my dumbfounded silence to ask with a dry mouth, "Kago, where did you get that child?"

"*My* child," he responded quickly. "My wife Osha, she cannot feed. Just cry and sleep."

Kago was looking at the child with such sadness in his eyes. I could tell he was having trouble finding the words.

"Osha sent me away from her longhouse," he stammered. "Something has made her sad and angry. She doesn't want me and she doesn't want our baby. My mother has gone to her and pleaded to let her help. But she turns away and only wishes to die."

The child made a small mewling sound, like a newborn kitten, and Kago put a finger to its cheek, stroking the baby with affection. He then slipped a knuckle into the infant's mouth, which generated energetic sucking.

"The chief, he sent for me," Kago continued. "Tells me the birth of the child made Osha sick. And our people are so weakened from illness that there is no other mother making milk. They want us to give up our baby for adoption to a tribe to the north. But this tribe, they are a warlike people and I don't trust them."

His eyes filled with tears as he put a hand over the infant's head.

"I know Osha is not ready to be mother. Still wild. Still beautiful."

Then he looked me straight in the eye.

"White friends keep baby."

Kago's English didn't contain the vocabulary necessary to explain any further the complex tribal laws by which this child's fate was determined.

He unwrapped a bundle from his pack containing a wooden scoop and a container of milk, along with various cloths and other implements of infant care. Patiently he demonstrated the method for pouring milk through the scoop into the infant's mouth, which the baby accepted with surprising accommodation.

157

Kago took Mary's hand and instructed her in various methods of infant wrapping and the intricate ritual of feeding.

"Kago," I protested. "We cannot care for the wee bairn. I am but a servant on the farm. How can Mary explain where the child came from? They wouldn't let her keep the child."

Both Kago and Mary were oblivious to my protestations as Mary focused solely upon the infant and Kago observed and instructed as best he could.

When Kago stood to leave us, he turned one last time to look at his wee child, laying his hand on the bairn's head, much as a pastor might do during the ritual of baptism. There were tears in his eyes, but before we could say another word, he turned and disappeared into the underbrush.

Chapter Twenty-Five

Walking through that forest with the babe in my arms felt like a dream, the light weight of the bundle making no sense at all, given the intricate detailing of ear and eye and the lively little fingers grasping and squeezing.

Jesus, Mary, and Joseph, how in the name of God am I to explain this?

Mary and I had argued about what to do. She wanted to take Kago's baby. I couldn't see how she could make up a story that her parents would believe. Why would she be alone so deep into the woods as to run across an abandoned papoose?

As I approached the house, nightfall starting to create shadows at the edges of the unfinished wood of the barn and darkening the path to the bunkhouse, John Brandon was escorting Master Fry to his buggy and Francis and Matthew were nearby securing the pens for the evening.

I must have been a sight, my face still bearing purple splotches from the tussle with Sam, as I approached Francis and Matthew with an Indian babe in my arms. At first they didn't look up from their work.

I stood awkwardly holding the child. Francis turned to see what I wanted.

"I was in the south woods checking the otter traps at the bend of Manada Creek. Walked on down past the dammed-up pond and thought I heard an animal yowling."

Francis peered into the bundle. "Holy Christ. It's a baby."

Matthew looked at the child, up at me, and back to the babe, open-mouthed.

Soon we had attracted a fair crowd, with heads popping out of the upper windows, including an anxious-looking Mary, who at my urging had returned to the farm well before me.

"What a sweet little face," Anne cooed. "Mother, come look!"

Elbowing through the admiring crowd, Mistress Brandon took charge immediately. "Good Lord, Alex, where did you get that child?"

"Abandoned in the forest, ma'am. Out past the bend in the creek."

"But why? By whom?"

"I don't know, ma'am. It was wrapped in this cloth and lying in the crook of a tree. Yelling its head off."

"Well, come here, little one. Why would anyone abandon you?" She was cuddling the wee babe and smiling down into the bundle. "Good heavens, Alex. The baby can't be more than a month old."

At that, the babe started wailing.

"This pouch, it was wrapped in the blanket with the child," I offered, handing over the feeding implements Kago had left us.

Mistress Brandon studied the funnel and the container of milk.

"It's an Indian. An Indian baby," she speculated. "Even though its skin is light."

The youngest Locke son peered into the bundle. "Mother, if it's an Indian baby, will they come here looking for it?"

"All I'm worried about right now is getting some milk into this child," pronounced the lady of the house, and she pushed through the gathering toward the kitchen house with Kago's baby.

Mary had joined the onlookers by that time and we both watched Mistress Brandon's back as she strode decisively into the kitchen.

"I should go help," Mary said, to no one in particular, as her father approached the gathering outside the pens.

"Master Fry tells me you boys are making reasonable progress with your lessons," John Brandon said to Matthew and the other Brandon and Locke boys.

"Father," Anne exclaimed. "Alex found an abandoned baby in the woods. Left in a tree. An Indian baby."

Mister Brandon turned to me with a discomfited expression. "What's this about, Alex?"

I repeated my story, which was beginning to sound more believable with each telling. "I didn't know what to do, sire. I hadn't held a wean since I kissed my baby sister Katie goodbye in Belfast. But I felt it would be wrong before God to leave the child there to be attacked by wild beasts."

Mary was watching me with wide eyes, as I made this earnest declaration to her father. She turned to him.

"Oh, Father, it's a lovely baby. Elizabeth is in the kitchen right now, trying to get it to take some milk."

"Well," grumbled the master of the house, "we're going to have to figure out what to do with it."

161

His forehead wrinkled as he considered the problem. He wasn't a man to make rash decisions, but I could see by the look on his face that this was a situation he didna' care to deal with.

Matthew moved closer to his stepfather.

"Is this a usual thing, for a tribe to abandon a child?" Matthew asked, looking to his stepfather's greater experience with native customs in the colonies.

"I've never heard of it before," Mister Brandon muttered. "And I don't welcome the thought that its tribe might come looking for the child."

Matthew looked as worried as his stepfather, so alike those two in how they reacted to any problem on the farm, brows furrowed as they leaned in together to weigh the options.

"James is going into Hanover tomorrow. I'm going to ask him to inquire about the fort they are building for the militia up the path to the gap. He said there would be a place there to lock up the natives they caught stealing off our farms and threatening the families down here in the valley. They might have some Indian women up there who could take care of this child. Matthew, before it gets any darker, could you ride over to the Catheys and ask James to stop by here to talk to me on his way into town?"

"Surely we can take care of the baby ourselves, Father. It wouldn't be right to turn an innocent child over to a bunch of rangers and prisoners," Mary protested.

Francis broke in. "Is it a boy or a girl?"

Mary and I looked at each other.

Chapter Twenty-Five

"I dinnae ken," I responded, it never having occurred to me to take a look.

Mary looked somber. "I'm going in to help with the baby."

And she was off to the kitchen.

Chapter Twenty-Six

The arrival of Kago's bairn on the farm changed everything. Mary no longer came to the clearing, since she had taken over much of the care of Polly, as Kago's daughter came to be called. And Kago, having deposited his babe with us, did not reappear. Mary adored the wee child and for the first time established a strong bond with her stepmother, who also loved Polly and felt her unusual arrival was a message from God that the Brandon family had a responsibility to raise her in the Christian way.

This English farm family of Brandons and Lockes shared one thing in common with Scots-Irish immigrants like me and Sam. We had come to a land of uncivilized natives who knew nothing of God or of the salvation that would come to those who accepted his holy son as their savior. Surely it was our duty to try to save them from eternal damnation.

The English of course had a firm solution for everything. For a child like Polly, they had a chance to give her something she would never have known in her native village, a chance for eternal salvation. The first step was a solid English name. Then the proper way to dress and speak. Somewhere at the end of a long line of transformation, a soul could be saved.

This should have been clear as day to me from the moment the child was given into our care. This was how I was reared, back on the farm in Ireland. Mary too, even though her faith was cloaked in Anglican ritual and mine in evangelistic Presbyterian. But to the two of us, there was something false, some kind of error of perception in this doctrine. An arrogance even. We knew Kago and we knew his heart and mind. Come to that, if the child grew up to be just like her father, would that be such a bad thing?

Elizabeth and Mary united in their campaign to keep the child in the family, much to the consternation of John Brandon, who didn't care for another mouth to feed and had misgivings about repercussions from the tribe that caused the child to be left in the woods.

My heart was heavy with the weight of responsibility. It was Kago's bairn left in my care, and not my own, but I knew of God's love for innocent children and how Jesus held open his arms saying, "Suffer the little children to come unto me for of such is the kingdom of heaven."

Would it not be a wicked sin to surrender the wee thing to the rough militia and their imprisoned savages? Who would walk with the child and comfort her when she awoke in the night? I prayed that Mary would have enough influence with Mister Brandon to convince him to keep the babe.

As a servant, I had no power over my own fate, much less that of an Indian babe. We were in the backcountry with no hospitals or charities to help us. Even the regular British soldiers had very little presence so far from the coast. The local rangers helped to keep the Indian problems under control, but they were not equipped to care for an infant.

Only the Catholic Church seemed interested in this problem, insisting that captured Indian children be turned over to them for proper Christian upbringing. But there were few Catholics this far west and virtually no orphanages, even if Mister Brandon had been willing to turn the bairn over to them, which was unlikely.

Kago didn't return to our meeting place. I so wished to talk with him, to find enough common words to better understand why his daughter had to be abandoned. The tribe did move around from season to season—Kago had taught us that much—but I didn't know whether his absence was part of their normal seasonal migration or whether it had something to do with the child.

I knew family was important to Kago. After my visit to his village for the false face healing ceremony, we had talked about families—his and mine.

"Why did you travel so far from your family, Alex?" he had asked, incredulous that I would willingly break the bonds of familial love and protection. "Your mother and father must grieve for you and your brother."

"Oh, aye, many tears were shed when we boarded the ship in Belfast," I responded. "But we were so poor and there was no future for us in Ireland. They wanted us to have a chance."

"Do they know you are servants now?" Kago could not get over the fact that we had given up our freedom to get a new start. To him, being a slave was the worst fate that could befall any man.

Chapter Twenty-Six

"We're not slaves, Kago. After four years of service, we will be free men. Sam and I are going to start a farm together. They are giving away land across the river."

His lips tightened and he wrinkled his brow at that notion.

"That is Indian land across the river. You would not survive a season there."

After wee Polly was given to us and Mary stopped coming to the clearing, I felt particularly forlorn. I had so many questions. Would they keep the babe? Had she thought about why Kago brought her to us? Did she love me?

When I passed her at the farm, I told her that Kago had not come again to the clearing.

"Can we speak?" I asked. She knew I meant more than the kind of talk we could have at the farm. "I miss you."

"But, Alex, I'm the one with the most responsibility for Polly. I mean, I wanted that. I want it. Kago would expect it of me. But I'm having trouble getting everything done. She wants to be fed all the time. And she wrinkles up her nose and gets frightfully angry at me if I don't respond quickly enough."

Mary, thinking about that demanding baby, smiled in a way that made it clear to me this child was occupying one hundred percent of her heart at this moment.

"Mary, please try to come to the clearing on Friday. I need to talk to you."

She came. We embraced in the privacy of our clearing, where we could be ourselves and let go of the formalities necessary when we ran into each other on the farm.

"Are you alright, lass? Is the family accepting the child?"

I couldn't define it exactly, but Mary had changed in some way. She seemed older, more settled.

She reached out and touched my face, tucking an escaped curl back behind my ear. "You are my best friend in the world, Alex. I miss our time together. But I'm worried that they will know about us—about our meetings and Kago and everything. Then they might decide to give away the baby. Or put her in the hands of the militia. I couldn't bear it."

Her eyes teared up and I took her in my arms and all was well in the world.

"You love the child, I know. But I love *you*, Mary Brandon. I'm never so happy as when I'm here with you, alone in the green forest, hearing the magic of your voice."

She pulled back and looked at me straight on. "And I love you too, Alex. But in a few more months you'll have to go back to Chester County. And every time I come here, every time I'm alone with you, it's going to be harder and harder to say goodbye."

My heart broke into little pieces with every word, but I knew that she spoke the truth.

Chapter Twenty-Seven

It was a surprisingly warm afternoon, the cicadas making a terrible racket that echoed through the still air. I led Sam down the lower path toward the forest clearing near the creek where Mary and I had so often met with our friend Kago. Neither Sam nor I had much to say. It felt all wrong to be bringing my brother to this place—our place, Mary's and mine—but I hadn't any choice in the matter.

Mary had approached us together that morning, out of breath with excitement. "I'm glad to have found you together. I have finally sorted through those papers in Father's study. And I'm quite sure of it now. Our families did business together back on the plantations in Ireland. More than 100 years ago. Thomas Brandon. Joseph McTurk. Father has walked me through our genealogy, and it all makes sense. Meet me at the clearing during Master Fry's lesson today. I'll bring the papers."

For me, it felt like an open acknowledgment that what we had together was over. She didn't appear to notice that she was sharing our secret place, the place of our sacred bond, with my older brother who not only hated the English but had hectored me privately for weeks about the dangers of seeing Mary alone.

Sam and I settled under the sugar maple and waited. "So this is where you meet her, eh?" Sam commented. "Very cozy."

"Come on, Sam. Let it go. Nothing improper ever passed between Mary Brandon and myself."

"But I told you, didn't I, that this was the same Brandon family?" Sam was self-righteous in his bitterness. "The same bloody English that cheated our great-grandfather. And I was right."

Before we could come to blows a second time, Mary arrived in the clearing with a pack around her shoulder.

"I can't wait to show you what I've discovered," she said with a smile, lowering her pack to the ground. "You know, I've been trying to get Polly to sleep in Father's study where it's quiet in the afternoon. With nothing to do but rock the cradle, I've been reading old letters. Brandon keepsakes going way back to our family's land grant in Ulster County. I didn't want Father to find me in there sorting through documents, so I grabbed this whole stack of papers."

Mary passed a handful of documents and letters to each of us and all was quiet in the clearing as we tried to decipher the meaning of these old records.

"Much of this is unrelated to our family's land grant in Ulster County," Mary said, breathless. "But keep reading."

Sam was able to put the pieces together because he had spent many childhood days in my grandfather's croft, hearing the old stories. He rifled through the papers, setting his eyes on one in particular.

"See this signature," Sam explained, showing me what appeared to be a page torn out of a log book. "That would be Old Thomas's second son, not nearly as greedy as James Brandon, but not inclined to miss an opportunity to increase his family's holdings either."

"And this patent, do ye see?" Sam queried, showing the document to Mary. "This is how your ancestors reclaimed the land that had been deeded to us, squeezing the family dry with quit-rents and penalties. So many broken promises."

Mary's curiosity was piqued by this improbable connection between our families, and she paid little attention to Sam's criticism of her ancestors.

Although none of us could decipher the meaning behind many of these old formal-looking papers, Sam's face took on a hard edge as he began to see the patterns of the Brandon plantation business.

I could see Mary was a little surprised at the intensity of Sam's resentment of the ill treatment of our forebears, all these years later. I could have told her he still bore grudges that felt fresh.

Sam continued the haranguing. "Do your papers show how James took possession of our family's cross?"

"What cross?" asked Mary distractedly, holding a letter with faded script up to the light.

"The McTurk cross," he asserted. "A relic that was in our family since our beginnings. And blessed by St. Francis himself."

"Sam, I wish you would let go of your romantic notions about our family's history. There was nothing grand about any of it. Never enough to eat. Nothing to call our own. The only cross I remember hung on the wall behind Ma and Da's bed—a cross of rough wood that Da had made as a child."

"Of course you never saw our family's cross. Nor did I. James Brandon stole it a hundred years before we were born," Sam insisted.

"Brother, you are too easily seduced by fairy tales," I retorted. "You don't even know what this cross looked like."

"Grandda told me exactly what it looked like. Not so different in size than the one that hung over the bed. But solid gold and embedded with red and blue gemstones. It was brought back to Scotland from the Crusades by one of our ancestors."

As Sam made this pronouncement, Mary, who had been preoccupied with deciphering faded calligraphy from a crumbling letter, looked up at Sam with shock.

Sam was still rifling through papers and I could see that Mary was disturbed by something. I took her gently by the arm and led her to the far side of the clearing.

"Are ye all right then, lass?"

Mary just shook her head in dismay. "I think we have your cross," she finally said.

Chapter Twenty-Eight

S am and I had been pulled from our regular work in the fields to assist Francis in repairing the farmhouse well, which had developed a rupture that threatened to contaminate the water supply. The Brandon farm was too far from the creek to rely on transported water for the family's needs so it was critical to repair the cracks in the mortar and rebuild the support structure around the well.

Being so close to the house, I hoped to have a chance to see Mary, but her sisters had fed the chickens and pigs and she didn't show her face all day.

As the sun settled lower in the sky, we pushed to get the interior work done before it was too dark to see what we were doing. Already the long drop below us was pitch black and the last rectangle of the day's light illumined the eastern side of the well where we were chipping away mortar. The sulfurous odor of mossy dank rocks was beginning to feel oppressive. It had been a long and arduous day and all three of us were dripping in sweat.

On his way in from the fields, Matthew stuck his head down into the well where we were working. "Francis, can I pull you out for a word?"

"We're trying to finish this patch before dark," Francis snapped. "Can't it wait?"

"I'm going to finish closing up the barn," Matthew replied. "Come catch me there when you're finished."

Francis was muttering to himself as we struggled to position the last rocks against one another in a way that would hold overnight as the mortar hardened. "Everything breaks down at once on this farm."

"This is going to hold just fine," I promised. "Sam and I will smooth out this section and close up for the night."

Francis was a capable farm hand and a reasonable man to work with, just like his brother, but he wasn't content with farm work the way Matthew was and when things fell apart it put him in a bad mood. But he gathered his bucket of mortar and spreader, nodding our way as he climbed out of the well.

Sam and I finished the grouting and checked the repair to make sure it would hold fast before climbing up to the surface, where we settled near the pump to clean our tools.

The last color was draining from the horizon and darkness settling in as Francis and Matthew passed nearby on the path to the house.

"She loves that child and I don't think she will ever forgive her father if he abandons it," Matthew said, his voice troubled. "She fears the baby will be neglected and abused at the fort."

"What choice have we got?" Francis argued. "We can't afford another mouth to feed. It might be different if the child were a boy. We could train a male child to work in the fields with the servants or sell his indenture in Lancaster. But an Indian girl could never pay for herself. We don't need another kitchen wench."

Chapter Twenty-Eight

They had stopped at the corner by the pens, wanting to finish their conversation before going inside.

"Look, Francis, our stepfather plans to take the child to the militia post up by the gap tomorrow. He's not even going to tell Mary. I want you to help me try to convince him to keep the baby."

"I don't agree with you on this, Matthew. I know you're sweet on Mary Brandon, but we've got the whole family to consider."

"And what about our Christian duty toward the child?" Matthew's voice had taken on a sharp edge.

"For now, I expect they'll put the babe with one of the squaws held at the gaol. When she's old enough, she'll be trained in honest work."

"Or sold off to a brothel or workhouse when she's ten," Matthew muttered in disgust. "Please, Francis, come help me reason with Father."

As their voices faded, I sat stock still, trying to hear more. My heart sank at the thought of Kago's child being abandoned to the control of the militia, with their cruel indifference and their disdain for the natives.

Did Mary know what they were planning? How could I get to her this late in the afternoon? Clearly neither of us was ready to take on responsibility for a child, and God knows Kago had no right to expect it of us, but I too felt an obligation to this child and was alarmed that she might be handed off to the ruffians that ran the local militia.

As the early evening shadows started to settle over the Brandon farm, I saw Anne gathering greens in the kitchen garden and hurried over to where she worked. Mary spoke often about her older sister and I knew how close they were. I didn't think Mary would have told

Anne about our friendship, but I knew she trusted Anne. I had to take the chance to approach her.

"Mistress Brandon," I addressed her from across the garden in a friendly fashion. "Could I speak to you for a moment, ma'am?"

Anne Brandon looked up from her work, surprised to be approached by one of the servants. She dropped her clipping tool into a basket and came to the edge of the kitchen garden where I stood.

"I'm very sorry to bother you, ma'am," I stuttered, "but I was wondering if I might ask you to tell your sister Mary that I need to speak to her when she has a moment?"

"Heavens, Alex, why don't you just go knock at the door?"

"Och, I would hate to bother her when she is busy preparing supper. I have located something she was looking for is all. If it wouldn't be too much trouble to just let her know that, ma'am."

"Alright, Alex, I will tell her."

I had scarcely ever spoken to Anne Brandon and I hoped she didn't find me impertinent in approaching her, but I was desperate to talk to Mary. I meandered about the kitchen garden after Anne went inside, praying she wouldn't wait too long to speak to her sister.

Mary came out of the kitchen door a few minutes later.

"Alex, what is it?"

"Lass, I'm sorry to pull you out of the house like this through your sister. But I had to talk to you tonight. Could we walk over by the barn for a moment?"

As I related the overheard conversation, Mary began to understand that her father was indeed prepared to abandon Kago's child and she almost sank to the ground. I took her arm to steady her.

"No," she protested. "Father wouldn't do that without speaking to me first. Elizabeth cares for Polly too. Surely she wouldn't let this happen. Matthew must have misunderstood."

I could see her mind sorting through the possible explanations for the conversation I had overheard. And I could see in her face a frantic need to find a different answer as she wavered between anger and fear and grief.

Finally, the realization that abandonment of the child could come to pass took hold. Her lower lip began to quiver and she fell into my arms with a sob.

Lord, I never loved Mary Brandon more than I did at that moment, weeping in my arms there in the farmyard for all the world to see.

"Oh, Alex, what are we to do? Kago trusted us with his child. We can't let them abandon her."

I had such high regard for Mary—for her courage and intelligence and high moral character—that it was unthinkable she should turn to me to solve an impossible problem. An outsider. A servant. With no power in this place and little understanding of how such choices were made. But how I loved holding her in her despair and how proud I felt that she looked to me for an answer, for a way to protect the child.

I took her arms and gently untangled her from our embrace. "Mary, your father respects you and will listen. You must compose yourself and go to him with a plan. I have seen the sparkle in his eye when he watches you. You must convince him that the values of your faith require your family to protect this child."

Chapter Twenty-Nine

I was up early to help Francis prepare for a long day in the forest cutting hardwood. The farmyard was still dark and cool, light from beyond the eastern hills just beginning to give shape to the house and orchard. But the roosters were awake and there was already activity inside the barn. I entered through the side door, figuring Francis would want my help to pack up the saws and axes.

The light from inside the barn spilled out from the open door across the still-dark farmyard, the faint odor of manure emanating from the stalls. Inside it was as bright as midday with lanterns hanging from each corner of the haymow ablaze at the corners of the barn. Francis was helping Mister Brandon load supplies into the cart, where his wife sat holding Kago's child. Mary stood before them weeping, her face puffy and red.

John Brandon sighed deeply, then dropped his pack in the back of the wagon and turned to take his daughter by the shoulders, looking her directly in the eye.

"Please, Father, don't take her away," she implored, glancing at Polly who was happily taking a bottle in Elizabeth's arms.

"Mary, I know this is hard for you. You've grown attached to the child. But it's better for Polly to make the break now before she becomes equally attached to you. We cannot keep her." Mister Brandon was gentle but absolutely resolved.

"You don't understand, Father. Polly is already attached to me. She depends on me to feed her and rock her. She will be hysterical when she can't find me." Mary's voice was tremulous and her breath ragged at the thought of the baby searching in vain among strangers for her familiar face.

"She will adjust," Mister Brandon said solemnly.

The still morning was shattered, as Mary wailed in grief and rage, tearing away from her father's grasp.

"Mary, I've had enough of this. As the head of this household, I've made the best decision I can for the well-being of this child, as well as the rest of the family. You are old enough to understand that. Go back to bed, daughter."

Mistress Brandon bore a look of dismay and had tears in her own eyes, but she said nothing.

"Where are you taking her?" Mary demanded.

"To the new fort."

"But why?"

"Because we can't afford to raise an Indian child, Mary. And it would be a danger to the family to keep her here at the farm. The militia has medical rangers and they will care for the infant until they can find a tribe that will take her."

"She'll be treated like a captive by any tribe that takes her. They aren't civilized, Father. They won't be kind because she's not one of their own."

179

"The child is more theirs than she is ours. They take captives from other tribes all the time. She will assimilate."

"No she won't. How could she? She's just a baby." Mary was getting more and more frantic, her voice breaking in anger and despair. "Is this what it means to be a Christian? Is it, Father?"

Mister Brandon just shook his head. "Good Lord, Mary. Is there anything you won't argue about? Get back to the house. Now."

Mary turned and ran out the door, just as Francis came in behind me.

"There you are," he said. "Come help me get the tools loaded."

After an exhausting morning felling trees and sawing logs, I stopped by the bunkhouse before the midday meal and discovered a note under my pillow.

> "Alex, please meet me at the usual place this
> afternoon when Master Fry starts his lesson."

Below the rapidly scrawled note was her signature.

> —Mary

When she came into the clearing, Mary looked like a changed person. She was sober and pale, with none of the liveliness I had come to know and love.

I went to her and held her, but she was still and angry and didn't yield to my touch.

She reached into a canvas bag and withdrew a gold cross encrusted with red and blue stones. She held it out to me as if giving a blessing, though there was a chill in the air as she placed the cross in my hands.

Chapter Twenty-Nine

I was so confused by what she was doing that I took the cross, turning it as the sun reflected off its golden surface. What did this mean? It felt like a ritual or sacrifice of some kind. Like our ceremony of blood kinship with Kago.

"It belongs to you," said Mary Brandon. And she turned and walked out of the clearing.

Book Three

Matthew Locke

A Sunday School Teacher

Salisbury, North Carolina, 1800

As the last stragglers put away their Bibles and slates, nodding respectfully to the septuagenarian Sunday school teacher and ducking out the classroom door, Matthew Locke pushed back from the massive oak desk, smiling to himself with a rueful shake of the head.

"Good Lord, how little they understand of the blessings they have inherited," he murmured.

James Cathey passed the boys in the hallway as they were leaving the Thyatira Presbyterian Church meetinghouse to join their families before Sunday morning service. He peered into the classroom where Matthew still sat, lost in thought.

"Are you ready to go, uncle?" he asked. "Your wife will be waiting with the family around by the sumac grove. The church must be half filled by now."

It still threw Matthew off pace to hear the family refer to his wife, a surprise to them all when he returned from his last trip to Philadelphia, marrying again at age sixty-eight after living contentedly as a widower for eight years after he lost Mary. Elizabeth Gostelowe, the widow of a skilled Philadelphia cabinet maker, didn't like living alone any better than he and was willing to leave her comfortable life in the city for the mountains of North Carolina to spend their last years in warm companionship. Mary, of all people, would have understood.

"Here I come," Matthew chuckled. "Slowly, mind you, after an hour with those rowdies."

James helped his uncle to his feet, still impressed by the willingness of this icon of the Revolution and elected Representative to Congress to serve the Lord by teaching a thing or two to schoolboys.

"I wasn't even reared in the Presbyterian Church, you know," the elderly teacher explained. "I was a vestryman over here at St. Luke's Episcopal. We were faithful Anglicans until after the war when loyalty to the Church of England somehow implied loyalty to King George."

A large clan of Lockes, Brandons, and Catheys laid claim to the pews in the front left section of the Thyatira sanctuary each Sunday morning. Nobody else would have considered occupying those places, given that James Cathey had donated twelve acres of land to the church, where the Sunday school building was still referred to as Cathey's Meeting House.

As Matthew and James walked out into the warm and breezy April morning, the old general exchanged friendly greetings and pats on the back with almost everyone he passed in the churchyard.

Though his step was now cautious and his erect figure crowned by a mantle of snowy hair, Matthew Locke had earned the respect of his friends and neighbors in Rowan County.

"General, I want you to meet my brother David, here with his family on their way to Tennessee," a jowly red-faced farmer said, pulling Matthew aside to shake hands. "We've known each other since the Regulator days, ain't we Matthew?"

"And not always in a fashion as friendly as today, Archie," Matthew added, gently elbowing the farmer as he reached out to shake hands.

The farmer turned to his brother. "Oh, he come around finally, him and his brother Francis the Sheriff, but he wasn't so friendly back then when us Regulators was tryin' to rein in the English governor."

"Well, I'll tell you what, Archie, I didn't take to mob rule back then and I still don't. I'm not sure you Regulators had it quite right, as far as what it meant to be a Patriot."

"But I guess we're in agreement today, ain't we, General? You not too high and mighty to come out on a boar hunt with Archie now and again, isn't that so?"

"After I get back from Philadelphia," Matthew assured him. "I could use some peace and quiet out in the woods, that's for sure."

"From what I hear, we're finally going to get rid of that weak excuse for a president."

"That's what I hear too, Archie. Adams is on his way out. And Jefferson will likely be the next president, thanks to the biggest Federalist of them all, Alexander Hamilton."

Hamilton's support of Thomas Jefferson over Aaron Burr in the

1800 presidential election was "the lesser of two evils" rather than a rejection of his own Federalist Party, even though his criticism had hurt John Adams's chance for reelection.

"Go figure," Archie added, scratching his head. "Well, sir, we appreciate all you do to look out for us farmers in the Congress up there, running back and forth to Philadelphia all the time. Brought back a new wife, I hear. But I gotta tell you, General, I attribute all your improvements, including joining the Presbyterian Church, to your late wife Mary, God rest 'er soul. Never knew a better woman."

Approaching his large extended family, Matthew couldn't help but think about all those who were no longer there—his indomitable mother; John Brandon, who had so willingly taken Matthew's family into his own; brother Francis and wife Anne Brandon; and of course his own beloved Mary, now gone these ten years.

A matron of middle years with a tremor in her voice but a warm smile stepped forward to greet Matthew with a kiss on the cheek, looking every bit the Philadelphian lady in a full-skirted gray dress with a laced bodice and linen kerchief matched with a modest head covering of the same material. He took her hand and led the family into the Thyatira Church, passing near Mary's tombstone which his new wife visited with him each Sunday after the service.

They had created their own caravan back in 1750—the whole clan of Brandons and Lockes and Catheys—travelling by Conestoga wagon with all their belongings, leaving behind the sheltered life they had built along Manada Creek, across the Susquehanna at Watkins Ferry, then down the Great Wagon Road through the Shenandoah Valley and into the hills of North Carolina. Land was cheap here in those days and he had bought 200 acres adjoining John Brandon's plantation on Grants Creek. But it was the fur trade where he made his money, he and Francis shuttling the old covered wagon back and forth to Charles Town in South Carolina, trading crops and furs and whiskey from the Moravian settlements and Irish villages in the backcountry to the English merchant ships docked in the port.

As the old Sunday school teacher looked back on all the years that followed—the Regulators and the war and all his passion to support a Jeffersonian democracy against the forces of Federalism in Congress—he wondered how often he had made the wrong choices. *Maybe it had been a mistake to vote against the Constitution back in '89,* he ruminated with a hint of regret. *I can already see the possibilities of what this nation may achieve as a united people.*

Matthew had quit listening to the sermon as his mind drifted back over a lifetime of memories. *We were still youngsters, Mary and I, when we came down here and started our life together, both of us soon swept up in taking care of a growing family. I was on the road in my Conestoga wagon with Francis most of the time, trading in the towns and villages and bargaining on the dock in Charles Town, leaving the child-rearing to Mary.* He chuckled to himself as he thought about Mary's youthful determination to get an education and assert her independence.

She was wildly independent and strong-willed in her youth, my Mary. She never lost that her whole life. I never thought she would need me the way I needed her. But somewhere between Manada Creek and another piece of fertile farmland here on Grants Creek off the Yadkin River in Rowan County, North Carolina, she decided she loved me. And she was the kind of woman who, once she made up her mind about such a thing . . . well, she was with you and always would be.

Now I'm so damn old. Don't know what keeps me going anymore. Better get the family cross out of the Bible and bring it up to my bedroom. Mary died with it in her hand.

As the minister droned on, Matthew glanced at the wooden cross behind the altar, wondering at the power such a religious symbol could have in a family's life.

Ah, my Mary, you were so sure the Brandons had no right to that cross. But who can understand the vagaries of fate that caused the cross to pass from one hand to another? I know this much. It brought you comfort in those final hours. And thus it became sacred to me.

How I miss you, my love. You haven't much longer to wait. I feel the last grains of sand sifting through the hourglass. I wager I'll see you again before the year is out.

Chapter Thirty

Lancaster County,
Colony of Pennsylvania, 1749

The day Father announced we were leaving London to make a new home in the American colonies, I was more interested in the queen cake Mother had made to celebrate my tenth birthday.

Throughout my childhood, my father John Locke had been a dashing figure who appeared and disappeared from our lives without notice, constantly running back and forth to Liverpool, Belfast, or one of Britain's remote colonies to manage the shipping business he ran out of London. When he was home, his loud laughter filled the house and our mother changed from matron-in-charge to another creature altogether—sweet and submissive and somehow in awe of our seafaring father.

From the perspective of a ten-year-old boy, every day in London brought a new wonder. The city was filling up with people who had left their farms to get work in the new brick factories with smokestacks that were beginning to line the Thames. Books and theater and music spilled out of every corner in the city. And England was on its way to becoming an empire, thanks to its dominance in shipbuilding, trading, and colonization of remote parts of the world.

But even though the merchant class in England was on the rise, everybody knew that real power and wealth came from being a land-owner. If you hadn't been lucky enough to be a first-born son of a landed aristocrat, you would never have a chance to secure a prosperous future for your family in England. Your children would have to make their way in the world by their wits and the sweat of their brow like everybody else.

According to Father, everybody had a shot at being a landowner in America, and a big one at that.

Mother wasn't so sure. I remember how she argued with him about the move.

"John, you're asking us to drop everything we know and travel halfway around the world to an uncivilized land, where our children will be at the mercy of savage Indians and wild animals. I don't want to be an immigrant."

"Not an immigrant, Elizabeth. A settler. The Pennsylvania Colony is part of England."

We had scarcely settled in Doylestown when he died, never having recovered from the illness he picked up during the journey.

I rarely dream of the ship anymore. The stench, the rolling dizziness below deck and Father weakening by the day, unable to keep a cup of tea in his stomach. But whatever fears beset Mother, she never let us know about them.

My older brother Francis stepped in after Father died and did all he could to act as head of our household. John and George were preoccupied and didn't want any part of that, but I still needed a father and was grateful to Francis for looking out for me, as he has done all these years. We're quite a bit alike, Francis and I—always trying to play the peacemaker, John would say—and I'm proud to be compared to him.

I can scarcely remember how we got from that frightful arrival in Philadelphia out to Lancaster County, to the tavern in Middletown that Mother took over from her cousin and to the good fortune that brought John Brandon into that tavern in search of a wife to take back to his farm. But I thank God every day for that good man and this rich land and the life we've built as a family here along Manada Creek.

I certainly did not expect to fall in love with my stepsister, Mary Brandon. She hated the idea of this new family. She wanted her mother back. Her resentment might have put some people off, but I saw right away that it was grounded in loyalty to her mother. Beneath the anger was a strong and beautiful woman. Someone who would stand by family through every kind of hardship.

I don't know when it happened exactly. When I started to love her. She was still a child when our parents married, then all of a sudden she wasn't. I had always been fascinated and sometimes irritated by her from the day we met—her quick wit, the unconventional things she thought and said, that mischievous look in her eye and her fleeting smile, quickly stifled, when she was teasing me. She turned from a strong-willed child into a beautiful woman overnight, waves of womanly emotion visible in her deep eyes, never any artifice about her, as if she paid no attention to such unimportant things.

And she was so smart, was Mary Brandon. I was sometimes shocked and always surprised to hear her opinions. Even though she had been raised on a frontier farm at the edge of William Penn's colony, she knew about the world and could talk about history or philosophy with the best of them.

We became friends right away. Having tried out all her far-fetched theories on her own family, she was glad to have a new set of stepbrothers and stepsisters to talk to and argue with. I could tell she liked me from the pleasure she took in teasing me, but that didn't mean she thought about me the same way I thought about her. Each time we talked, she lingered in my thoughts afterward and I knew almost from the first that I wanted something more from her. But, with my slow tongue and shyness, I despaired of ever winning her affection.

Chapter Thirty-One

I left Sam and Alex to stow the spreader and harrow from the morning field work and hurried back to the farmhouse. On Fridays we had only a half-day to complete a full day's work in order to make time for our studies with Master Fry.

He was a pale, spindly man, Master Fry, lacking in both humor and social graces, but he had completed university in Scotland so was considered suitable as a tutor. I was not convinced that Master Fry's lessons yielded sufficient value to justify the cost of a half-day's work for six of us each week. But John Brandon insisted.

"Lads, take out your slates and transcribe these sentences. 'The reluctant adversary made manifest his displeasure.'" He read each sentence slowly but with perfect diction, as if speaking to a rebellious child or a moron. "'Maria coughed into her kerchief before collapsing back onto the thin mattress.'"

We had of course learned basic skills of reading and calculation as children before we left England, and John Brandon instructed the whole family in matters of history and world events. Master Fry was tasked with improving our writing skills, as well as introducing elementary Latin and logic.

Mary had ceased her incessant complaining about exclusion of the womenfolk from our lessons, but I couldn't help but envy her freedom from these tedious exercises. I knew better than to think of Mary Brandon during lessons. But it amused me to think about how disappointed she would be with the tedium of recitations in contrast to the romantic notion of education she had built up in her own mind.

There was so much about Mary Brandon to admire. Being married to someone like that, why every day would be a new adventure, if only to discover what farfetched idea she would wake up to each morning. Starting a new day beside Mary. How I would love to watch her sleep, vulnerable and lost in dreams, her soft skin so near my own. I would reach my hand under the quilt and move slowly down the curve of her waist . . .

"Matthew, did you hear the question?" Master Fry's high-pitched but insistent buzzing finally breaking through.

"Excuse me, sire, but could you repeat it?" I stammered.

That elicited a round of sniggers from my brothers, as Francis discretely opened my Latin book to the correct page.

"Third person singular. 'He loves.'"

"Amat," I rejoined, horrified at the thought the tutor could have been reading my mind.

Of all the useless things Master Fry taught us, Latin grammar was the worst. Perhaps if we could study Julius Caesar's battle strategies, there would be something worth learning.

At the conclusion of an interminable afternoon of lessons, I slipped past George and William to complete afternoon chores in the house and check in on Mother, who had been feeling poorly for a couple of days.

The family had been in an uproar since one of the servants had come across an abandoned Indian babe in the forest. I guess I understood why Alex couldn't have left the child there to starve or be consumed by wild beasts. But this addition to the crowded Brandon farmhouse had caused no end of trouble and consternation, especially since Mother and Mary were catering to the baby like two mother hens protecting the same newly hatched chick.

As I passed along the upstairs corridor, delivering wood to each hearth, I could hear three female voices raised in acrimony inside the bedroom which Anne and Mary shared, the door having been left ajar. Complaining loudest was the Indian babe, whom we called Polly, her outrage echoing throughout the house.

"Mary Brandon, for God's sake quit trying to force the bottle into her mouth when she is too distraught to drink," Mother scolded, attempting to wrench the child from Mary's arms without success.

"She has taken no milk since midnight," Mary insisted, close to tears.

Having borne and fed seven children of her own, Mother shook her head in dismay at the willful determination of her stepdaughter as the child continued to wail.

"Please, Mary, just let me walk with her for a moment."

Mary released the infant and Mother began to walk about the room, cooing and patting and jiggling the little bundle, as Polly gradually calmed herself.

"But she must eat to live," Mary argued.

"Think about the child, my dear. She has been torn from her mother, from the warm milk of a mother's breast, to this place so strange and unfamiliar to her. It's more important to make her secure in our affection. She will become hungry after she feels safe."

The pine boards of the farmhouse floor creaked as Mother paced between Anne's spinning wheel and the small writing table holding Mary's quill and ink.

I doubted that Mother understood the depth of Mary's mourning for her own mother or her resentment at being forced to accept a substitute. After Father's death, whatever fear or despair or longing Mother may have felt, we saw only her fierce determination to provide for us. What tears she spilled for Father were shed in private. She could not have afforded to return to England if she had wanted to.

I wondered whether her marriage to John Brandon grew out of tenderness and longing such as I felt for his daughter, or whether it was just another practical means of survival, like the tavern in Middletown.

"Look, Mary," Mother said softly as she lay the sleeping infant in the cradle, "I see that you love this child. But it is not ours. You should not become so attached. We probably cannot keep her."

Mary's voice was harsh and ragged as she spoke. "You don't want Polly because she's Indian."

Mother was still for a moment. "Actually, Mary, I think she's a lovely child. But surviving out here is not a question of what I want or don't want. Your father bears the weight of many responsibilities. Don't make it harder for him than it already is."

Chapter Thirty-One

Mother's tall angular frame and slender figure belied her fifty-six years. She was a handsome woman, towering above Mary Brandon, a healthy glow in her cheeks from work in the kitchen garden. If she appeared harsh or intimidating to Mary, I knew it was a veneer she had found necessary in her early years here without the support and comfort of a husband in a land still wild and without institutions to protect a woman on her own.

I sighed and continued my rounds, resolved to the prospect that the two ladies most dear to me in the world would likely never feel any real affection for each other. Mother might not have possessed the soft demeanor that Mary associated with her own mother, but I knew she would fight to her last breath for those she held dear and would include Mary in that fierce protective love if only given half a chance.

As I returned the wood sling to its place beside the smokehouse, my stepfather called me over to the blacksmith shed which we used to repair equipment and shoe the horses.

The hut was small, dark and hot, the glow from embers in the raised brick hearth casting bursts of red and gold on the rough walls. There was scarcely room to move about, with barrels of nails, files, and scrap iron cluttering the floor, along with buckets of water at the ready for any unintended flare-ups. For my own part, I preferred to be out in the fields. But I knew ironworks were essential to keeping our ploughs and shovels in working order, not to mention nails and latches, shoes for the horses, and pots for the kitchen. And I was determined to do all I could to support the efforts of my stepfather to keep our farm productive.

"Matthew, I want you to see to the repair of this flail before we start in the flax field tomorrow after lunch. You remember how to shape the metal bands, do you not?"

"Yes, I think I can manage. I will find you if I run into trouble," I assured him, speaking with more confidence in my blacksmith skills than I felt.

"At least you can escape the yowling from the nursery," he added with a shrug.

"Mother and Mary are in earnest competition to provide mothering to the foundling Indian child," I said offhandedly.

He shook his head with a mix of irritation and resolution, running fingers through a head of still-full hair, just beginning to gray around the temples.

"Well, I suppose that's the way God made women to feel. But I wish Elizabeth would return to her bed. She has not been well, you know. And all this to-do about an abandoned Indian child is damned inconvenient when you're trying to manage a farm."

"Mary is in love with that child," I observed. "She surprises me a little—with her independent spirit and her passion for learning, always with her head in a book or writing to one of her aunts in Philadelphia or London. I've never really thought of her as the motherly type."

John Brandon raised one eyebrow and studied me with amusement. "I think she'll make a very strong mother, Matthew. She'll rear smart children and protect them as surely as your own mother has done. And, anyway, she's pretty as a picture, my Mary. What man wouldn't want her?"

For some reason, his question brought to mind the specter of young Alex Turrentine and I felt a wave of despair. John Brandon would of course have no idea about Mary's interest in the field hand. As I stood there speechless, John Brandon laughed.

"You're taken with my Mary, aren't you Matthew?"

For the life of me, I couldn't think of a response to this inquiry, hoping he couldn't read my mind as I stood before my stepfather open-mouthed.

He laughed and patted me on the back, passing toward the door. "If you don't inform my daughter of your interest, Matthew, you may find somebody else has turned her head."

Chapter Thirty-Two

It had been a long day in the fields, and I was starving. By the time our evening supper rolled around, I was more than ready to get off my feet and concentrate on filling my stomach with a bowl of Mother's venison stew and a glass of cider.

Mother ran the kitchen with ease and efficiency, having managed a popular tavern in Middletown before moving to the farm to oversee the Brandon-Locke menagerie. So with dusk approaching, I was surprised to see my sisters and stepsisters standing around the front porch speaking to one another in low voices instead of carrying out Mother's orders in the kitchen.

Anne pulled me aside as I approached the house. "Matthew, you should see to your mother upstairs. Her consumption is worse and Father fears pernicious anemia. We're going to take care of supper, but it will be late this evening."

I could hear her deep rattling cough before I entered the bedroom. My stepfather was pacing the room with a furrowed brow as Mother tried to catch her breath to complete instructions she was giving to Mary. Her face was inflamed and damp with sweat and her voice cracked as she tried to speak, lacking adequate breath to carry her words.

The window curtains were drawn, making the bedroom with its single small window appear even darker than it was. My stepfather's books and writing table were in his study downstairs so their bedroom contained little beyond Mother's dressing table holding a pitcher and a small mirror, two side tables by the bed, one with a lit candle, and a carved chest of drawers brought over by Mother from England.

"Mary," my mother was almost whispering, "I mustn't touch the baby with this putrid sore throat, and I don't want you in here either. You must take charge of Polly until I'm better and, for heaven's sake, don't bring her into this sick room."

My stepfather eased her back onto his pillow. "Elizabeth, I'm sending Matthew for the doctor over by Harris's Ferry. You are unwell and faring more poorly by the day."

"Oh, John," she responded wearily, "don't do that. I don't need the quackery of that apothecary to recover from this fever. Anne is making me a potion of tea and molasses. Mary, remind her to boil the rhubarb in lavender water first."

Mary waited for me outside the bedroom, the babe in her arms.

"Matthew, could you ask Father to move the bassinet into my room?" Mary implored. "What if Polly comes down with the fever?"

"It's Mother we should be concerned about," I muttered irritably. "The child is fine."

I took our fastest wagon, with our sorrel colts Spanker and Raleigh in front, to find my way to Doctor Stumpf in Paxtang, against my mother's objections. She had her own theories about powders and potions and did not appreciate the curative measures offered out here on the frontier, generally consisting of copious amounts of blood-letting and purging. Mother had learned about contamination and quarantine from her uncle back in London and, no matter how many doctors out here told her it was so much poppycock, she was insistent about keeping herself apart from the rest of the family during the illness.

Doctor Stumpf's office served first and foremost as the region's primary apothecary shop. Even though it was getting dark by the time I arrived, the doctor's office was busy with customers. Located near the popular ferry stop where traders and travelers crossed the Susquehanna River, it was easy to spot the freshly painted white storefront, a sign posted atop the lintel in large black stenciled letters: APOTHECARY.

I was anxious about Mother and annoyed to be kept waiting while Doctor Stumpf examined waiting patients, tended to customers seeking medical advice, and sold elixirs over the counter.

Please, God, let her be well soon, I prayed silently. *I've already lost one parent in this colony. I don't know what would become of us if we lost another.*

The apothecary shop was packed full of interesting implements and I occupied myself studying the array of curatives as Doctor Stumpf packed up his case for the trip out to our farm. At one end of the shop, a red brick fireplace was crammed with black pots, pitchers, and kettles of every shape and size. Hanging from the fireplace arch were spoons and stirring sticks positioned on either side of a horseshoe. An entire wall behind the counter was lined with little wooden drawers, each neatly labelled with the abbreviated name of an herb or powder, arranged in alphabetical order. On the workbench above the drawers were scales, mortars and pestles, measuring cups and spoons, and in a separate glass-front case were syringes, minute vials of liquid in small cases, and tools for cutting and extraction. Herbs hung both inside and outside the window to dry out. And on the high shelves, white porcelain canisters with blue design and Latin lettering held some of the most frequently prescribed potions.

Doctor Stumpf was a big man with sandy hair and a few stray whiskers on his chin, well past the prime of life. He talked all the way from Paxtang to the farm. Like many of the doctors in this part of the Pennsylvania Colony, he qualified to practice medicine by virtue of trial-and-error learning, in the same way lawyers qualified by having "read" the law. There weren't many university-trained physicians outside Philadelphia and Mother wasn't alone in preferring her own medicinal recipes to those of the local apothecary.

"We got pestilence all over the valley this year. But I guess it could be worse. I hear Philadelphia is overrun with yellow fever—again," he complained in a heavy German accent. "They lost ten people in that village near Second Mountain."

I felt like he was talking for the sole purpose of keeping us both awake as the dark woods swept past our wagon. The crescent moon shed enough light to outline the forest perimeter, which had been cut back to clear the road for wagons and horses. Though there must have been farmhouses behind the stands of softwood, the night was black in the distance as far as the eye could see, and I felt the emptiness of this vast forested continent, so long without human habitation other than wandering tribes of Indians.

"If they keep letting people into this colony, we're going to need more doctors, that's for sure. I write up every meeting with every patient in this register of mine—the dates, the symptoms, the treatment, and how well the patient fared—and I've now got eight volumes on my shelf. If I ever get time to study my registers, I'll be able to provide some important case studies to the big hospitals."

He was waving his bound register in the dark, pleased to have a captive audience to hear his theories of medicine.

"I am now trying a new formula of astringent citrus juice and saffron with a teaspoon of laudanum, which has eased the suffering of many and which I expect will settle your mother's dark humors."

I wanted to share the apothecary's optimism about the likelihood that his potion could cure Mother's ague. I was of course grateful that he was willing to head out into the country with me in the dead of night. But the experimental nature of his curative formulas gave me about as much confidence as I got from the local preacher.

The farmhouse was quiet when we entered, gently pushing open the heavy front door, the stairs creaking as we ascended. I was concerned that waking Mother in the middle of the night might not be the best thing for her health. But when I led Doctor Stumpf into the bedroom, the flickering candlelight illuminated Mother's figure propped up on her pillow, looking miserable, a distinct rattle that could be heard from the hallway sounding with each breath she took. She was clutching a cup of tea which filled the room with scents of brandy and honey, my stepfather in vigil at her side.

Chapter Thirty-Two

In his hand was the small gold cross that he hid in the compartment at the back of the Brandon family Bible, brought out in times of crisis. It gave me a shock to see him there in the dark, holding the cross. The reality that we might lose her struck me in the gut.

I remember when I first saw the cross. We were at a wake for our cousin's child, stillborn over at the Cathey farm, shortly after we joined the Brandon family. My stepfather held the cross as he gave the blessing over the small body. "Christ in heaven, take this child into your protective arms. Shelter him in peace for all eternity." As he touched the dead infant with the shimmering gold cross, he said, "And may your cross guide his steps into eternal glory."

My stepfather looked up when he heard us enter the sickroom, laying the cross on the table next to the candle.

"Thank you, doctor, for coming out to us so late in the night," he said, rising to shake Doctor Stumpf's hand.

"Your servant, sire. Now let me take a look at Mistress Brandon if you please," replied the apothecary.

After checking her pulse and peering ponderously into her mouth and nose and ears, the doctor listened attentively to Mother's heart and lungs, then made the extraordinary request for access to the chamber pot in order to smell the urine for signs which only he could discern. After each exploration, he recorded careful notes in his medical history register. Self-styled tools of weight and measurement were extracted from his medical bag, along with an assortment of needles, knives, and razors.

Once his ministrations were complete, the doctor turned to my stepfather and myself with instructions to provide towels, hot water, and a basin for blood-letting, not bothering to respond to Mother's protestations.

"It is essential to remove as many of the impurities in your fluids as we can, my dear," he intoned, patting her on the arm. "Contaminated humors are being carried in your blood and will continue to multiply until removed and replaced by new blood." As he removed a razor, lancet, and scraper from a shell-covered carrying case, he completed his tutorial. "Breathing the vein is necessary to tamp down the inflammation that is making you sick."

"But, doctor," protested my mother, "I will be further weakened by the light-headedness that comes afterward."

"Now, now, Missus Brandon," he murmured absently, spreading the cloth under her outstretched arm, tied tightly with a cloth strip to make the veins swell, as he sharpened the triple-edged lancet with which he would make the incision.

As my mother's blood dripped with satisfyingly regular plops into the retainer, Doctor Stumpf kept up the patter of medical theory that had entertained me on the long drive out to the farm.

The bleeding seemed to go on forever, our blue-patterned porcelain tureen almost filled to the brim with thick burgundy emanations from Mother's forearm. I was tired and fretful, fearing for my mother's health, and not looking forward to another back-wrenching trip to the river. Mother kept her eyes closed during the procedure, making clear her distaste for an invasion she deemed unnecessary, but bending to her husband's will as she must.

I was worried about her. So many of our family and friends out here had been lost to fever, epidemic, intestinal infection, abscess, and childbirth. I had experienced the death of one parent and had no desire to lose this one.

As Doctor Stumpf was concluding his business with my stepfather by the front door, he ordered strict usage of his purging formula for at least three days. My stepfather and Doctor Stumpf had agreed upon the quantity of farm goods to be paid for the doctor's services and I was sent to the chicken coop to gather poultry and eggs and to the cellar for apples and berries, which were laid in the back of the wagon.

By the time I rolled back into the farmyard after my second trip to Paxtang that night, the sun was fat and round as it ascended above the eastern horizon.

Chapter Thirty-Three

Mother's illness weighed on us throughout the planting season, with so much work to do in the fields and an extra infant to care for in the house. But as the weather began to warm up and the days stretched longer, she regained a bit of color in her cheeks and took over management of the kitchen again. Her relationship with Mary was transformed by their common affection for the native child in our care and for the first time I saw a closeness developing between them.

Dinnertime at the Brandon farmhouse was a boisterous affair, our big clan clustered round the table, my stepfather at the head and Mother at the foot. The chatter, laughter, and general chaos of our family meals enlivened the whole farm—raised voices, clattering dinnerware, peals of mirth, and sharp rebukes drifting outward from the cracks and crevices of the two-story clapboard farmhouse. We worked hard to keep the farm going, each and every Brandon and Locke on our feet from daybreak to dusk, even seven-year-old Lizzy. The family dinner was our time to relax and reward ourselves after a hard day's work.

But peace in the Brandon household had been ripped asunder by my stepfather's insistence upon finding a more permanent home for the Indian child. He and Mother had endured an emotional day, delivering the baby to the fort that housed the local militia. Tensions were high, Mary locked away in her room all day, and our meal was served late.

The long oak table held an oil lantern at each end and, in between, the house servants had placed platters of pork butt from the smokehouse, potatoes from the cellar, and fresh greens from the garden behind the kitchen house. The lively chatter that usually paused when the head of the household took his seat to offer the blessing, failed to resume as dishes were passed and plates filled.

In spite of hunger pangs and a table laden with savory fare, a gloomy silence hung over the room like smoke trapped in a misty hollow. It was no surprise that Mother, recently recovered from her illness, looked tired after a long day on the road. In my stepfather's absence, the farm work had fallen behind schedule and the dinner bell sounded a half-hour later than usual. But I was certain that the unusual silence had more to do with the gossip that had filled the farm all day. The Indian child Polly had been delivered up to the militia stationed at the new fort, to be cared for by native women held there as captives.

Mother held her chin up as she directed the children to their seats, but I could see weariness in her eyes from the events of the day and a lingering pallor in her cheeks. Though Mother ruled the roost with an iron fist and my stepfather rarely challenged her authority inside these four walls, neither she nor any of us would take our seats until he had done so first.

My stepfather seemed diminished this evening, his rugged features pale as he took his place at the head of the table, eyes fixed on the pewter place setting in front of him instead of scanning the room for one of us to reprimand or praise or tease. Placement of the infant with the militia couldn't have been easy, given the affection of his wife and daughter for the child, but I understood that his quick action was intended to circumvent further bonding which would make the inevitable fracture even harder on familial harmony.

Launching into the blessing immediately, as chairs were still scraping the pine floorboards, he prayed, "Heavenly Father, bless this food and the grace by which it was provided to the nourishment of our bodies."

Instead of the usual "Amen" and on to realizing that long-awaited nourishment, he stopped mid-prayer, and the awkward silence made me wonder whether I should open my eyes to determine whether the family was still there. When I finally cracked open one eye, I saw that my stepfather still had his eyes closed in silent contemplation and several of the children had yielded to curiosity as I had, regarding him with concern.

Most notably, Mary Brandon, at the far end of the table next to Mother, had remained on her feet and was regarding her father with a look of fury, her eyes red from weeping and her hair disheveled, making no pretense of participating in the ritual.

Our stepfather, after a lengthy pause, resumed the blessing. "Guide our footsteps, Holy God, on a path of righteousness. Thy will be done in all things and not our own, that we may discern what is holy and good through the example of thy son Jesus Christ, in whom we place all hope and trust and in whose name we pray. Amen."

As chairs scraped and serving ladles clattered, Mary still stood, arms crossed, observing her father with an icy glare, until Mother stood beside her and took her wrist, gently easing her toward her chair. I noticed that Mother kept her hand on Mary's arm, patting and caressing in the manner one might try to calm a nervous filly.

Mary's attention was focused entirely on her father and it took a moment for her to realize she was being urged to her seat by her stepmother. She then turned to Mother with fury.

"How could you?" Mary whispered loudly, withdrawing her arm and turning away from Mother's anxious ministrations. "I thought you cared about Polly. At least you made a good show of it, just like you do with the rest of us."

"Child . . ." Mother tried to interject.

"I'm not your child, any more than Polly was. You're not my mother. My mother is dead. You pretend to love us, just like you pretended to love Polly. But you got rid of her the first chance you got."

Mary's voice was growing louder and more argumentative, and Mother looked down the table at her husband for help.

"Mary, go to your room this minute," he snapped. Seeing Mother close to tears at Mary's anger and knowing what a wrenching separation it had been for both of them, John Brandon was as furious as his daughter.

Mother had worked hard to be attentive and kind to the Brandon children, addressing their needs as scrupulously as those of the seven of us whom she had borne. But what would I know about what goes on in a mother's heart? She and Mary hadn't all the years together that we Lockes had. I didn't think Mother ever really expected she would take the place of Mary's own mother. But I knew that she too loved the Indian babe. It wasn't fair of Mary to blame her.

We often gathered in the parlor after supper, but tonight my stepfather retired to his study right after our meal so it was clear there would not be a discussion this night about the state of English imports into the colonies. Francis and I had joined in a chess match while Anne and Margaret talked quietly on the settee over their needlework. William and George were in the corner, puzzling over a particularly vexing assignment from Master Fry. Mother had taken her leave for the evening and Mary was nowhere to be seen.

"I know precisely what you have in mind, Matthew," Francis grinned as he moved his rook to the edge of the board with a flourish. "It will do you no good."

Having expected and awaited this very scheme, I moved my knight into position to force a sacrifice.

Considerable racket was coming from my stepfather's study next to the parlor as cabinet doors slammed.

"Stepfather is in a rare fit of pique today, is he not?" I wondered aloud, given the uncharacteristic temper he had shown at the table.

"Well, of course he is," Francis replied. "Mary behaved abominably at dinner, lashing out at Mother in front of everyone. Can you imagine what our father would have done in the face of such insubordination?"

I couldn't disagree with Francis's reaction to Mary's tantrum. However much she cared for the Indian child, John Brandon deserved better from his daughter. But her grief was so apparent and sincere that I couldn't bring myself to criticize her nor did I care to hear her judged by my brother. I studied the chess board without responding.

"Oh, of course," Francis teased. "You would never find a fault with pretty Mary Brandon, would you?"

Before I had a chance to respond to this provocation, my step-father came into the parlor and asked in an agitated voice, "Did one of you take the family cross?" Everyone looked up in surprise, since the cross had remained in its assigned pocket in the back of the leather-bound Brandon family Bible since we had joined this family, except when my stepfather took it out for special occasions.

"I think I saw it at Mother's bedside when she was taken with the ague last week," I volunteered. "Perhaps it was left upstairs."

"I'm sure I returned it to the Bible," muttered my stepfather, turning to go up the stairs to search.

When he returned empty-handed, we began a discussion in earnest about which servants had access to the house and the possibility of a thief in our midst.

"Richard, you and William are to organize a complete search of the property at daybreak tomorrow. Francis and Matthew will assist you. I want the house searched top to bottom, the slave quarters, the bunkhouse, the barn."

He shook his head in dismay. "I can't believe one of our own people would take it. That cross has been in this family for over a hundred years. My God, can you trust no one?"

Since John Brandon had taken on the role of father to our family, he had been a steady, powerful figure in my life, someone to look up to and a man I aspired to emulate. It is a fearful thing to travel so far from one's homeland and to lose a father in the process. I hadn't forgotten my father, not for a minute. I was no longer a child when John Brandon came to Middletown to court my mother. But not a day passed that I didn't thank the Lord for this strong and principled man who took on responsibility for our large family.

He showed an interest in me from the very beginning, teaching me the principles of running a farm profitably, of seeking knowledge, and of growing into manhood on a solid foundation of devotion to God and family.

It was unsettling to see him so rattled by events of recent days— Mother's illness, the bitter conflict with Mary over abandonment of the Indian child, and now betrayal from within and loss of a family treasure that was his comfort in times of trouble. I noticed that he put his sons Richard and William in charge of the search and wondered whether that implied suspicion that the thief might be one of his stepchildren.

At daybreak the next morning, Richard organized the search and sent me with William to the bunkhouse and barn to look for the missing cross among the goods of our indentured servants and hired field hands. Most of the hands were already awake when we entered their sleeping quarters.

"I must ask all of you to wait outside while we search your quarters," William announced, stretching to exercise his authority while clearly embarrassed to imply suspicion of men with whom we had worked shoulder-to-shoulder throughout the growing season.

Chapter Thirty-Three

Most of the servants were up and washing at the cistern or having bread and hot tea from a kettle warmed over the open fire in front of the bunkhouse, but a few were still in bed. All looked at William and myself in surprise but dragged themselves up and out as he directed. Sam Turrentine was pulling his younger brother out of bed and bore an unpleasant expression as though our taking possession of our own bunkhouse were an inappropriate intrusion. Alex was not fully awake, but I saw him speak to his brother in a low voice with a look of alarm. Sam picked up his day pack, but William instructed him to leave everything in the bunkhouse.

The bunkhouse was a small, rustic one-room log structure with a single window on the east side, so the thin early morning light cast one dusty rectangle of brightness into the cramped sleeping quarters. The servants stood just outside the door, questioning each other about possible causes of such a search, as the ascending sun began to take the chill off a disturbing morning.

There were so many immigrants working in the Pennsylvania Colony under indenture that I hadn't given much thought to their precarious status. It had always seemed to me like another kind of apprenticeship. But these boys, many of whom were younger than we were when we came to America, looked worried and anxious, as though their very future were at risk. I felt bad for them and wished someone other than I had the duty to conduct this search.

The servants had few possessions, so it was only a matter of minutes before my search of Sam Turrentine's pack unearthed the stolen cross. Feeling the outstretched arms of the ancient relic tucked inside a cotton handkerchief, I didn't need to remove the cross to know it had been found. "Here it is," I pronounced, studying the relic with awe and reverence, as if for the first time, as I removed the cloth wrap.

William came over and sat on the floor beside me, caressing the gold cross. We were both lost in silent thought.

"What will happen to Sam?" I asked.

"Father will have to turn him over to the authorities," William opined.

"What in God's name would have possessed him to come into our house and steal? How did he even find it?"

As we contemplated the gold cross, a shadow blocked the morning light from the door.

"Sam didn't do it. It was me. My fault. I . . . I just put it into his pack. For safekeeping." Alex Turrentine was standing before us, cheeks aflame and a look of alarm on his face.

And fast on his heels was his elder brother, pushing Alex aside and assuming full responsibility himself.

"You'll both have to come up to the house with us," William instructed them. "My father will want to talk to the two of you."

Chapter Thirty-Four

I pulled Spanker off the road onto a path toward an old stone structure tucked into an oak grove, identifiable only by the churchyard cemetery laid out nearby. The colt whinnied with delight now that our trip from the farm was near its conclusion. Even though I had made several trips by wagon to Harris's Ferry to deliver goods for shipment down the river, I had never seen this part of the settlement at Paxtang. In spite of the bucolic setting, I knew this would be an unpleasant day. I would have chosen to be anywhere else but here if my stepfather had given me any choice in the matter.

John Brandon had invited me into his study last night, asking that I close the door behind me.

"Matthew," he said with a serious look on his face, "I must ask you to do a thing for me tomorrow. There is to be a hearing to determine the fate of Sam and Alex. I had planned to be there, but your mother is still doing poorly and I dare not leave her. William and George have to complete the fencing. You must go to Paxtang and represent the family."

I had wondered where Sam and Alex were and hoped my stepfather hadn't turned them over to the British militia.

"Are they to be tried, then, for theft?"

"Not in a court of law. The Presbyterian Church handles local matters which involve members of their congregation. The Turrentine boys were active members of a congregation down in Chester County, so the local presbytery was willing to hear the case."

Although the English colonial authorities had established courts of law in the eastern part of Pennsylvania, there were not many official British courts this far west. As a result, the network of Presbyterian churches in Pennsylvania resolved most legal disputes that arose among their own church communities.

I had ridden Spanker down to Paxtang alone, worrying the whole time about what would be required of me. I hadn't been in the room when my stepfather questioned the servants and he wasn't particularly helpful about what to say to the church officials.

"If they ask, just tell them what you know about the boys and what happened, Matthew. It wouldn't be right if no one from the family who had employed them showed up."

There was a surprising amount of activity around the church so early on a Tuesday morning. Four dusty horses were tied to the post in front of the church and a couple of small farm wagons were parked in the shade of a big chestnut. Three farmers, looking uncomfortable in their Sunday meeting clothes, were huddled up nearby, debating the durability of the new flails and sickles that had just arrived in Lancaster.

The Paxtang Church was the oldest and most prosperous of the three churches in the Donegal Presbytery. Even though they had finally built a Hanover Church for the Scots-Irish communities near our farm at Manada Creek, the elders in the presbytery had decided to hear this case at Paxtang, where a session meeting was already calendared.

As I was tying Spanker to the post on the shady side of the church, a portly gentleman with a craggy face, bushy eyebrows, and a deep Scottish accent approached me.

"Well then, you must be Mister Brandon's stepson Matthew," he offered, extending his hand. "I am Reverend John Elder and I will be presiding over today's session. We are in your debt for coming over to assist today."

I could scarcely complain to the old gentleman that it was my stepfather whom he should thank since the decision to participate had hardly been my own.

"Let me show you around," he said, directing me toward the church. "We were in a log meetinghouse for many years, similar to the Hanover Church, before we could afford to build this one. I gather your family are Church of England?"

"Yes, though we have plenty of cousins of your persuasion. But our roots are mainly in England," I responded.

"Och, well, the English, they call us Scots-Irish and other ill-mannered names, but I guess we're all immigrants now, aren't we?"

The old stone church was a remarkably impressive structure for this part of the world, with local gray-white stone on the exterior wall, brick oven arches around the tall windows, and a high-pitched roof. As we stepped inside, the morning sun slanted through multiple arched windows onto whitewashed walls and hardwood pews installed on two levels of sparkling sanctuary.

Near the polished oak altar at the front of the church, with a car-
peted step in front where the faithful could kneel to pray when they
came up to take communion, two tables were set up and people were
milling around them, studying papers and chatting among themselves. Some of the pews were occupied by onlookers. I could see that
our former servants Sam and Alex, the homespun shirts they worked
in freshly washed and ironed for this appearance, were seated in the
second row and were conferring with a serious-looking gentleman
dressed in Sunday attire.

"I will be conducting the session," Reverend Elder said. "This
matter will be taken up first, after a few items of business pertaining
to this church, and we should have you out of here before noon."

I regretted being here at all, especially as I observed the Turrentine
brothers nervously awaiting the outcome of this hearing to know
their fate. Sam was studying the floor, head in hand, while Alex
watched the businesslike hubbub on the raised platform behind
the altar wide-eyed. The theft of a small family cross would not be
important enough for their case to be referred out to the courts of
the colonial authorities, but if it were, the boys could well wind up in
a militia prison.

I had worked with both Sam and Alex over some months now,
found them to be honest, hardworking, and reliable. I was puzzled
that they would come into the house and steal from us, given everything I knew about their character. It was a disappointment. But
at the same time, I was not prepared to see their lives destroyed.
Now that I was here, I felt extremely nervous that I might do or say
something that could influence the outcome. Wasn't it just like John

Brandon to ask me to be here to represent the family, without mentioning that he expected me to be a witness at a public trial?

Reverend Elder slipped into a pew near the back of the church and patted the seat beside him.

"We're proud to be spreading the word of God out here on the frontier," he said in a low voice, "where the constant threat of attack from the natives weighs heavily on the settlers. This sanctuary is a place where a farmer can find some inner peace and inspiration after a hard week in the fields," he beamed, extending his arm proudly over the sacred space. "Like the whole Presbyterian movement, we've had our quarrels relating to the Great Awakening. But we're an Old Side church and an Old Side presbytery, and we believe it is the immigrants who will make this a great land, one grounded in the traditions of our faith."

My stepfather had forewarned me that the Paxtang minister had a reputation as something of an eccentric and in particular as someone who saw the native population as a barrier to Christianizing the continent. In the local broadsheets, he had been openly critical of what he saw as the "soft" Quaker approach to the Indians.

The old preacher sat with me quietly for a few minutes.

"I must go finish preparations for today's session," he said, patting my knee. "When I call you up, there will be some questions for you. Just tell us truthfully all you know about this episode and you will then be excused."

I was glad to have a few minutes to collect my thoughts. I was not accustomed to speaking before a group of people and hoped I wouldn't appear too nervous. This was not a church of my own faith, but I nonetheless took comfort in the quiet that always settled upon me in a house of worship. My own Anglican Church with its beautiful rituals always left me with a feeling of gratitude for our family and the bounty of the earth and a kind of optimism that things would work out as they should. But today my thoughts were scattered and I didn't feel confident that I knew what was right in such an awkward situation.

When we had searched the servants' bunkhouse and found the cross in Sam's pack, the Turrentine boys were embarrassed and worried about what it would mean for them. But neither of them said a thing to explain why they would steal from a family who was helping them work off their indentures.

A fly landed on my wrist, content to rest there since I was too distracted to shake it off. I watched as it preened itself, taking a brief spin in the air from time to time before returning. But my thoughts were elsewhere. *Given Mary's fondness for Alex, would she ever forgive me for being here? And what if my testimony should be biased by my competition with Alex for Mary's affection?*

Mary didn't know about any of this. Her father had insisted on discretion. The day we found the cross, he made the decision on the spot. James Cathey was asked to take custody of the Turrentine brothers and to use his Presbyterian connections to turn this matter over to the church, which regularly took responsibility for problems in the Scots-Irish community.

After James left with Sam and Alex in his wagon, my stepfather gathered Richard, William, Francis, and myself in his study.

"This unpleasant business with the servants stops here. I don't want it gossiped about on the farm. In particular, I don't want to worry

Elizabeth about it since her health is still fragile. If anybody asks, the Turrentine boys are working over at the Catheys' for a while."

"What are you going to tell Mary?" I asked, knowing she would notice Alex's absence.

"I have asked Mary to devote herself to Elizabeth's care for now. Dr. Stumpf tells me yellow fever is spreading in the valley. I want Elizabeth to stay in bed until she fully recovers. Mary has the responsibility to keep her there."

I couldn't help but hope that this forced confinement would heal the rift between Mary and my mother.

"I will speak to Mary when the time is right," he assured me.

Chapter Thirty-Five

As I watched the session meeting unfold behind the altar of the Paxtang Church, I wondered about these men acting as a court of law in judgment of Alex and Sam. They weren't trained in the law, but I could see they were taking seriously their duty to perform justice, stiff and awkward in their dark Sunday coats.

As the pastor implied, being called Scots-Irish by the English wasn't meant as a compliment. But here they were—both the accused and the court spawned by the poverty and oppression of Northern Ireland. And trying their damnedest to build a rule of law into everyday life at the outer edges of the colony.

And maybe that's what this new world was all about when you got right down to it.

I wasn't given to praying except when prodded to do so by my stepfather at the dinner table. But I felt deeply the responsibility of bearing witness against these poor servants—even though one of them seemed to have captured my Mary's heart. I took a deep breath and closed my eyes.

Chapter Thirty-Five

"Oh God, let me say the right thing. You know my heart and the love I have for Mary. And should she choose Alex over me, I would surely find that hard to bear. But I do not wish to cause harm to these men who stand here accused."

One of the members of the local congregation, a tall, gaunt figure in a coat too large for his frame and an unkempt beard, was calling the meeting to order. Reverend Elder began with a lengthy prayer, then introduced two other pastors who were here for the session. The secretary who would record the minutes of the meeting joined the others at one of the tables positioned in front of the altar. After some discussion about past minutes and meeting protocol, Reverend Elder stood up and described the theft that had occurred at our farm.

"Because these two brothers, indentured to Mister John Brandon over at Manada Creek, are members of the Fagg's Manor Church down in Chester County and have been attending the Hanover Presbyterian Church up here, this dispute falls within our presbytery. Since the session here at Paxtang was the first one coming up, we decided to hear the case at this church. You boys will have a chance to say your piece, but first I want to hear from Matthew Locke, who is here representing the Brandon family. Could you come up here to the table, Mister Locke?"

I walked to the front of the church and stood in front of the clergy assembled at one of the tables.

"Explain to us, if you would be so kind, how you came to bring Samuel and Alexander Turrentine to work on your farm?"

"We were just ready to bring in the crops last fall when one of our servants—Willie McKenzie—was taken by the Indians while he was out working one of the fields by himself. We knew it was the Indians since he left his water jug behind and the Indians planted a big stake with feathers right there in our field."

"And we all know, don't we, what likely became of him? Did you ever get your servant back?"

"No, we've not heard a word of him since. But my stepfather got in touch with a friend down in Chester County to look for somebody to come in on short notice and work for us a few months. These brothers were indentured to two different farmers down there. John Brandon picked up their indentures for a season of service on our farm."

The pastor took the Brandon family cross from a pack and laid it on the table. In this sacred space, as the morning light struck it, I was moved by how simple and beautiful it was, and so closely identified with the Brandon name and legacy that it was appalling to me to think that our servants would have tried to steal it.

"And is this the cross that was stolen?"

"Yes, it has been in the Brandon family for many years and was always kept in my stepfather's study in a compartment in the back of the family Bible."

"Was it typical for your servants to be in the main house?"

"No, not really. But we treat our servants like part of the family and from time to time they join us for supper in the kitchen or do chores inside the house."

"Had these two boys given you any trouble before?"

"No, not at all. They were good workers and had always complied with our rules. Well-liked on the farm. But when my stepfather discovered the cross was missing, he insisted upon a complete search of the property. I was surprised they had taken it."

After I returned to my seat, the reverend called up the Turrentine brothers.

"I know that you two boys were active members in Fagg's Manor Church down in Chester County," he said. "And even though you came to the colonies without your parents, I believe you were raised in a God-fearing household in Ireland. Can you explain why you took this cross from the Brandon family Bible?"

Sam and Alex looked at each other and it was clear to me that they had not reached agreement on how to respond to these claims. In his usual way, Sam clammed up, glaring as his younger brother stepped forward.

"Sire, we regret any behavior that has caused trouble to Mister Brandon or his family," Alex said. "They treated us kindly and fairly during our term at the farm."

The session elders who were sitting at the table with the inquisitor watched the young immigrant with skeptical eyes. They were dressed in their Sunday clothes and were taking seriously their moral prerogative to keep the members of their Presbyterian flock on a righteous path. This boy didn't seem appropriately humbled by the sin he had committed in breaking the trust owed to the master of the house and in particular in risking his eternal soul by stealing an icon that symbolized the ultimate sacrifice made by our Lord.

Alex didn't seem a bit chagrined at the circumstance in which he found himself, which didn't surprise me, knowing him to be a cheerful person who was not lacking in self-confidence. But as he was beginning to launch into praise of our family's treatment of the servants, there was some kind of exchange going on behind me near the entry to the sanctuary and I turned to see Mary Brandon enter, accompanied by her cousin Andrew Cathey.

Disregarding her cousin's effort to keep her quiet at the back of the church until an appropriate opening, Mary marched resolutely to the front of the church where Sam and Alex were standing and approached the table where Reverend Elder and his colleagues were seated. Alex stopped speaking and looked at her with alarm.

Mary was out of breath and distressed as she turned to the clergy and said, "I gave them the cross. They didn't steal it."

This caused considerable turmoil among the assembled session, as Mary was reprimanded for breaking into the inquiry and was made to explain who she was and by what right she had come forward to speak.

"I gave it to them, don't you see? I took it out of Father's Bible and brought it to them in the clearing. It belonged to their family first."

"Slow down, young lady. By what authority do you interject yourself into this session meeting?"

Mary looked at the elder with determination and fury. "By the authority of what's fair and true. Isn't that what this church is supposed to be doing? My father was mistaken. And so was his father. This isn't our cross. It never was."

Alex turned to her and put his hands on her shoulders, in a way that would have been inappropriate even if this hadn't been a church or an inquiry into thievery by indentured servants of their master's personal property.

Chapter Thirty-Five

"Mary," he said softly. "Go home. You don't need to do this."

Mary removed Alex's hands and looked as mad at him as she was at the authorities.

"Oh yes I do, Alex. Why didn't you tell them I gave you the cross? It belonged to your family long before my greedy ancestors stole it." Her voice shook with emotion and I could see from where I was sitting that, in spite of her valiant effort to control herself, tears had begun to glisten on her cheeks.

At this point, Reverend Elder stepped forward and took Mary gently by the arm, encouraging her to sit and offering a handkerchief. She wiped her eyes, cleared her throat, and straightened to her full height.

"May I speak to you, sirs, of what I know about this cross?" Mary inquired politely, having regained some equilibrium.

After consulting among themselves, the church leaders let her speak.

"After Alex and I became friends, we talked of our families, how they came to America and everything. We discovered that we had ancestors in Northern Ireland at the same time—during the development of the plantation system by King James. Alex's ancestors were among many Lowland farmers brought in from Scotland to work the plantation fields, drawn to Ulster County with the promise of land ownership. My ancestors, the Brandons, in connection with their membership in a London guild, received a land grant in Northern Ireland and became wealthy on the proceeds."

She walked to the table and picked up the cross.

"This cross had been in Alex's family for many generations. It was taken from them by my forebear James Brandon, the son of Old Thomas, who took advantage of Anglican bias and claimed everything of value the Turkingtons had, including this cross. The name was Turkington there in Ireland, by the way, not Turrentine. I found the papers and everything," at which point she dumped a pile of documents onto the table where the pastors were sitting.

Reverend Elder stood and signaled to me. "Mister Locke, could you come forward to the table, please?"

"Ladies and gentlemen, I am adjourning the meeting until two o'clock this afternoon, to give the disputing parties a chance to read these papers. Mistress Brandon, Mister Locke, Samuel and Alexander, please meet me in my study in fifteen minutes."

Mary reached out and touched my shoulder. "Matthew, could I speak to you outside?"

Mary said nothing until we were alone in an oak stand near the cemetery entrance. She was still shaking from the emotion of her testimony and furious with me.

"Matthew, how could you and Father deceive me so? Why didn't you tell me you were coming here to testify against Alex and Sam? It was a false accusation that could ruin their lives. What about the so-called values you're always claiming to believe in? And why would you not have spoken to me about this? It was dishonest of you. And cowardly. I am so tired of being treated like a child in my own family."

I was so taken down by this rebuke that I scarcely knew what to say. I could see in her lovely dark eyes that she hated me and would never forgive me.

"Mary, I'm sorry if you feel I was hiding something from you.

Your father was planning to be here until yesterday. He didn't want you to be involved. He knew you would be upset. I scarcely had time to understand what was going on."

"I thought we were friends," she said. "I thought I could trust you."

How could I respond to such a statement?

"You *can* trust me," I said tentatively.

"You knew of my friendship with Alex. You should have told me."

"Mary, I don't know what's in those papers nor do I understand the nature of your relationship with Alex. Why would you take your father's cross and give it away—with no discussion and no explanation? What were you thinking of? It was wrong."

She knew I was right. She swallowed hard and her eyes shone, but she didn't cry. She closed her eyes and nodded, not wanting to discuss it with me further. "Let's go in," she said finally.

After an hour in Reverend Elder's office, all of us reading papers and discussing their implications, the minister leaned back and stretched.

"I think I've heard enough. I want to suggest a resolution of this dispute, which I would like to present to the reconvened assembly when they return. But first let us pray together."

All in the room dropped their documents on the table, lowered their heads, and closed their eyes.

"Heavenly Father, we are convened here in your house to resolve a worldly dispute, to resolve it in a way that follows the model set by your son—that is just and merciful and forgiving. Be with each person in this room, Holy Father. Give us wisdom to do your will, fill us with the Holy Spirit, guide us toward the path you would have us take. And let us go forth from this place to save souls and to lead lives touched by the spirit and the light. Amen."

As he was speaking, my mind wandered, worrying about the fate of Sam and Alex. They had endured so much hardship to make their way to Pennsylvania. And they were prepared to take the blame for a theft they did not commit.

Why did so many people pull up stakes to come to this unsettled land? And by what right? Reverend Elder seemed to be fair enough in seeking resolution of our family's dispute. But what about this tension between the natives and the poorest of our immigrants? And, whether you're the early arriver or the immigrant, does might make right? Whose land is this anyway?

The minister picked up the ancient relic. "It's a lovely old cross," he said. "I think I'm going to keep a little of its magic with me after this day is done. I hope each of you will do the same."

"Mary," he said, handing her the cross and pushing the documents in her direction, "return this cross to your father. Whatever the circumstances of its passage into your family's hands, it is not your place to give it away. 'Honor your father,' as the Good Book says.

"Samuel and Alexander, even though you did not steal the cross, the bonds of trust have been broken with this family. I have been in communication with the Chester County farmers who held your indentures. McClaskey and Dickey are willing to take you back early. You were wrong to accept the cross Mary brought to you, but I think you are good boys who have a chance to make your way in this world and be successful. I am not recommending expulsion from the church and will commend you to the pastor at Fagg's

Manor with the expectation that he will welcome you back into their congregation."

His decision was stated in such a manner that no further discussion was invited. Mary was staring at the cross the pastor had placed in her hand and Alex was staring at Mary, as if memorizing her face. I saw a tear come to her eye and I wondered if she loved him.

"Boys," said Reverend Elder as he rose, "Mister McEvans here will drop you at your places down in Chester County on his way back to Fagg's Manor. I want you to come back into the sanctuary and take your place at the witness table as I recount our determination to the congregation."

As he escorted Sam and Alex out of the room, I saw Alex turn and look at Mary. I could see that he loved her. Mary looked dazed and confused. As the pastor led the boys down the hall, Mary remained in her seat, studying the cross and turning it in her hands.

I followed the Cathey wagon home, stopping when James pulled over for a rest. But Mary kept to herself and I could see she was grieving about the church's decision and angry that she could do nothing to change it.

Chapter Thirty-Six

It was the second consecutive summer of drought. Even though we had trenched irrigation channels from Manada Creek to the fields, the creek was running so low that only a trickle made its way clear to the barley and wheat fields. We studied the skies first thing each morning, hoping to spot a cloud formation that portended rain, the life blood of a farm.

We had cousins outside Lancaster who had devised a raised reservoir to catch rainwater. If we had a cistern like that here on the farm, we could have reaped the beneficence of last fall's heavy rain that breached the banks of Manada Creek. As it was, we had to haul buckets of well water up to the house just to fill our big oak bathing tub which was shared by the entire family. Everybody else on the farm bathed in the creek.

Far more critical was the survival of our crops and fruit trees. We counted our blessings to be in this vast land of fertile soil and branching waterways which gave most farmers access to a nearby creek or river. But our chances at survival ebbed and flowed with the weather, and it didn't take much to tip the balance between prosperity and disaster.

Chapter Thirty-Six

I was supervising two of the field servants in the orchard and saw my stepfather walking with old Abraham through the barley patch near the eastern stone wall. There was a healthy demand for barley back at the distilleries in Philadelphia and Baltimore, so we hoped at least to get the barley crop down the river before fall harvest started in earnest.

"When you get to the end of the row next to the well," I instructed the boys, "take the buckets back to the shed. I'm going out to the barley patch to talk to Mister Brandon."

My stepfather was crouched next to Abe as they studied a mass of small winged insects flittering around the thin brown bunch grasses.

"Sho lookin' poorly," Abe muttered as he fingered the grass.

John Brandon raised himself wearily from the ground as I approached. "Were you able to get enough water around the fruit trees?"

"We won't finish until tomorrow," I explained. "You can barely wet one tree with a bucket, the way the ground soaks it up. By the time we get to the end of a row, the first ones look dry again. No matter what we do at this point, the fruit is going to be too small to ask full price."

"I know," he said, shaking his head. "Same with the grain, if there's anything left after the bugs get finished with it."

He put his hand on my shoulder and walked with me out of earshot of Abe. "Did you see the broadsheets over in Hanover about land down in the Carolinas? They're practically giving it away. And with two bad harvests here, I don't see how we're going to get through another winter. That's a milder climate down there, lots of streams jumping with fish, and good tillable soil. I'm sure the meadows will have to be cleared, but they aren't full of stone like we have here."

I had come to trust my stepfather's instincts on the subject of farming, but I couldn't imagine pulling up stakes on a farmstead we had put so much work into. Mother had regained her health, but I worried about the strain it would cause her to uproot the family from the place that had become our home.

"Don't say anything about this yet, Matthew," he said as we walked toward the house, leaving Abe to bring in the ox cart. "I don't want the family in an uproar until I'm sure about the Carolinas. But I need someone to help me make this decision. Maybe I'll take you with me over to see Jim Cathey. He has been thinking about this for a while now."

Mary Brandon was on the porch, watching as her father and I approached the house. She had kept her distance from me ever since the Turrentines left. And she hadn't been the same person since the Indian child was turned over to the British militia at the fort. There was nothing I could do to change how she felt about me. But that didn't stop my heart from skipping a beat whenever I sat near her at dinner or passed her in the yard.

As my stepfather pushed open the front door, Mary reached out and grabbed me by the arm. "Can I talk to you for a moment, Matthew?"

We walked together past the barn and toward the chicken coop on a path that led into the forest. She was quiet until we were well past the farmyard.

"Matthew, I don't know how to begin. But I need your help." There was a vulnerability in Mary's voice I had never heard before.

Chapter Thirty-Six

"Can I trust you?"

She had turned to face me and was holding my shirt by the sleeve, a look of desperation in her deep eyes. The thought that she might need me, whatever the reason, warmed me. "Mary, of course you can trust me," I promised, taking her hand from my shirt and holding it in my own.

She looked at me quizzically, the hint of a smile slipping over her face so quickly I couldn't be sure that's what it was. The thing I had always loved most about Mary Brandon was her honesty and fearlessness, and those brown eyes of hers were now studying me with such intensity I had to laugh.

"You won't admit it, but I think you do trust me, Mary Brandon," I posited. "You've dragged me out here to the edge of the forest to tell me your secrets."

"Ah, of course," she said, in a teasing voice I hadn't heard in months, "you are my brother after all."

"I am not your brother."

"All right, then," she said. "Come with me to the clearing and I will explain everything." She turned on her heel, and I followed her swift steps down the trail and into the forest.

I had been down this path many times and was familiar with several grassy patches along the way to the deer blind. This part of the woods was usually moist and green with mossy logs and volunteer ferns, but the trees were as dry as the fields and our feet crunched over dropped needles and dried out leaves as we made our way deeper into the forest. The trail branched this side of the creek and Mary led me down the lower path to a sandy dell surrounded by sumac and maple, with an opening to the sky that invited sunlight into the clearing.

She turned to me, placing her hands on both arms and looking me straight in the eye.

"It's about Polly. She wasn't really abandoned. Alex didn't find her. She was . . . she was put into our care."

It took me a moment to understand what she was saying. "Polly? What do you mean 'put into our care'? Whose care?"

I was trying to grasp the meaning of what Mary said, but hearing Alex's name threw me off balance. A terrible thought flashed through my mind that she and Alex had conceived a child together.

It was nonsense, of course, and I knew that not even Mary Brandon could disguise a pregnancy and childbirth from her whole family. But my resentment and jealousy of Alex Turrentine, who had so captivated Mary's attention, still simmered.

As I stood looking at her, trying to understand what she was saying, an even greater shock ran through me from head to toe as an armed Indian stepped from behind a bush, positioning himself close enough to Mary to remove her scalp with the swing of his axe.

I reached out and pulled Mary away from him and put myself between her and the Indian, wishing desperately that I had brought along my shotgun, then turned to face the attacker, reaching for the knife in my belt. The Indian, quicker than I, extracted his own blade.

From behind me, I could hear Mary's voice as if in a dream, arguing, explaining herself, trying to get between me and the native. "Matthew, wait, he's a friend. It's Kago."

As the Indian and I faced each other with weapons drawn,

Mary ran between us and held the Indian by the arms, just as she had held me.

"No, Kago, friend, *nua*, my brother. Stop."

The Indian returned the knife to his strap, eyeing me suspiciously and stepping back, waiting quietly without moving until I did the same. As he stood watching, Mary turned, took me by the arm and guided me to sit on the ground. She did the same with the native, who sat opposite me with legs crossed and dark eyes that never left me.

As she told me the story of how Alex Turrentine and Kago had become friends and how she discovered their meeting place in the forest, I began to understand how the bond between Mary and Alex took hold. I always knew there was something between them, and was jealous of it, excluded from the secrets they would share as they passed one another in the farmyard going about their daily chores.

"We became very close, the three of us," Mary explained. "Kago is smart. He always tried to explain to us the risk to his tribe's way of life from the white man. He wanted to learn from us. And we wanted to learn from him."

As Mary described their meetings in the clearing, the Indian would break in from time to time expanding upon Mary's description with words of his own which were spoken in very competent English. At one point when she was describing Kago's tribal affiliation, he held out an arm to silence her and said, patting his chest, "Kagogararo."

Then the Indian reached over and took Mary's bare arm and laid it upon his own, wrist to wrist, in a gesture that was shockingly intimate and could have meant instant death to an Indian in a white town or village.

"We are blood brothers," he said with fierce determination, holding their wrists together with his other hand and turning to me to make sure his point was understood. He then took her hand in both his own and looked into her eyes, which were starting to glisten with emotion.

He was of the Conestoga people, a nomadic tribe that moved seasonally in and out of the mountains near our farm. After the loss of many of his kinsmen from disease brought by the white man, the tribe was dwindling. More and more of them were moving south of Lancaster to an area called Conestoga Town, near the river, but they came back north to hunt seasonally.

"So much death among our people. My wife Osha, she lost mother, father, sister, whole family. Always sad. Too many sick and too many killed. No milk for baby. 'Baby die too,' she told me. 'You take.' I didn't know what to do. So I brought our baby to my white friends. Alex and Mary. Our tribe went south. But now . . . " He was quiet for a moment, trying to gather his thoughts. "We think about our child. She is of my people, not the whites. My wife . . . her heart cries . . . she needs her baby."

As Kago spoke, Mary's eyes didn't leave her friend. She wrapped herself in her own arms, tears beginning to slide down her cheeks. Her voice was choked and very quiet as she said to him, "Oh, Kago. I'm so sorry. Father wouldn't let me keep her."

Mary turned to me, her face wet with tears. "Matthew, this is all my fault, don't you see? Kago had come to us before Alex left. But then everything happened so fast. I wasn't even told that Alex and Sam had been sent away until the day of their hearing in Paxtang."

I was at a loss for words. I had known a few natives who worked in the loading dock at the gristmill or in the garden at church, but they were a quiet people who didn't feel at their ease around whites. It was both astonishing and at the same time so like Mary Brandon to have had a deep relationship with a native where they treated each other as equals and intimate friends.

The Indian held Mary's hand as she wept and waited patiently for her to regain her composure.

"You'll find my baby, Mary? Take her back from soldiers."

"Matthew will help us, won't you Matthew?" she asked, turning to me. "You said I could trust you, and I do."

This left me speechless. I had no idea how I could help with such an earnest and utterly impossible request. But Mary was looking at me as if I could solve all the problems of the world, and I would have done anything to justify her confidence.

The Indian looked up at me. "Mary trusts you. So I also trust."

He then rose to his feet, greeting each of us gravely with a nod of thanks. Then to Mary, "My friend, when you have my daughter, leave your mark for me. Then we go south with my people."

The Indian slipped into the forest as quietly as he came. Mary and I were both still. She looked at me and started to say something but then stopped herself.

"Mary, even if we could reclaim the child, do you think it's the right thing—for her, I mean?" I asked. "You heard what he said. Their people are dying."

Chapter Thirty-Seven

J ohn Brandon was bent over his register of accounts, a tallow candle burning on the rough desk to augment the illumination from two high windows. He had not changed out of his work breeches and homespun shirt, as he would normally do in the evenings before supper, since we had just completed the midday meal and he would return to work in the fields this day. He periodically dipped his goose feather quill into the black ink pot as he recorded income and expenses from this month's trade.

"Come in, Matthew," he urged in response to my tap on the door. "You said you wished to speak to me?"

My stepfather's study was furnished simply with a desk and shelves hewn from lumber on the farm that had been split and shaped at the sawmill for the purpose of being made into furniture. Though we were not wealthy, John Brandon, unlike most of the farmers on the Pennsylvania frontier, had a large collection of books and a separate room for his private affairs from which he managed the business of the farm.

I pulled a chair up to his desk as he snuffed out the candle. With the new taxes that had been imposed on both beeswax and tallow candles, we burned them only as needed.

Mary had argued that we should speak to her father together about the Indian child, but I convinced her that we would be more likely to enlist his support without the emotion that sometimes sprang up between the two of them.

"It concerns Mary," I said, jumping right into a well-rehearsed appeal.

A knowing smile warmed my stepfather's face. "I expected you would be coming to see me, Matthew. It has been clear to me for some time how you feel about my daughter. And, you must know that it's a relief to me that your affection for Mary has remained steadfast, in spite of her theatrics relating to the Irish servant boy. Such romantic fantasies are common in young women of this age and must be forgiven in Mary's case as an affliction derived from reading too many books of fiction."

I was not prepared for the conversation to take this particular turn and cleared my throat awkwardly before continuing.

"Sir, it is something else I come to speak to you about. But it does concern Mary, and Alex Turrentine as well. Did she ever explain to you why she took the cross?"

My stepfather rubbed his forehead wearily. "She has a tendency to overreact to everything, Mary does, and she dreamt up a cock-eyed notion that our cross had been improperly taken from the servants' family back on the plantation in Ireland. There's no reason to believe that was the case, in spite of the conclusions Mary drew from my papers."

"Irrespective of the cross's provenance," I responded, "I don't think Mary would ever have acted so rashly had she not been so angry and upset about the Indian child."

John Brandon sighed and shook his head. "That's what I mean about Mary. She has many wonderful qualities, my daughter, but she is given to excess emotion. It was absurd for her to insist we adopt an abandoned Indian child. My wife was much taken with the child as well and shed tears at the fort when we left her, but she understood and accepted my decision. Surely Mary does not propose that we establish a charitable home for abandoned Indian children here on our small farm?"

"That's just it, sir. I have now come to understand that the child was not abandoned. It was given to Mary and Alex Turrentine for caretaking when the native parents were unable to care for it."

John Brandon raised an eyebrow and waited for me to continue.

"She and Alex had become friendly with a young brave from the Conestoga tribe who found his way to the farm over the Swatara Gap in Blue Mountain. They apparently conducted lessons together to learn more about each other's language and culture," I explained, trying to make it sound like a perfectly natural and commonplace practice.

I knew most people would find their little learning circle in the woods not only unusual but quite socially improper. And my step-father could well throw up his hands in fury at his daughter, not to mention myself as the messenger. Instead, he began to chuckle to himself, shaking his head in dismay.

"Well, son, if it were anyone but Mary, I would swear you were making this up. But it's just the kind of thing my daughter might get herself mixed up in."

I continued my narrative, having avoided an explosive reaction so far. "I met the Indian yesterday," I recounted. "He stepped out of the bushes into the clearing near the deer blind, scaring me half to death. Mary had asked for my help without forewarning me that we were meeting up with an Indian. They are fast friends, it seems. And the Indian and his wife are hoping to get their child back."

John Brandon rubbed his face in a mix of exasperation and amusement.

"And so she's got you running to me on her behalf, does she, Matthew? And could I ask you why you would put yourself out and risk your good standing in this household on behalf of my impulsive daughter, an Indian boy who can't decide whether he wants his child or not, and an Irish servant who, best as I could make of it, was trying to win my daughter's affection while stealing my property? My God, Matthew, you must really love the girl."

This speech left me open-mouthed and without words. I could feel a flush of embarrassment turning my face red.

"And, by the way, Matthew, how do you propose I extract this child from the militia, having turned her over to the warden at the fort? I don't even know if the child is still there."

After yesterday's meeting with Kago in the forest, I had thought much about what the Indian had said, particularly with regard to the impact of European immigration upon his tribe and indeed his whole race. To us, the American colonies represented a chance to get a new start and to free ourselves from oppressive systems of government that favored the few over the many. We immigrants were proud of bringing modern ingenuity from a more advanced civilization to natives who lived in abject poverty without any understanding of what education and science and great literature and music could bring to their lives.

I understood that the Indians bore hostility toward the white farmer, but I had attributed that to their tribal warlike nature. It had never occurred to me that there could be in their mind a real loss of something valuable as we settled this land.

In trying to explain this to my stepfather, I'm not sure I succeeded in opening his eyes to the plight of the natives. What he did understand was that my assistance in returning the child to its parents might well earn me Mary's gratitude. And I'm pretty sure John Brandon had placed his hopes on a match between Mary and myself. For my own part, I must confess I would have done pretty much anything to win her affection.

Had our paths crossed in England as a result of our parents' marriage, it would have been unseemly to consider a union within the same family. But out here, there were few opportunities to form social bonds with other young people of the same age. And a solid marriage was essential to building a life of security and safety so far from civilization. I knew my stepfather wanted to see his daughters wed. And while I would never pursue marriage with Mary unless she too found it desirable, I certainly wasn't going to walk away from a chance to win her gratitude—and, with any luck, her heart.

"When you brought us here to this farm on Manada Creek— Mother and a half-dozen more mouths to feed," I began, "I knew right away that good fortune had finally returned to our family. I don't know what would have become of us back there in Middletown, chasing each other around the tavern."

"With the mother you've got, Matthew, you would have got along just fine there on the river. But the moment I met your mother, I knew she would make a fine wife and a good mother to my children. And so she has done."

"But Mary still longs for her own mother," I reminded him. "And she's not sure about any of us Lockes to this day, myself included."

"She is an independent-minded woman, like your mother. And, in my opinion, the man who wins her heart will be fortunate indeed."

I was beginning to feel uncomfortable with the direction of this conversation, and not just because my stepfather was steering the topic away from the problem at hand.

"Well, sir, I'm sure of this. She will make up her own mind about who she gives her heart to. And, for the moment, I just want to help her keep a promise to a friend, a promise that she holds sacred, I believe."

John Brandon agreed to write a letter to Lieutenant Scott at the garrison where Polly had been placed, though he warned me that she could well have been removed from the fort by now.

He even consented to let Mary join me on a pilgrimage to attempt to reclaim the child.

Chapter Thirty-Eight

We set out from the farm the next morning just as the sun's imminent arrival was beginning to cast a dim light that outlined the barn and smokehouse. Both Mary and I had been up well before daylight, finishing our morning chores before the trip up Blue Mountain. I had tapped on her door to make sure she was up and we scurried around in the darkened house, whispering to each other as we threw together bread and cheese for our packs, just as if we were heading out for a day of hunting or fishing together.

"Here, put this into the cart," she instructed, handing me her pack, which I tossed with a thud into the back. "Shhh . . . You're going to wake everyone up."

She was wearing her scarlet woolen cape, eyes flashing with excitement as we headed out on our adventure, partners in a worthy cause and happy to be together.

You could see the gap in the ridge as we approached the fort, which had been built in a location most likely to deter Indian incursions from the other side of the mountain. It was a misnomer to call it a fort since it was hardly more than a small dirt clearing containing a few rough log buildings and encircled by wooden poles with pointed tops placed close together to protect the inhabitants from attack.

Since the British Regulars stationed in the coastal regions of the colony were not numerous enough to protect the frontier, local able-bodied males between the ages of sixteen and sixty were expected to provide service as citizen-soldiers in the local militia. The Provincial Council of Pennsylvania would appoint a local volunteer, or even sometimes a British soldier, to act as officer of a militia post with responsibility to fill the muster rolls with citizen-soldiers and to maintain order. The militia was made up of farmers and merchants and carpenters, a constantly changing crew of locals who did their time to keep the settlers safe. They fought the Indians when need be, and in the process they learned to fight like the Indians.

The gate was open as our cart approached the militia station and we drove in and pulled up in front of the log building that served as headquarters. A surprising number of people were milling about, many of them Indians who may have once been captives but now helped to maintain the camp. The interior of the fort had been stripped of trees and grasses, so it was dusty, as were its inhabitants, both native and white.

Mary remained seated in the cart as I stepped down to introduce myself to the man who emerged from the shelter. He wore dirty and torn breeches over scraped boots covered in dust. He eyed us suspiciously from what little could be seen of his creased and sun-scraped face, which was almost entirely obscured by a wild, unkempt beard.

Before uttering a word, he spat a mottled glob of liquid chewing tobacco into the dirt.

"What're you here for?" he muttered, looking us over.

"I am Matthew Locke," I explained, "here on behalf of my step-father John Brandon." My first instinct to extend my hand was suppressed by a quick assessment of the man in charge.

"Lieutenant Scott," he replied without welcome.

I had expected to be taken into the militia quarters, but Scott didn't concern himself with the protocols of hospitality.

"This spring Mister Brandon brought an abandoned Indian infant here to the fort," I explained. "We've since discovered the parents of the baby and they have asked for our help in finding their child. Here is my stepfather's letter."

With a look of irritation, Scott snatched the letter from my hand and gave it a cursory look.

"Do ya think we've got nothin' better to do than keep track o' redskin whelps? They drop 'em like rabbits in the tents over there."

The post had a barrack with a dirt floor and rough-hewn log walls where many of the men slept, as well as a gaol where they locked up a few. But many of the inhabitants, including most of the native Indians, had erected tents and lean-tos all along the edge of the encampment, just inside the protective walls of the fort. They had dug latrines and cooking pits and most of them willingly gave up the shade and water of more spacious accommodations for the safety of the garrison. Some of the natives were there as captives, but they were passive and quiet and didn't appear to pose any risk to the militia or others who came and went around the fort.

Chapter Thirty-Eight

"Were you in charge here when Mister Brandon and his wife brought the child?"

He spat another wad of tobacco juice into the dirt.

"Not as I recall."

"Could we speak to some of the Indians who live here?" I asked.

"You can do whatever you like, but most of 'em won't understand a word you say."

Mary and I left the cart tied to the hitching post and made our way among the squalid tents. An elderly squaw, sitting cross-legged and clothed in a ragged skirt with a rough blanket wrapped around her shoulders, was mashing paste with a pestle in a stone mortar, flies resting on her arm and circling the pasty substance.

Mary was quiet and I could see she was shocked by the circumstances of the natives and horrified that Polly had been deposited in such a place.

"Are you sure you'll even recognize the child?" I wondered.

"Of course I will," she insisted impatiently.

Mary's attention was drawn to a female of middle years carrying two baskets through the settlement, the first white woman we had seen at the garrison. Mary turned away from me to intercept the woman.

"Excuse me, ma'am, do you speak English?" Mary inquired.

"Aye, I do," the woman responded.

"I'm seeking a baby Indian girl who was left here almost two months ago. She would be maybe three months old by now. My parents brought her here as an abandoned child." Mary's voice was tremulous.

"Come with me. I must deliver these vegetables, but I know someone we can talk to." Mary fell in step with the basket carrier and I followed them further into the encampment. Mary and I waited outside as the woman stepped into various tents and lean-tos, dropping off produce.

After emptying her basket, she stopped in front of a tent with a tidy garden in front, peering inside and beckoning an Indian woman to come out. The two of them spoke in a tongue I could not understand, then the basket carrier took Mary by the arm and I followed them to a larger enclosure nearby. She bade me wait outside and took Mary into the tent.

With the tent opening secured behind them, I was left out in the heat and dust for a good long while, wondering whether Mary was safe. After a long wait, the basket carrier emerged without Mary.

"She will be out before long," the woman assured me. "She must take the time to know the baby's caretaker and see that the child is at ease with her."

As I stood in the heat and dust, I heard a commotion from inside the tent. Then Mary emerged with a child in her arms, pursued by a young woman with a dirty face and an exposed breast. Mary spoke to the Indian girl forcefully in a tongue I could not understand, invoking the name of her friend Kagogararo several times. The native grabbed Mary by the shoulder, turning her back toward the tent, beside herself with fury, arms flailing, her hand raised to Mary in a threatening manner.

I moved Mary and the child out of harm's way and began to explain as gently as I could under the stressful circumstances that we were returning the child to its rightful Indian parents. The native was not to be placated, however, and responded with a heated outburst that rose in pitch to a kind of mournful wail.

A bearded figure was moving rapidly toward us from my right and before I could utter a sound Lieutenant Scott had struck the Indian woman in her gut with the butt of his rifle, driving her to the ground with a soundless exhalation of breath.

Mary wailed in horror at the assault, and I tried to reach out to the native who lay prostrate on the ground.

"Shut your mouth, you redskin shite," he shouted. "You make one more move and I'll slit your throat."

Mary and I stood speechless and terrified.

Scott turned to us with a sneer. "Now, get the hell out of here before somebody gets killed."

Mary was shaking as I helped her and Polly into the cart. We were almost back to the farm before either of us felt calm enough to speak.

I reached out and took her hand. "It was the right thing to do, Mary. The child should not have been left in that place."

Chapter Thirty-Nine

I followed Mary down the path by Manada Creek, the Indian child in her arms. As we walked, Mary carried on a continuous conversation with the infant, as if she could be understood, speaking in the high voice of a child herself.

"Listen to the bird singing, Polly . . . It's way, way high up in the tree . . . Oh, the happy little birdie . . . So beautiful, just like you . . . I love you, sweet girl . . . Don't ever forget that."

Mary had been preoccupied with the child since we returned from the fort, savoring their time together. I was stunned by the depth of feeling that can develop between a woman and an infant, even one who is not her own.

Kago was waiting for us in the clearing. Sitting beside him was a striking Indian maid with deep eyes and a worried expression. She jumped up when we arrived and took the child out of Mary's arms, studying the babe from head to toe, her face softening and beginning to glow. Then, as Mary watched, she began to walk around the edge of the clearing, singing softly to her daughter in words we could not understand, her eyes never leaving the child's face.

Kago, I think, understood, even as his wife celebrated the return of her child, that Mary was mourning her loss. He gently put a hand on each of Mary's shoulders, speaking softly to her.

"You have given us back our life, my friend," he said, looking into Mary's eyes. "We will remember your name to Great Spirit all the days of our lives. Our child will grow up hearing stories about a white girl named Mary who loved her."

After the Indian family departed, Mary turned back toward the farm, walking resolutely and dealing with her loss in her own way. I reached out to touch her sleeve but she recoiled. She would not be comforted by me or by anyone.

In the days that followed, Mary grieved and kept to herself. The rest of the family was preoccupied with the stunning news that we were going to sell the farm and head south to the fertile hills of North Carolina.

We had been hearing rumors for months about the availability of rich farmland in the Carolinas which could be purchased for a pittance. Settlers from the north of Ireland, as well as England and Germany, continued to move into the Susquehanna Valley, so we could ask a good price for our small farm at the foot of Blue Mountain. And with that money we could buy farmland in Carolina sufficient to provide separate land grants to each of us.

Though I had known this move was coming, my stepfather often using me as a sounding board to grapple with difficult decisions, it was not a change I welcomed. Our little piece of rolling farmland along Manada Creek was our home, the first place that had felt like home to me since we left London. And how long ago that seemed.

I didn't relish becoming a migrant again, having to make my way among strangers in a new place. Even though our large family, together with the Cathey clan from across the creek, would constitute its own village, I was keenly aware of the dangers of travel through unsettled parts of the colonies and the risk from unfriendly natives and wild animals. But I saw John Brandon's dilemma. As my generation of Brandons and Lockes was reaching maturity, ready to start our own families, the Pennsylvania farm was too small to allocate parcels to all. And nearby land had become too expensive to increase our stake.

I had to think about my future and the family I hoped to have. I knew perfectly well who I hoped to have that family with, but I doubted that Mary Brandon wanted any part of it.

When my stepfather invited me into his study for a heart-to-heart talk, my worst fears were realized.

"Son, you are of an age to find a wife and start your own family. Your mother and I want to see you settled before you have to take on more responsibility for the new property in Rowan County. I know your heart has been leaning toward Mary for a long time. But she is strong-willed and does not always yield to my guidance. We're wondering, your mother and I, if you would consider Anne for a wife?"

My stepfather had been watching me carefully as he offered up this proposal. I must have appeared as blank-faced as the village idiot as I attempted to consider and respond to such an unexpected proposal.

Anne Brandon was kind, compliant and thoughtful, and pleasing to the eye as well. I respected her and liked her, but I had never felt for her the yearning or heart-pounding emotion that filled me every time I was in the company of her younger sister.

"Sir, I . . . Anne is surely intended for my brother Francis, who must also wed," I stammered.

My stepfather looked perturbed. I felt sure this idea of a match between Anne and myself had been generated by my mother who understood well Mary's stubbornness and had probably concluded she would refuse to marry me.

"Anne and Francis are too much alike," he explained patiently. "And there seems to be little progress in their courtship. It's true that Anne is a bit older than you, but not so much really, and she is still of age to begin bearing children. She would make a good wife, Matthew. Anne is modest and frugal and she would strive always to make her husband happy."

I had never for a moment considered Anne Brandon as a wife and was so ill-prepared for such a suggestion that I could not find words to respond. Among the million wild thoughts that were crossing my mind was a profound sadness that Mary must have made it clear to her father that she would never have me for a husband.

In the days that followed, my thoughts returned again and again to what it was my parents were asking of me. I had deep respect for my stepfather, grateful for all he had done for my family. And I'm sure, were I in his place, I would use every means at hand to find a match for an older daughter of marriageable age.

I was tending to the horses before setting out for a day in the fields when my mother and Anne came into the barn.

"Matthew, I want you and Anne to go over to Jim Cathey's and help with the apples. They need extra hands this morning. He will send a bushel back with you."

"But I was going to work with Francis on that irrigation ditch to the barley field," I protested.

"John is going to work with Francis this morning," Mother assured me. "You'll be back by mid-afternoon."

Anne didn't look any happier than I was to be sent on this mission. As I turned the cart toward the Manada Creek ford, Anne broke the silence between us.

"This isn't to do with having apple pie for supper tonight, is it?"

I was amused to discover that Anne shared a bit of her sister's candor.

"Did your father speak to you, then?"

"No, your mother. 'Divide and conquer' is their motto. Was it Julius Caesar who said that?"

"So it was," I rejoined. "As he undertook his campaign in Gaul."

"Look, Matthew, you need not worry yourself about this. They are fretting about the fact that I may soon be regarded as a spinster and thus will have lost my market value. It's so much stuff and nonsense. And, anyway, I'm too old for you."

Anne smiled ruefully, shaking her head with resignation.

"That's not true at all, Anne. It's just that I've always assumed you and Francis would wed. I think he expects the same thing. He's just too reserved to do anything about it."

"And I guess you believe Mary will eventually realize you're too good a catch to pass over," she responded, lifting an eyebrow.

"Oh, Mary . . . That's something else altogether. I'm not sure she ever wanted me. In any event, it's perfectly clear she'll never forgive me for standing by while Alex and Sam were sent away. Not that I was sorry to see them go. Or that I could have done anything about it. Anyway, I wouldn't want to marry someone who didn't find it agreeable."

"That was a fine speech, Matthew. But I don't believe it for a minute."

"Oh, don't you, sister Anne? Well, you may be surprised when I come courting."

I winked at Anne and she laughed heartily. And it struck me that this fine-looking stepsister of mine would not be a bad choice for a wife.

In the days that followed our apple-picking duty at the Cathey farm, Anne and I continued to enjoy a warm and lively friendship that would last a lifetime. She never took seriously my earnest consideration of her as a mate, but we enjoyed teasing each other about our shortcomings in the art of romance and developed a true friendship.

I guess it was obvious to everyone in the family that Anne and I had become more friendly. While we were not intentionally trying to stir up jealousy, we had a few good laughs about our parents' keen interest in our friendship, not to mention the consternation on the faces of Francis and Mary when a look of complicity or irrepressible laughter passed between us at the supper table.

Just weeks before we departed for North Carolina, Mother organized a big picnic on the Cathey side of the creek for our families and friends to feast on supplies we couldn't take along, to transfer some goods too big or too perishable to transport, and to say goodbye to old friends. It was a time for toasts and shared memories, a blessing from the pastor and music by three fiddlers from nearby farms.

Nobody loved a celebration more than Mary Brandon, and she was a vision that day in a yellow sundress with little white flowers around the neck and a bonnet with matching yellow ribbon.

Mary, of course, was excited about our move, looking forward to seeing the Shenandoah Valley and passing over the great rivers she had heard about. I could see her across the meadow, stopping to chat with aunts, uncles, and cousins who had settled in groups onto blankets and were sipping cider and enjoying the music.

Anne was teasing me about Mary's vexation at what she felt to be a budding romance between Anne and myself.

"Well, you explained to her, did you not, Anne, that we are merely good friends trying to defend ourselves against parental schemes designed to increase their population of grandchildren?"

"No, of course I did not," Anne laughed. "Miss 'Mary Mary Quite Contrary' can think what she likes. It's good for her to be wondering where she stands for a change. Sorry, Matthew, but I haven't had many chances to make my little sister jealous and I am enjoying this quite a bit."

Anne's remarks gave me a jolt of pleasure. Jealous? Mary? Surely not. But the mere thought of it moved me across the meadow to where Mary was in lively discussion with Cousin Richard, the yellow ribbon around her bonnet dancing in the breeze.

"Greetings, Richard. It's the end of an era here in the Pennsylvania countryside, isn't it? This valley has been a fine home for all of us over these years," I said, already feeling nostalgic.

Chapter Thirty-Nine

"Aye, that it has, Matthew."

I took Mary's arm, with a nod to my cousin. "I'm going to borrow my little sister here for a few moments, cousin. Pleasure to see you."

Before Mary had a chance to resist, I tucked her arm into mine and headed back toward the firepit.

"Your little sister, my foot," Mary protested, attempting unsuccessfully to extricate her arm from mine.

"Oh, come on, Mary, walk with me for a bit."

"And what do you think Anne will say when she sees you walking with me arm-in-arm?"

"What would you expect her to say?"

"Since you are courting my older sister, I do not think you should be so friendly."

"Why Mary Brandon, are you jealous of my friendship with my sister Anne?"

"Of course I'm not," she protested, again attempting to pull away as I held tight to her arm.

"I am not courting your sister. But I do admire her and I enjoy her company. And she and I have had to fend off furious efforts by the parents as of late to make a match. That has brought us closer in friendship. But, Mary, she has always known it's you I love."

I was surprised at my newly discovered presence of mind to make such a bold declaration and I didn't stop to gauge Mary's reception.

She was quiet then as we walked under the bright Pennsylvania sky. And she didn't try to pull away.

Chapter Forty

The mountain roads were so narrow we had to pull aside every time we passed a wagon going the other direction. Not that we saw travelers heading north all that often. It seemed the whole of Pennsylvania was moving south toward the Carolinas. We forded dozens of streams and ferried across wide rivers that would be the life blood of the farmers who settled nearby. As we approached rivers or rolling valleys, the trail opened up and we could see the line of covered wagons winding down in front of us like spilt cream cutting through the fertile green meadows.

There were six wagons in our group alone, stuffed to the brim with the most precious belongings of the Brandon-Locke-Cathey families, the remainder having been sold off or given to neighbors. Family members travelled in farm wagons that had been rigged up for the journey with metal frames and stiff white canvas coverings to protect against the dust and dirt and rain that pelted the caravan. We were especially proud of the new Conestoga wagon purchased from a master German artisan in Lancaster. Pulled by six heavy horses and loaded with most of the household furnishings and farm implements of all the families in our caravan, the bed of the wagon was bowed in the middle to hold goods in place over the bumpy terrain and caulked with tar to keep it dry over river crossings. We were a sight to behold and the envy of many a fellow traveler along the wagon road.

Leaving hadn't been easy. As we pulled out of our little community of farms fed by Manada Creek, I could see a look of grim determination on my stepfather's face as he snapped the reins briskly to move his team out before tears were shed. As farmers, this land was as much a part of us as an arm or leg and it felt somehow unnatural and wrong to leave behind the fields that had sustained us all these years.

But as we rolled along the familiar road into Lancaster and then across the Susquehanna into unknown territory, the Great Wagon Trail became our new home and the ever-moving landscape and rhythms of life on the trail became normal to us.

Most of us were weary after a few days of jostling and dirt and supper cooked over an open fire. The exception was Mary Brandon who was excited to see new places and curious about all the people we met at the waystations and campsites where all of us migrants enjoyed the mutual protection of fellow travelers.

"Can you see the Potomac yet, Matthew?" Mary asked, leaning up from the wagon bed where she and Anne and two of our cousins were passing the hours with needlework and gossip.

"Not yet. Do you want to come up and sit with me for a while?"

Mary gave me her hand and I steadied her as she made her way up from the covered bed to the driver's bench. It could be dusty up front, but this morning the air was clear and fresh and Mary inhaled deeply, the scents of pine and honeysuckle permeating the forest.

I had not yet grown accustomed to Mary's touch and the simple act of guiding her to the bench, her soft hand in my own, my arm around her waist as she pulled up beside me, gave me the most inexplicable feeling of joy. In her usual way, Mary was interested in every new thing we passed. My tendency was to look back and mourn what we had lost. Not Mary Brandon. It was always the future, and everything ahead of us seemed sparkling and magical when seen through her eyes.

The bumping and lurching through rugged mountainous terrain was surprisingly less tedious when I could look out of the corner of my eye and distract myself with a glimpse of Mary's porcelain skin, her shiny brown locks swept by the breeze as she chatted amiably about a creature seen scurrying through the underbrush or an unusual bend in the river.

It felt as though we had been on the road for endless weeks, but we had scarcely begun the long journey down through the Appalachian Mountains to the hills of Carolina. The Great Wagon Road had been the main north-south Indian path for generations before our people sailed to America from all parts of Europe. But today the Indians were mostly contained in the west and this trail was now the white man's road, stretched wider by wagon wheels. The Indians, and even the deer and buffalo and wolves, had fled into the forests and valleys to escape the constant rumble of wagons, punctuated by the flash of gunfire as the menfolk tracked dinner meat for their families camping along the trail.

Eager to see the country we were passing through, Mary was making it a habit to join me on the driver's bench for hours each day.

Chapter Forty

For me, those hours in conversation with her were the happiest I had known. She asked about everything—the vegetation, the birdsong, and the rights and wrongs of the new civilization that was being overlaid upon this once nearly empty land.

"Look at the expanse of this valley, Matthew. Isn't it beautiful? Maybe we should stop and make our home right here."

"We can't afford land in Virginia," I countered. "But your father assures me we will find streams and hills and valleys just as lovely in North Carolina."

"I hope we're not too late to the Carolinas to lay claim to good farmland," she calculated. "Uncle Jim came back from his journey with tales of fertile land lying fallow and available for almost nothing. Father will be sorely disappointed if we arrive to find all the land sold off."

"He won't be the only one," I rejoined.

"Matthew, ever since the ferry deposited us on this side of the river, I couldn't help but wonder whether Kago and Osha and Polly mightn't be nearby. They were going to travel south too this month. Maybe they are on a parallel path closer to the ridge line."

"You miss her, don't you?" I asked, knowing the answer.

"I was all she had for a while. It's a different kind of feeling, being needed like that. She was such a lively, engaging child. Each time I came to pick her up, she would reach out to me, eager to be in my arms. Your mother loved her too, but Polly was never quite content unless she was with me."

"We did the right thing, Mary. I could tell how much Osha and Kago love her. She belongs with her own people."

"Do you think Osha is a good mother? You know, before, even before Kago brought Polly to us, something was wrong. That's why he turned to us."

"Did you see her face? She's a mother. I think the love of a child is something a mother always has inside. When I first met Kago, I couldn't understand what he was trying to say about Osha and how upset she had been about the death all around her. But when I saw her with the child, I knew that's where Polly should be."

Mary reached over and took my hand. "Thank you, Matthew. Without your help, we never would have gotten her back from the fort."

Mary was holding my hand in her lap and didn't remove it as we rode along, her face flushed with emotion as she remembered this child she had loved. As for me, I was as happy as a man could be. I wanted to stop time and remain forever in that moment, riding through the dappled sunlight of a pine-scented forest with the warm softness of Mary Brandon's hand in my own.

Mary lifted my hand and moved it back to my knee with a pat.

"I'd better not let Anne see me holding hands with you," she confessed, a teasing note in her voice. "She's back there hearing a lecture from our aunt about why she must now marry your brother."

"I don't think arranged marriages are a good idea," I insisted. "But it's true that Anne and Francis would make a good match. And who else are they going to meet on the wagon trail—or on a remote farm in Carolina for that matter?"

"People shouldn't have to marry if they choose not to," Mary snapped.

Chapter Forty

"And if your father chose a husband for you, Mary, are you saying you would refuse?"

"Of course I would refuse."

Mary was, as always, trying her best to assert control over her own destiny. It's one of the things that made me love her. She had never approved of her father's marriage to my mother, thinking of it as a betrayal. In point of fact, her father had been widowed longer than my mother and it was us Lockes who might have been offended by our mother's hasty marriage to John Brandon.

I assumed my mother and my stepfather had given up on Mary's taking a liking to me. Why else would they have tried to make a match between Anne and myself? I probably should have tried harder with Anne. But who can understand the ways of the heart? All I knew was that my heart started to pound whenever trouble-some young Mary needled me with her quick wit. I couldn't keep up with her, that's for sure. But I was sure of one thing. Every mile along this road was brighter when she sat by my side.

The trail had just turned away from the sunny green valley we had been passing through into another deeply forested stretch of winding road and I couldn't see the expression on Mary's face.

"Luckily for your father, Anne is not as hard-headed as you are. And anyway, you should be glad if she agrees to marry Francis. It won't be appropriate for you to accept a husband until your older sister is married off."

Mary exhaled with an audible sound of exasperation. "What on earth makes you think I want to be married?" she spluttered grumpily.

"All girls hope to marry someday. With you, I've seen already how much you want to be a mother. And what a wonderful mother you will be. And anyway, you would be a burden on your father if you didn't find a husband."

"I would never be a burden on Father. I can do all kinds of things to help him run the farm," she protested.

Her stubborn insistence upon self-sufficiency made me wonder whether she would ever need me or anyone else.

"You didn't seem to be immune from matters of the heart when Alex Turrentine was around," I sniffed with more bitterness than I intended.

The last thing I had intended to do was to bring Alex into the lovely day Mary and I had been sharing. In fact, I hoped never to hear his name again. But I hadn't been blind to her infatuation with him. She had risked estrangement from her father to try to save Alex and his brother from prosecution. And she had, after all, stolen her father's most precious icon through some misplaced sense of justice going back a hundred years.

"Don't you dare speak to me of him," she insisted, glaring at me with a cold eye. "You know perfectly well that he did nothing wrong."

"He and Sam have left the colony, you know," I stated with some satisfaction. "They couldn't maintain that cabin in Mifflin County because of the Indians."

She was quiet then, refusing to look my way, punishing me for bringing up a sore subject. But she wasn't the type of girl to pout and soon moved on to sharing her thoughts on the next topic of colonial controversy that crossed her mind.

When we stopped for the evening, circling our wagons in a defensive position in the event of Indian attack, we split into groups to prepare for the evening meal—gathering wood for the campfire, hunting squirrels or rabbits, collecting fruits or berries. We always did our chores in groups of three or four, the threat from Indians or wild animals never far from our minds. But I was able to pull Mary aside before she left with her cousins to bring up water from the creek.

"Mary, I'm sorry. I shouldn't have said what I did. Please come and walk with me," I implored her.

We followed a cleared path down toward the creek where clear water bubbled over stones of black and amber, bright green moss growing up the bank toward a stand of wild fern.

"I've no right to belittle your relationship with Alex. He and Sam were treated unfairly, both by our family and by fate, having been born into poverty and desperation. You and I were more fortunate. I worked with Alex all the time and I liked him fine. But I didn't like the way he looked at you and I won't apologize for that."

"Are you saying you were jealous, Matthew?" Her tone was lighter, even though she was chiding me.

I gave her a sidelong look, but didn't answer the question, hoping she wouldn't notice the warm flush on my face.

She continued to grumble about politics and I was just as happy to leave off the question of my jealousy.

"You know perfectly well, Matthew, that the Brandon family has no right to that cross and never did have. Our ancestors were part and parcel of the English gentry who looted Ireland to fatten their own pocketbooks."

"I don't think Alex cared half as much about that cross as you did," I insisted. "And think about your father. The Brandon cross, whatever its provenance, has been a comfort to him all these years, including those long months when he was mourning your mother."

"You always defend Father," she complained, "no matter how wrong he may be. He didn't like the idea that I was close friends with a servant, an indentured Ulster Scot of the lower class."

"You underestimate him, Mary. John Brandon is not the kind of man who judges others so harshly. He is working as hard as he can to give his family—and mine—an opportunity to prosper. And it's not easy."

She was studying me. "You're a lot like him, you know."

"Good," I replied cheerfully. "Maybe you could try to be a little easier on both of us."

She was riding up front again the next day and I was careful not to bring up Alex's name again.

"I've been talking to Francis," I told her. "Once we get our home-steads going, we're going to set up a trading business to sell furs from the backcountry in the port of Charles Town. The extra wagon we bought for this trip won't be needed for everyday farming and we hope your father will let us use it for our trading business."

I was excited about the prospect of creating our own business in the developing colonies of the South. Francis had worked out all the details and I could see there was money to be made in moving goods from the farming communities to the ports where ships were constantly coming from England, loaded with manufactured goods, and returning from the colonies with our own exports.

"But Father said each of you would get your own farms near Salisbury," she argued. "How do you think you can run a farm and be riding the trade routes to Charles Town at the same time?"

"In the Carolinas, not only is land cheap, but so are slaves to tend it," I was quick to reply.

She was quiet, thinking about what I had said.

"I don't like the notion of owning slaves," she stated with a furrowed brow. "They didn't choose to come here."

"Oh, I suspect they are better off here than where they came from," I countered. "Abraham and Bella are quite content with us and with their lot in life, I would say."

"How would you know that, Matthew? Have you ever asked them? Would they dare tell you the truth?"

It was so like Mary. Never accepting anything at face value. Always challenging what everybody else accepts as just the way things are. I had to shake my head.

"Mary Brandon, what makes you so sure you're right about everything?"

"And what makes *you* so willing to go along with whatever is easiest, even if it's wrong?"

I pretended to ignore her combative remark, but in truth I never ignored a single thing Mary said to me. She had a fertile mind and a moral compass that defied the customs of the day and of our remote and constrained life as farmers in an unsettled wilderness.

But it wasn't just because of her contrarian bent that I loved Mary Brandon. It was something much harder to understand—a joy in her presence and a breath that caught in my throat every time we touched.

When we stopped that evening, I again asked her to walk with me, even though it was clear our family was beginning to notice the time we spent alone together. It was not like me to shirk responsibility to set up camp. But at the time, everything else was secondary to my desire to be alone with Mary.

"Well, we'd better move quickly then," she laughed, "or Father will find chores for us to do."

We ducked down the nearest path and congratulated ourselves for getting away.

"Shhh," she warned. "Don't make so much noise or they'll come looking for us."

She took my hand and we walked quickly together along the quiet path, thick with pine needles. She was feeling playful and I couldn't have been happier if my life depended on it.

Once out of earshot, we stopped under a red maple and Mary held up her arms in adulation of the green, silent forest and its teeming world of flora and fauna.

"Oh, isn't it grand to be out of that wagon and here in the cool, quiet forest?" she exalted.

I walked over to her and put my hands on her shoulders, moving slowly, ever so slowly, closer until our lips touched.

"I love you, Mary Brandon. I have loved you from the first day I crossed Manada Creek on the way to your farm, all of us crammed into the back of your father's wagon. Your family came pouring out of the house to see what was going on, shocked by the Locke invasion. I saw you at once, before I even got out of the wagon. You were all I ever wanted, and I shall never be a happy man until the day you become my wife."

She didn't give me an answer that day. But her eyes told me everything I needed to know. And it was clear to me then, as witnessed over the next forty years we spent together, that whatever God meant me to make of my life, she would be by my side.

The Great Wagon Trail

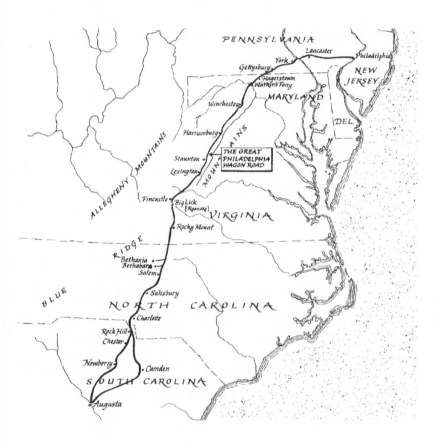

Courtesy of The Dietz Press, Richmond, Virginia

Genealogy Continued

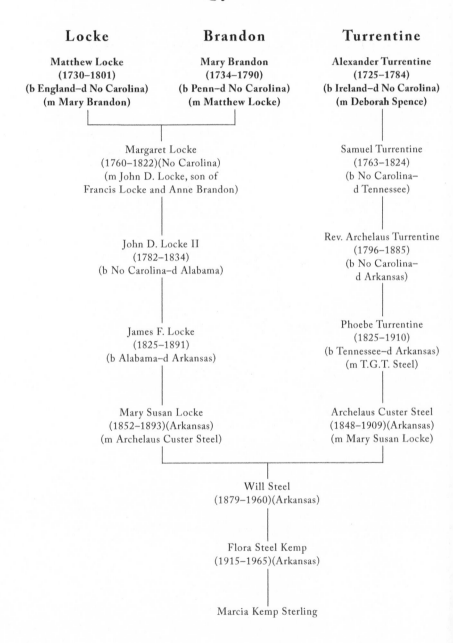

Locke	**Brandon**	**Turrentine**
Matthew Locke (1730–1801) (b England–d No Carolina) (m Mary Brandon)	Mary Brandon (1734–1790) (b Penn–d No Carolina) (m Matthew Locke)	Alexander Turrentine (1725–1784) (b Ireland–d No Carolina) (m Deborah Spence)

Margaret Locke
(1760–1822)(No Carolina)
(m John D. Locke, son of
Francis Locke and Anne Brandon)

Samuel Turrentine
(1763–1824)
(b No Carolina–
d Tennessee)

John D. Locke II
(1782–1834)
(b No Carolina–d Alabama)

Rev. Archelaus Turrentine
(1796–1885)
(b No Carolina–
d Arkansas)

James F. Locke
(1825–1891)
(b Alabama–d Arkansas)

Phoebe Turrentine
(1825–1910)
(b Tennessee–d Arkansas)
(m T.G.T. Steel)

Mary Susan Locke
(1852–1893)(Arkansas)
(m Archelaus Custer Steel)

Archelaus Custer Steel
(1848–1909)(Arkansas)
(m Mary Susan Locke)

Will Steel
(1879–1960)(Arkansas)

Flora Steel Kemp
(1915–1965)(Arkansas)

Marcia Kemp Sterling

Afterword

In an age when genetic matches can be found online and family trees expand effortlessly through the research of others, it's hard to ignore the fact that bits and pieces of our ancestral DNA continue to surge through our own veins and to shape who we are.

When the daughter of James Locke married the son of Phoebe Turrentine in an Arkansas frontier town just after the Civil War, two pioneer families with intertwined histories were finally made one. Like most American settlers, the Lockes and Turrentines who bought parcels in the southwest corner of Arkansas were younger children of large families who had moved westward for cheaper land.

Most of the families who settled in Arkansas during the years before the Civil War had been on their way to Texas, where land was being practically given away in order to increase the population of Texas and bring a new Confederate state into the union. Farmland had opened up in Arkansas in large part because of the forced relocation of native tribes to Oklahoma in the shameful episode of American history called the "Trail of Tears."

Tangled Roots

The Turrentine family was headed for Texas in the fall of 1837, and was camped out near Arkadelphia when a severe storm brought a big pine down onto their camp, killing two boys and breaking Jim Turrentine's leg. Jim was saved only because of the strength of Old Nelse, a slave brought with the family from Tennessee, who was able to lift the tree. The family decided to stay put in Arkansas.

Jim Locke and his wife Kit ran a boarding house in Paraclifta, where folks stayed when they came to the Sevier County Seat to argue about land boundaries or settle a tax lien. Many of their boarders became personal friends. Young Doctor George Todd was so close to Jim and Kit that they named their firstborn son George Todd Locke, a decision they regretted when George left Arkansas during the Civil War to serve as a doctor for the Union Army at the urging of his sister Mary Todd Lincoln, who was married to the President. Uncle Jim, as my mother called him, was a descendant of Mary Brandon and Matthew Locke, as well as Anne Brandon and Francis Locke.

Phoebe Turrentine married another pioneer of Scots-Irish heritage, Thomas George Tucker Steel, who had come into Little Rock on a flatboat from Virginia and became an itinerant preacher, or circuit rider, for the Methodist Church. During a time when lawyers didn't go to law school for their training, this family produced a number of country lawyers who "read the law" and then answered questions before the local bar in order to qualify as attorneys. When post–Civil War reconstruction changed county lines and dismantled a system of agriculture based on slave labor, these families spread out over the state, but many of their progeny have stayed with the practice of law over the centuries.

Afterword

Those of us who are descendants of the Turrentine-Steel union owe a debt of gratitude to a slave called Gib, whose quick response saved Phoebe's life when she was a child. Gib was the blacksmith on the Steel farm. Little Phoebe was playing around Gib's forge with a piece of iron in her mouth, when she stumbled and swallowed it, nearly choking to death. Gib grabbed her by the ankles and shook until the iron was dislodged.

Before the Turrentines moved to Arkansas, Gib had been the property of a Tennessee neighbor of theirs, and he was married to an enslaved woman owned by the Turrentines. Jim Turrentine's offer to buy Gib, or alternatively to sell his wife to the neighbor, was initially rejected. Only after much arguing and weeping was the neighbor finally convinced that his valuable property would be rendered worthless without his wife, and a deal was struck.

Written documentation of such stories is replete in my family's history—stories of heroic feats by enslaved men and women, told and re-told over the generations. Whether such romantic notions as the "heroic slave" or the mutual loyalty between slave and master ever translated into commitment to reject the system of enslaved labor that supported the agricultural South cannot be known.

The settlers of Lockesburg, Arkansas, like those who inhabited most of Appalachia and much of the southern United States, were of Scots-Irish heritage, descendants of the great flood of immigrants from Northern Ireland in the 1700s escaping war and famine. These "Ulster Scots," as they were often called, were a different group from the poor urban Catholic Irish who entered the American cities a hundred years later. The Scots-Irish were Protestant farmers from

Scotland, recruited by the English to the Northern Ireland plantations to help control the rebellious natives in that part of Ireland, most of whom were Catholic. The "Troubles" from that effort continue to plague Northern Ireland to this day.

This story is fictional, but it is based on real people and what we know of their lives. It is unlikely that Matthew and Francis Locke ever met Samuel and Alexander Turrentine, even though both sets of brothers arrived in Philadelphia at about the same time in the mid-1700s. All four of them lived in the Pennsylvania Colony for less than a decade before loading up and following the Great Wagon Road through the Shenandoah Valley and down into North Carolina, the Brandons and Lockes settling near Salisbury and the Turrentines near what is today Raleigh.

After Samuel and Alexander Turrentine worked off their indentures, they remained in Chester County, registering as tax-paying free men there in 1753 and 1754. They had acquired a "wheat patch" on the other side of the Susquehanna River in Mifflin County on Kishacoquillas Creek, a tributary of the Juniata, and built a cabin there. But the French and Indian War broke out and Mifflin County became a dangerous place for settlers. By 1761, each of the Turrentine brothers owned land in North Carolina. They must have left Pennsylvania in a hurry, abandoning buried treasure at their cabin consisting of two mattocks for working the soil and a bottle of whiskey.

Matthew and Francis Locke were historic figures in North Carolina in the Revolutionary War era. They made their money in the 1760s, running a line of Conestoga wagons from the hill towns and villages of the Carolinas to Charleston, trading animal skins and farm products for wine, fabrics, and manufactured goods from England. In the lead-up to the Revolutionary War, Matthew was Treasury Commissioner of the Colony of North Carolina, member of the North Carolina Senate and House of Commons, Brigadier General during the war, and elected Representative from North Carolina to the new United States Congress after the war. His brother Francis was also a significant figure in government and politics during this time.

Matthew and Mary are buried in the Thyatira Churchyard near Salisbury, North Carolina, a reflection of their transition from Anglican/Episcopal roots to Presbyterianism.

Matthew's Last Will and Testament passes some 800 acres of land to his sons. To my own ancestor, his daughter Margaret, he gave "my Negroe boy Stevan, in consideration that my old Negroe man Peter be by her supported during his life, also one hundred dollars in cash to be paid by my executors."

Every family has its own narrative, and the storyteller in mine was my maternal grandfather Will Steel, a Texarkana lawyer and judge who was born in Lockesburg, Arkansas; his mother was a Locke and his paternal grandmother a Turrentine. That's why we always thought of ourselves as part of the great Scots-Irish 18th century immigration to America and why the Lockes and Turrentines and Steels stay vivid in the family imagination, though they were only three of our sixteen great-great-grandparents.

None of us would be here, after all, if John Brandon had not made a trip down to the Susquehanna—we know not for what purpose— where he met Elizabeth Locke. Having been left a widow with seven children to support in a land that was not yet home to her, Elizabeth wound up managing a tavern in Middletown, near what is today Harrisburg, Pennsylvania. When she met the widower Brandon, her family joined his on their farm near Hanover, Pennsylvania, in what was then part of Lancaster County, now in Dauphin County northeast of Harrisburg.

Elizabeth's sons Francis and Matthew married John's daughters Anne and Mary, respectively, and in the next generation Matthew and Mary's daughter Margaret married Francis and Anne's son John. So the intermingled blood of five of the characters in this story—Francis Locke, Matthew Locke, Anne Brandon, Mary Brandon, and Alexander Turrentine—was passed to my siblings and myself through our mother.

As to the changes in the Turrentine name over the centuries, there's no clear evidence that the Turrentine brothers' surname had evolved from McTurk in Scotland to Turkington in Northern Ireland to Turrentine in the colonies. I have seen copies of their indentures and "Torrentine" was the name transcribed on those documents, which had clearly evolved to Turrentine by the time they purchased land in North Carolina. But Turrentine family genealogists have found no record of that name in the county of their birth, whereas there are lots of Turkingtons. Transcription errors of this kind were common at immigration centers throughout American history.

The speculation that the Scottish name McTurk could have derived from a slave brought back to the British Isles from the Crusades is pure poetic license. But of course in Scotland the prefix "Mc" like the French "De" and the Dutch "Van" developed in the Middle Ages to identify a person by either the birthplace or the given name or occupation of his forebears. In England and Scandinavia, such identifying tags were often tacked onto the end of a surname in the form of "ton" or "son." And during the Crusades, the term "Turk" was often ascribed to the variety of Islamic tribes who battled the Christian crusaders from the West for control of the holy city of Jerusalem.

Family Bibles served as a daily source of instruction, as well as containing records of births, deaths, and marriages, throughout the early centuries of American life. The cross itself is a literary device in this story, but it is symbolic of the way DNA, family values, and family narrative get passed down.

This is my family's story and, while it is a work of fiction, I have tried to reflect accurately the circumstances of each of my ancestors to the extent I know them. Mary and Matthew and Alex were real people who lived lives of joy and pain like all of us and whose legacy lives on in the generations that followed.

Acknowledgments

I owe a debt of gratitude to my first and best editor, critic, and supporter Nat Sterling, who helped me make final edits by patiently reading this manuscript aloud—one chapter a day during tea time—and provided great advice as this story came together.

I was assisted by a group of excellent readers who, because of their literary expertise and friendship, provided thoughtful and valuable input on the manuscript. Thanks so much to Carol Allen, Jeanie Ardell, Ann Dye, Joan Skurnick, Judith Steiner, Jennifer Sterling, and Anita Stewart. I'm also grateful for the invaluable feedback from my writers' group who offered editorial suggestions and critical input as the story developed, including Holly Brady, JoAnneh Nagler, Julia Weiner, Ron Ost, and Richard Abramson. And special thanks to Andrew Dyrli Hermeling for sharing his expertise about 18th century interactions between the settlers and native peoples in the Pennsylvania Colony.

The cover art is by Texarkana artist Thomas Hinton (1906–1975), and my thanks go to his niece Betty Miller Jones and her daughter Valorie Jones for once again permitting me to use one of his wonderful paintings to create a book cover that evokes memories of family and childhood.

Discussion Group Topics and Frequently Asked Questions may be found at:

www.MarciaKempSterling.com

About the Author

 My love of writing, which took on a practical bent during my career as a lawyer, has become a source of satisfaction during retirement. When coupled with a passion for history and curiosity about ancestry, my literary interests have included personal heritage and the part my forebears might have played in the flow of history.

This focus has now led to two books, the latest of which, *Tangled Roots*, takes place in the colony of Pennsylvania during the mid-1700s and is told in the fictional voices of three of my ancestors.

Prior to becoming a writer, I had an unusually interesting professional life, doing legal transactional work for technology companies during a time of explosive growth in Silicon Valley.

Between graduating from Vanderbilt with a degree in French literature (it never having occurred to me I'd have to earn a living) and starting Stanford Law School fifteen years later as a single parent of two young children, I found my way to California at the peak of the hippie revolution.

I've been a newspaper reporter in Houston and partner in a Silicon Valley law firm, a high school teacher and executive of a software company. I've advocated for the U.S. software industry in Washington and Brussels and Beijing as Chair of the Business Software Alliance, chaired the administrative board of the Palo Alto United Methodist Church, and led encounter groups and Al-Anon groups and support groups for spasmodic dysphonia and neurofibromatosis.

I live in Palo Alto, California, with my husband Nathaniel Sterling, former Executive Director of the California Law Revision Commission. Every summer Nat and I host Cousin Camp for our seven children and their families, including our ten grandchildren.